OUTSTANDING
NEW YORK ... AUTHOR ... NOVICH'S

ONE FOR THE MONEY

"[Stephanie Plum] is a Jersey girl with Bette Midler's mouth and Cher's fashion sense. Who could resist this doll?"
—*The New York Times Book Review*

"Of the current lineup of female detectives, almost all of them tediously feisty and quirky, she's the only one you'd want to eat pizza with."   —*Entertainment Weekly*

"Comes roaring in like a blast of very fresh air . . . Goes down like a tall, cool drink."   —*The Washington Post*

"Evanovich has crafted a heroine for today, tough, vulnerable, resourceful, and impulsive."   —Nora Roberts

"Many writers create good characters, but to create hilariously funny ones virtually bristling with believable sexual electricity—that's an achievement. Janet Evanovich accomplishes that in her delightful *One for the Money*."
—*USA Today*

"Plum's funny, first-person narration . . . and the tangible sense of place lift [this] above the crowd."
—*Miami Herald*

MORE . . .

"Evanovich's writing is full of sharp humor and Stephanie is an inspired creation." —*Trenton Times*

"First novels this funny and self-assured come along rarely; dialogue this astute and raunchy is equally unusual . . . A delightful romp." —*Publishers Weekly* (starred review)

"A smartly paced debut with an irresistible heroine who, despite trouble getting her man, will have readers hooked by page three. Trenton is about to become the comic mystery's most improbable hot spot."
—*Kirkus Reviews* (starred review)

"A wonderful sense of humor, an eye for detail, and a self-deprecating narrative endow Stephanie Plum with the easy-to-follow believability that accounts for her appeal as a heroine . . . A witty, well-written and gutsy debut."
—*Library Journal*

TWO FOR THE DOUGH
"Stephanie Plum . . . is back with her pepper spray, stun gun, up-to-here hair, and out-to-there attitude . . . That girl has some class." —*The New York Times Book Review*

"While Janet Evanovich's wry humor and quirky characters are reminiscent of Elmore Leonard, she puts a feminist spin on this inventive and fast-paced thriller, which places it in a class by itself." —*San Diego Union Tribune*

"*One for the Money* was great fun; so's *Two for the Dough* . . . I'm more than ready for *Three to Get Deadly*."
—*Orlando Sentinel*

"[In] *Two for the Dough* . . . a truly gritty, ethnic, very complex Trenton, New Jersey, comes across beautifully."
—*Boston Sunday Globe*

"The sharp repartee and Stephanie's slightly cynical but still fond relationship with her family and the burg hold a treasury of urban-style charms." —*Publishers Weekly*

THREE TO GET DEADLY

"Another rollicking chapter in the madcap career of Janet Evanovich's sassy bounty hunter."
—*The New York Times Book Review*

"The redoubtable Stephanie is a character crying out for a screen debut." —*Publishers Weekly*

"*Three to Get Deadly* marks the delightful return of brassy Stephanie Plum, fashion-challenged bounty hunter."
—*Seattle Times/Post-Intelligencer*

"Janet Evanovich's screwball thrillers offer up a wonderful heroine for the '90s . . . In lots of scenes you're likely to laugh out loud . . . Evanovich always picks just the right detail and makes 'the burg' come alive. It's a very small world . . . a world that's rich with comic possibilities, and the author triumphantly mines every single one." —*Detroit Free Press*

"*Three to Get Deadly* . . . proves just as funny and fast-paced as its predecessors." —*Orlando Sentinel*

FOUR TO SCORE

"Laughs, action and imaginative characters . . . Evanovich is a clever writer, and her hero's self-deprecating sense of humor and witty observations about life on the seamy side are contagious."
—*Chicago Tribune*

"Stephanie is a one-woman riot on her own, but with her intrepid assistants, she's a war zone. It's one of the funniest reads of the summer with lots of wisecracks, bizarre characters, steamy sex and an attitude as big as all outdoors."
—*Dallas Morning News*

"She makes the reader laugh out loud on one page and fret the next. *Four to Score* is a Plum choice." —*USA Today*

"This 'crime novel' had me laughing out loud . . . To put it in Jersey-speak, you'll piss your pants reading it."
—*Mademoiselle*

"*Four to Score* gathers momentum and carries readers along in a hilarious missing-person quest . . . Plum is anything but plummy-voiced: She delivers wisecracks in a vernacular that has the bite of salsa . . . [The] pace is breakneck."
—*Boston Sunday Herald*

HIGH FIVE

"*High Five* is a fun romp through the wilds of New Jersey. Evanovich delivers the hilarious characters her fans adore, while refreshingly different Stephanie is at her best."
—*USA Today*

"[The characters] are so full of quirky American life, like a Preston Sturges ensemble, that it's hard not to like them as much as Evanovich obviously does. Plum herself is terrific fun."
—*The Washington Post*

"The witty dialogue and crazy plot twists make you laugh almost non-stop as you speed through *High Five* . . . Evanovich is the master of snappy dialogue. Her offbeat characters seem perfectly at home in Trenton. Her plot never lags, just escalates as the hilarious shenanigans pull you along at breakneck speed."   —*San Francisco Examiner*

"Fans of Evanovich's previous books in this series will be happy to see Steph hanging with the usual suspects . . . Steph has a spunky, earthy appeal—like a hot dog at the beach with a few grains of sand."   —*People*

"As for the hot-stuff heroine: in Ranger's words to his protegée, after she innocently causes a barroom riot, 'You never disappoint.' "   —*The New York Times Book Review*

"If you're new to the Plum novels, *High Five* may well send you in search of the others. Few mystery writers are as entertaining as Evanovich when it comes to dialogue and character description."   —*Newark Star-Ledger*

HOT SIX

"[Evanovich's novels are] among the great joys of contemporary crime fiction."   —*GQ*

"Outrageous characters are the author's specialty…the humor is nonstop . . . a romantic triangle adds some tantalizing allure."   —*Entertainment Weekly*

"[Stephanie Plum's] sleuthing efforts on Ranger's behalf lead to run-ins with the rambunctious army of cops, killers, and rival bounty hunters Evanovich gleefully puts on her tail. Luckily for Stephanie, the inventive mind that got her into this giddy mess is clever enough to dig her out of it."
                                        —*The New York Times Book Review*

"There are enough cars exploding, guns firing and scary break-ins to keep any mystery buff satisfied, while Stephanie's entertaining sex life . . . and running commentary are laugh-out-loud funny."   —*New York Post*

"Non-stop laughs with plenty of high jinks."   —*USA Today*

"An appealing detective, a love interest, a little danger and a lot of laughs . . . a classic screwball detective story."
                                                  —*Dallas Morning News*

"Stephanie Plum [is] Trenton's most adorable, least reliable bounty hunter . . . On the day this Jersey tomato decides to diarize, look to your laurels, Bridget Jones."
                                                  —*Philadelphia Inquirer*

SEVEN UP

"A madcap comic mystery—Jersey-girl style."
                                                  —*The New York Times*

"Expect a laugh per page . . . Bottom line: Plum Pick."
                                                  —*People*

"If you like your summer reads hot and sassy, try *Seven Up*."
                                                  —*Boston Herald*

"[*Seven Up*] is funny, sexy, scary."   —*Booklist*

"Edgy romance triangle, the loopy family relationships, [and] the bounty-hunting jobs that skate between absurdity and genuine tension."   —*Denver Post*

"Evanovich continues . . . her successful formula . . . [she] provides a beginning that illustrates all that is right with this series and an ending that ties the story together, gives us a dose of reality, and leaves us with a cliffhanger."
                                                  —*Chicago Tribune*

HARD EIGHT

"Evanovich does it again, delivering an even more suspenseful and more outrageous turn with the unstoppable Stephanie . . . waiting for *Nine* will be tough."
—*Publishers Weekly* (starred review)

"The things Evanovich does so well—family angst, sweet eroticism, stealth shopping, that stunning mix of terror and hilarity—are done better than ever here."
—*Booklist* (starred review)

"Keeps up Evanovich's standards for over-the-top situations." —*Chicago Tribune*

"A must read . . . readers will want to finish this delightful work in one sitting." —*Midwest Book Review*

"Well plotted and cleverly resolved . . . her wickedly funny characterizations and the intriguing love triangle are what keep her readers coming back for more." —*Bookpage*

"Just when you think that the adventures of Plum and company can't get any funnier or more convoluted, Janet Evanovich proves you wrong—nobody does it better!"
—*RT Bookclub*

ONE FOR THE MONEY

JANET EVANOVICH

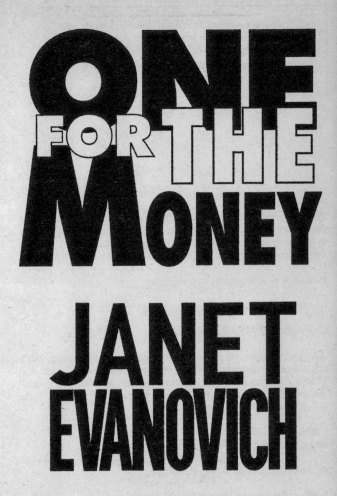

St. Martin's Paperbacks

This is a work of fiction. Names, characters, places, and incidents are products of the author's imagination or are used fictitiously and are not to be construed as real. Any resemblance to actual events, locales, organizations, or persons, living or dead, is entirely coincidental.

Published by arrangement with Scribner

ONE FOR THE MONEY

ISBN: 0-312-99045-6
EAN: 80312-99045-9

Printed in the United States of America

Scribner hardcover edition published 1994
St. Martin's Paperbacks edition / April 2003

St. Martin's Paperbacks are published by St. Martin's Press, 175 Fifth Avenue, New York, NY 10010.

15 14 13 12 11 10 9

This book is for my husband, Peter—with love.

ACKNOWLEDGMENTS

The author wishes to acknowledge the invaluable assistance of the following people: Sergeant Walter Kirstien, Trenton P.D.; Detective Sergeant Robert Szejner, Trenton P.D.; Leanne Banks; Courtney Henke; Kurt Henke; Margaret Dear; Elizabeth Brossy; Richard Anderson, Gilbert Small Arms Range; David Daily, Fairfax County P.D.; and Roger White. With special thanks to my agent, Aaron Priest; to Frances Jalet-Miller; and to my editor, Susanne Kirk, and her assistant, Gillian Blake.

ONE

THERE ARE SOME MEN WHO ENTER A WOMAN'S LIFE and screw it up forever. Joseph Morelli did this to me—not forever, but periodically.

Morelli and I were both born and raised in a blue-collar chunk of Trenton called the burg. Houses were attached and narrow. Yards were small. Cars were American. The people were mostly of Italian descent, with enough Hungarians and Germans thrown in to offset inbreeding. It was a good place to buy calzone or play the numbers. And, if you had to live in Trenton anyway, it was an okay place to raise a family.

When I was a kid I didn't ordinarily play with Joseph Morelli. He lived two blocks over and was two years older. "Stay away from those Morelli boys," my mother had warned me. "They're wild. I hear stories about the things they do to girls when they get them alone."

"What kind of things?" I'd eagerly asked.

"You don't want to know," my mother had answered. "Terrible things. Things that aren't nice."

From that moment on, I viewed Joseph Morelli with a combination of terror and prurient curiosity that bordered on awe. Two weeks later, at the age of six, with quaking knees and a squishy stomach, I followed Morelli into his father's garage on the promise of learning a new game.

The Morelli garage hunkered detached and snubbed at the edge of their lot. It was a sorry affair, lit by a single shaft of light filtering through a grime-coated window. Its air was stagnant, smelling of corner must, discarded tires, and jugs of used motor oil. Never destined to house the Morelli cars, the garage served other purposes. Old Man Morelli used the garage to take his belt to his sons, his sons used the garage to take their hands to themselves, and Joseph Morelli took me, Stephanie Plum, to the garage to play train.

"What's the name of this game?" I'd asked Joseph Morelli.

"Choo-choo," he'd said, down on his hands and knees, crawling between my legs, his head trapped under my short pink skirt. "You're the tunnel, and I'm the train."

I suppose this tells something about my personality. That I'm not especially good at taking advice. Or that I was born with an overload of curiosity. Or maybe it's about rebellion or boredom or fate. At any rate, it was a one-shot deal and darn disappointing, since I'd only gotten to be the tunnel, and I'd really wanted to be the train.

Ten years later, Joe Morelli was still living two blocks over. He'd grown up big and bad, with eyes like black fire one minute and melt-in-your-mouth chocolate the next. He had an eagle tattooed on his chest, a tight-assed, narrow-hipped swagger, and a reputation for having fast hands and clever fingers.

My best friend, Mary Lou Molnar, said she heard Morelli had a tongue like a lizard.

"Holy cow," I'd answered, "what's that supposed to mean?"

"Just don't let him get you alone or you'll find out. Once he gets you alone . . . that's it. You're done for."

I hadn't seen much of Morelli since the train episode. I supposed he'd enlarged his repertoire of sexual exploitation. I opened my eyes wide and leaned closer to Mary Lou, hoping for the worst. "You aren't talking about rape, are you?"

"I'm talking about lust! If he wants you, you're doomed. The guy is irresistible."

Aside from being fingered at the age of six by you-know-who, I was untouched. I was saving myself for marriage, or at least for college. "I'm a virgin," I said, as if this was news. "I'm sure he doesn't mess with virgins."

"He specializes in virgins! The brush of his fingertips turns virgins into slobbering mush."

Two weeks later, Joe Morelli came into the bakery where I worked every day after school, Tasty Pastry, on Hamilton. He bought a chocolate-chip cannoli, told me he'd joined the navy, and charmed the pants off me four minutes after closing, on the floor of Tasty Pastry, behind the case filled with chocolate éclairs.

The next time I saw him, I was three years older. I was on my way to the mall, driving my father's Buick when I spotted Morelli standing in front of Giovichinni's Meat Market. I gunned the big V-8 engine, jumped the curb, and clipped Morelli from behind, bouncing him off the front right fender. I stopped the car and got out to assess the damage. "Anything broken?"

He was sprawled on the pavement, looking up my skirt. "My leg."

"Good," I said. Then I turned on my heel, got into the Buick, and drove to the mall.

I attribute the incident to temporary insanity, and in my own defense, I'd like to say I haven't run over anyone since.

DURING WINTER MONTHS, WIND RIPPED UP HAMilton Avenue, whining past plate-glass windows, banking trash against curbs and storefronts. During summer months, the air sat still and gauzy, leaden with humidity, saturated with hydrocarbons. It shimmered over hot cement and melted road tar. Cicadas buzzed, Dumpsters reeked, and a dusty haze hung in perpetuity over softball fields state-wide. I figured it was all part of the great adventure of living in New Jersey.

This afternoon I'd decided to ignore the August buildup of ozone catching me in the back of my throat and go, convertible top down, in my Mazda Miata. The air conditioner was blasting flat out, I was singing along with Paul Simon, my shoulder-length brown hair was whipping around my face in a frenzy of frizz and snarls, my ever vigilant blue eyes were coolly hidden behind my Oakleys, and my foot rested heavy on the gas pedal.

It was Sunday, and I had a date with a pot roast at my parents' house. I stopped for a light and checked my rearview mirror, swearing when I saw Lenny Gruber two car lengths back in a tan sedan. I thunked my forehead on the steering wheel. "Damn." I'd gone to high school with Gruber. He was a maggot then, and he was a maggot now. Un-fortunately, he was a maggot with a just cause. I was behind on my Miata payments, and Gruber worked for the repo company.

Six months ago, when I'd bought the car, I'd been looking good, with a nice apartment and sea-son tickets to the Rangers. And then *bam*! I got laid off. No money. No more A-1 credit rating.

I rechecked the mirror, set my teeth, and yanked up the emergency brake. Lenny was like smoke. When you tried to grab him, he evaporated, so I wasn't about to waste this one last opportunity to bargain. I hauled myself out of my car, apologized to the man caught between us, and stalked back to Gruber.

"Stephanie Plum," Gruber said, full of joy and faux surprise. "What a treat."

I leaned two hands on the roof and looked through the open window at him. "Lenny, I'm going to my parents' house for dinner. You wouldn't snatch my car while I was at my parents' house, would you? I mean, that would be really low, Lenny."

"I'm a pretty low guy, Steph. That's why I've got this neat job. I'm capable of most anything."

The light changed, and the driver behind Gruber leaned on his horn.

"Maybe we can make a deal," I said to Gruber.

"Does this deal involve you getting naked?"

I had a vision of grabbing his nose and twisting it Three Stooges style until he squealed like a pig. Problem was, it'd involve touching him. Better to go with a more restrained approach. "Let me keep the car tonight, and I'll drive it to the lot first thing tomorrow morning."

"No way," Gruber said. "You're damn sneaky. I've been chasing after this car for five days."

"So, one more won't matter."

"I'd expect you to be grateful, you know what I mean?"

I almost gagged. "Forget it. Take the car. In fact, you could take it right now. I'll walk to my parents'."

Gruber's eyes were locked halfway down my chest. I'm a 36B. Respectable but far from overwhelming on my 5' 7" frame. I was wearing black spandex shorts and an oversized hockey jersey. Not what you would call a seductive outfit, but Lenny was ogling anyway.

His smile widened enough to show he was missing a molar. "I guess I could wait for tomorrow. After all, we *did* go to high school together."

"Uh huh." It was the best I could do.

Five minutes later I turned off Hamilton onto Roosevelt. Two blocks to my parents' house, and I could feel familial obligation sucking at me, pulling me into the heart of the burg. This was a community of extended families. There was safety here, along with love, and stability, and the comfort of ritual. The clock on the dash told me I was seven minutes late, and the urge to scream told me I was home.

I parked at the curb and looked at the narrow two-story duplex with its jalousied front porch and aluminum awnings. The Plum half was yellow, just as it had been for forty years, with a brown shingle roof. Snowball bushes flanked either side of the cement stoop, and red geraniums had been evenly spaced the length of the porch. It was basically a flat. Living room in front, dining room in the middle, kitchen at the rear. Three bedrooms and bath upstairs. It was a small, tidy house crammed with kitchen smells and too much furniture, comfortable with its lot in life.

Next door, Mrs. Markowitz, who was living on social security and could only afford closeout paint colors, had painted her side lime green.

My mother was at the open screen door. "Stephanie," she called. "What are you doing sitting out there in your car? You're late for dinner. You know how your father hates to eat late. The potatoes are getting cold. The pot roast will be dry."

Food is important in the burg. The moon revolves around the earth, the earth revolves around the sun, and the burg revolves around pot roast. For as long as I can remember, my parents' lives have been controlled by five-pound pieces of rolled rump, done to perfection at six o'clock.

Grandma Mazur stood two feet back from my mother. "I gotta get me a pair of those," she said, eyeballing my shorts. "I've still got pretty good legs, you know." She raised her skirt and looked down at her knees. "What do you think? You think I'd look good in them biker things?"

Grandma Mazur had knees like doorknobs. She'd been a beauty in her time, but the years had turned her slack-skinned and spindle-boned. Still, if she wanted to wear biker shorts, I thought she should go for it. The way I saw it, that was one of the many advantages to living in New Jersey—even old ladies were allowed to look outlandish.

My father gave a grunt of disgust from the kitchen, where he was carving up the meat. "Biker's shorts," he muttered, slapping his palm against his forehead. "Unh!"

Two years ago, when Grandpa Mazur's fat-clogged arteries sent him to the big pork roast in the sky, Grandma Mazur had moved in with my parents and had never moved out. My father accepted this with a combination of Old-World stoicism and tactless mutterings.

I remember him telling me about a dog he'd had as a kid. The story goes that this dog was the ugliest, oldest, most pea-brained dog ever. The dog was incontinent, dribbling urine wherever it went. Its teeth were rotted in its mouth, its hips were fused solid with arthritis, and huge fatty tumors lumped under its hide. One day my Grandpa Plum took the dog out behind the garage and shot it. I suspected there were times when my father fantasized a similar ending for my Grandma Mazur.

"You should wear a dress," my mother said to me, bringing green beans and creamed pearl onions to the table. "Thirty years old and you're still dressing in those teeny-bopper outfits. How will you ever catch a nice man like that?"

"I don't want a man. I had one, and I didn't like it."

"That's because your husband was a horse's behind," Grandma Mazur said.

I agreed. My ex-husband had been a horse's behind. Especially when I'd caught him flagrante delicto on the dining room table with Joyce Barnhardt.

"I hear Loretta Buzick's boy is separated from his wife," my mother said. "You remember him? Ronald Buzick?"

I knew where she was heading, and I didn't want to go there. "I'm not going out with Ronald Buzick," I told her. "Don't even think about it."

"So what's wrong with Ronald Buzick?"

Ronald Buzick was a butcher. He was balding, and he was fat, and I suppose I was being a snob about the whole thing, but I found it hard to think in romantic terms about a man who spent his days stuffing giblets up chicken butts.

My mother plunged on. "All right, then how about Bernie Kuntz? I saw Bernie Kuntz in the dry cleaners, and he made a point about asking for you. I think he's interested. I could invite him over for coffee and cake."

With the way my luck was running, probably my mother had already invited Bernie, and at this very moment he was circling the block, popping Tic Tacs. "I don't want to talk about Bernie," I said. "There's something I need to tell you. I have some bad news. . . ."

I'd been dreading this and had put it off for as long as possible.

My mother clapped a hand to her mouth. "You found a lump in your breast!"

No one in our family had ever found a lump in their breast, but my mother was ever watchful. "My breast is fine. The problem is with my job."

"What about your job?"

"I don't have one. I got laid off."

"Laid off!" she said on a sharp inhale. "How could that happen? It was such a good job. You loved that job."

I'd been a discount lingerie buyer for E.E. Martin, and I'd worked in Newark, which is not exactly the garden spot of the Garden State. In truth, it had been my mother who had loved the job, imagining it to be glamorous when in reality I'd mostly haggled over the cost of full-fashion nylon underpants. E.E. Martin wasn't exactly Victoria's Secret.

"I wouldn't worry," my mother said. "There's always work for lingerie buyers."

"There's *no* work for lingerie buyers." Especially ones who worked for E.E. Martin. Having held a salaried position with E.E. Martin made me as appealing as a leper. E.E. Martin had skimped on the palm greasing this winter, and as a result its mob affiliations were made public. The C.E.O. was indicted for illegal business practices, E.E. Martin sold out to Baldicott, Inc., and, through no fault of my own, I was caught in the house-cleaning sweep. "I've been out of work for six months."

"Six months! And I didn't know! Your own

mother didn't know you were out on the streets?"

"I'm not out on the streets. I've been doing temporary jobs. Filing and stuff." And steadily sliding downhill. I was registered with every search firm in the greater Trenton area, and I religiously read the want ads. I wasn't being all that choosy, drawing the line at telephone soliciting and kennel attendant, but my future didn't look great. I was overqualified for entry level, and I lacked experience in management.

My father forked another slab of pot roast onto his plate. He'd worked for the post office for thirty years and had opted for early retirement. Now he drove a cab part-time.

"I saw your cousin Vinnie yesterday," he said. "He's looking for someone to do filing. You should give him a call."

Just the career move I'd been hoping for—filing for Vinnie. Of all my relatives, Vinnie was my least favorite. Vinnie was a worm, a sexual lunatic, a dog turd. "What does he pay?" I asked.

My father shrugged. "Gotta be minimum wage."

Wonderful. The perfect position for someone already in the depths of despair. Rotten boss, rotten job, rotten pay. The possibilities for feeling sorry for myself would be endless.

"And the best part is that it's close," my mother said. "You can come home every day for lunch."

I nodded numbly, thinking I'd sooner stick a needle in my eye.

• • •

SUNLIGHT SLANTED THROUGH THE CRACK IN MY bedroom curtains, the air-conditioning unit in the living room window droned ominously, predicting another scorcher of a morning, and the digital display on my clock radio flashed electric blue numbers, telling me it was nine o'clock. The day had started without me.

I rolled out of bed on a sigh and shuffled into the bathroom. When I was done in the bathroom, I shuffled into the kitchen and stood in front of the refrigerator, hoping the refrigerator fairies had visited during the night. I opened the door and stared at the empty shelves, noting that food hadn't magically cloned itself from the smudges in the butter keeper and the shriveled flotsam at the bottom of the crisper. Half a jar of mayo, a bottle of beer, whole-wheat bread covered with blue mold, a head of iceberg lettuce, shrink-wrapped in brown slime and plastic, and a box of hamster nuggets stood between me and starvation. I wondered if nine in the morning was too early to drink beer. Of course in Moscow it would be four in the afternoon. Good enough.

I drank half the beer and grimly approached the living room window. I pulled the curtains and stared down at the parking lot. My Miata was gone. Lenny had hit early. No surprise, but still, it lodged painfully in the middle of my throat. I was now an official deadbeat.

And if that wasn't depressing enough, I'd weakened halfway through dessert and promised my mother I'd go see Vinnie.

I dragged myself into the shower and stumbled out a half hour later after an exhausting crying jag. I stuffed myself into pantyhose and a suit and was ready to do my daughterly duty.

My hamster, Rex, was still asleep in his soup can in his cage on the kitchen counter. I dropped a few hamster nuggets into his bowl and made some smoochy sounds. Rex opened his black eyes and blinked. He twitched his whiskers, gave a good sniff, and rejected the nuggets. I couldn't blame him. I'd tried them for breakfast yesterday and hadn't been impressed.

I locked up the apartment and walked three blocks down St. James to Blue Ribbon Used Cars. At the front of the lot was a $500 Nova begging to be bought. Total body rust and countless accidents had left the Nova barely recognizable as a car, much less a Chevy, but Blue Ribbon was willing to trade the beast for my TV and VCR. I threw in my food processor and microwave, and they paid my registration and taxes.

I drove the Nova out of the lot and went straight to Vinnie. I pulled into a parking space at the corner of Hamilton and Olden, extracted the key from the ignition, and waited for the car to thrash itself off.

I said a short prayer not to be spotted by anyone I knew, wrenched the door open, and scuttled the short distance to the storefront office. The blue and white sign over the door read "Vincent Plum Bail Bonding Company." In smaller letters it advertised twenty-four-hour nationwide service. Conveniently located between Tender Loving Care Dry Cleaners and Fiorello's Deli, Vincent Plum catered to the family trade—domestic disturbances, disorderlies, auto theft, DWI, and shoplifting. The office was small and generic, consisting of two rooms with cheap walnut paneling on the walls and commercial grade rust-colored carpet on the floor. A Danish modern couch upholstered in brown Naugahyde pressed against one wall of the reception area, and a black and brown metal desk with a multiline phone and a computer terminal occupied a far corner.

Vinnie's secretary sat behind the desk, her head bent in concentration, picking her way through a stack of files. "Yeah?"

"I'm Stephanie Plum. I've come to see my cousin, Vinnie."

"Stephanie Plum!" Her head came up. "I'm Connie Rosolli. You went to school with my little sister, Tina. Oh jeez, I hope you don't have to make bail."

I recognized her now. She was an older version of Tina. Thicker in the waist, heavier in the face. She had lots of teased black hair, flawless olive skin, and a five-o'clock shadow on her upper lip.

"The only thing I have to make is money," I said to Connie. "I hear Vinnie needs someone to do filing."

"We just filled that job, and between you and me, you didn't miss anything. It was a crummy job. Paid minimum wage, and you had to spend all day on your knees singing the alphabet song. My feeling is, if you're going to spend that much time on your knees, you could find something that pays better. You know what I mean?"

"Last time I was on my knees was two years ago. I was looking for a contact lens."

"Listen, if you really need a job, why don't you get Vinnie to let you do skip tracing? There's good money in it."

"How much money?"

"Ten percent of the bond." Connie pulled a file from her top drawer. "We got this one in yesterday. Bail was set at $100,000, and he didn't show up for a court appearance. If you could find him and bring him in, you'd get $10,000."

I put a hand to the desk to steady myself. "Ten thousand dollars for finding one guy? What's the catch?"

"Sometimes they don't want to be found, and they shoot at you. But that hardly ever happens." Connie leafed through the file. "The guy who came in yesterday is local. Morty Beyers started tracking him down, so some of the prelim is already done. You've got pictures and everything."

"What happened to Morty Beyers?"

"Busted appendix. Happened at eleven-thirty last night. He's in St. Francis with a drain in his side and a tube up his nose."

I didn't want to wish Morty Beyers any misfortune, but I was starting to get excited about the prospect of stepping into his shoes. The money was tempting, and the job title had a certain cachet. On the other hand, catching fugitives sounded scary, and I was a certifiable coward when it came to risking my body parts.

"My guess is, it wouldn't be hard to find this guy," Connie said. "You could go talk to his mother. And if it gets hairy, you could back out. What have you got to lose?"

Only my life. "I don't know. I don't like the part about the shooting."

"Probably, it's like driving the turnpike," Connie said. "Probably, you get used to it. The way I see it, living in New Jersey is a challenge, what with the toxic waste and the eighteen-wheelers and the armed schizophrenics. I mean, what's one more lunatic shooting at you?"

Pretty much my own philosophy. And the $10,000 was damned appealing. I could pay off my creditors and straighten my life out. "Okay," I said. "I'll do it."

"You have to talk to Vinnie first." Connie swiveled her chair toward Vinnie's office door. "Hey Vinnie!" she yelled. "You got business out here."

Vinnie was forty-five, 5' 7" without his lifts, and had the slim, boneless body of a ferret. He wore pointy-toed shoes, liked pointy-breasted women and dark-skinned young men, and he drove a Cadillac Seville.

"Steph here wants to do some skip tracing," Connie said to Vinnie.

"No way. Too dangerous," Vinnie said. "Most of my agents used to be in security. And you have to know something about law enforcement."

"I can learn about law enforcement," I told him.

"Learn about it first. Then come back."

"I need the job *now*."

"Not my problem."

I figured it was time to get tough. "I'll make it your problem, Vinnie. I'll have a long talk with Lucille."

Lucille was Vinnie's wife and the only woman in the burg who didn't know about Vinnie's addiction to kinky sex. Lucille had her eyes firmly closed, and it wasn't my place to pry them open. Of course, if she ever *asked* . . . that'd be a whole other ball game.

"You'd blackmail me? Your own cousin?"

"These are desperate times."

He turned to Connie. "Give her a few civil cases. Stuff that involves telephone work."

"I want this one," I said, pointing to the file on Connie's desk. "I want the $10,000 one."

"Forget it. It's a murder. I should never have

posted bail, but he was from the burg, and I felt sorry for his mother. Trust me, you don't need this kind of trouble."

"I need the money, Vinnie. Give me a chance at bringing him in."

"When hell freezes over," Vinnie said. "I don't get this guy back, I'm in the hole for a hundred grand. I'm not sending an amateur after him."

Connie rolled her eyes at me. "You'd think it was out of his pocket. He's owned by an insurance company. It's no big deal."

"So give me a week, Vinnie," I said. "If I don't get him in a week, you can turn it over to someone else."

"I wouldn't give you a half hour."

I took a deep breath and leaned close to Vinnie, whispering in his ear. "I know about Madam Zaretski and her whips and chains. I know about the boys. And I know about the duck."

He didn't say anything. He just pressed his lips together until they turned white, and I knew I had him. Lucille would throw up if she knew what he did to the duck. Then she'd tell her father, Harry the Hammer, and Harry would cut off Vinnie's dick.

"Who am I looking for?" I asked Vinnie.

Vinnie handed me the file. "Joseph Morelli."

My heart flipped in my chest. I knew Morelli had been involved in a homicide. It had been big news in the burg, and details of the shooting had been splashed across the front page of the Trenton *Times*.

VICE COP KILLS UNARMED MAN. That had
been over a month ago, and other, more important,
issues (like the exact amount of the lottery) had replaced talk of Morelli. In the absence of more information, I'd assumed the shooting had been in the
line of duty. I hadn't realized Morelli'd been
charged with murder.

The reaction wasn't lost to Vinnie. "From the
look on your face, I'd say you know him."

I nodded. "Sold him a cannoli when I was in high
school."

Connie grunted. "Honey, half of all the women
in New Jersey have sold him their cannoli."

TWO

I BOUGHT A CAN OF SODA AT FIORELLO'S AND
drank while I walked to my car. I slid behind the
wheel, popped the top two buttons on my red silk
shirt, and stripped off my pantyhose as a concession
to the heat. Then I flipped open Morelli's file and
studied the photos first—mug shots from Morelli's
booking, a candid picture of him in a brown leather
bomber jacket and jeans, and a formal pose in a
shirt and tie, obviously clipped from a police pub-
lication. He hadn't changed much. A little leaner,
perhaps. More bone definition in the face. A few
lines at the eyes. A new scar, paper thin, sliced
through his right eyebrow, causing his right eyelid
to droop ever so slightly. The effect was unsettling.
Menacing.

Morelli had taken advantage of my naiveté not once, but twice. After the scene on the bakery floor, he'd never called, never sent me a postcard, never even said good-bye. And the worst part of it all was that I'd *wanted* him to call. Mary Lou Molnar had been right about Joseph Morelli. He'd been irresistible.

History, I told myself. I hadn't seen the man more than three or four times in the past eleven years, and each time had been at a distance. Morelli was a part of my childhood, and my childish feelings for him had no place in the present. I had a job to do. Plain and simple. I wasn't out to avenge old injuries. Finding Morelli had nothing to do with revenge. Finding Morelli had to do with the rent money. Yeah, right. That's why I suddenly had this knot in my stomach.

According to the information on the bond contract, Morelli lived in an apartment complex just off Route 1. This seemed like a good place to start looking. I doubted Morelli would be in his apartment, but I could question his neighbors and see if he was picking up his mail.

I set the file aside and reluctantly squeezed my feet back into my black heels. I turned the key in the ignition. No response. I gave the dash a hard shot with my fist and let out a grunt of relief when the engine cranked over.

Ten minutes later, I pulled into Morelli's parking lot. The buildings were brick, two-story, utilitarian.

Each building had two breezeways. Eight apartments opened off each breezeway, four up and four down. I cut the engine and scanned for apartment numbers. Morelli had a ground-level rear apartment.

I sat there for a while feeling stupid and inept. Suppose Morelli was home. What would I do, threaten to tell his mother if he didn't come peaceably? The man was up for murder. He had a lot at stake. I couldn't imagine him hurting me, but the possibility of being mortally embarrassed was extremely high. Not that I've ever let a little embarrassment stop me from forging blindly ahead on any number of dumb projects . . . like my ill-fated marriage to Dickie Orr, the horse's behind. The memory cued an involuntary grimace. Hard to believe I'd actually married a man named Dickie.

Okay, I thought, forget about Dickie. This is the Morelli plan. Check out his mailbox and then his apartment. If I got lucky (or unlucky, depending on how you looked at it), and he answered his door, I'd lie through my teeth and leave. Then I'd call the police and let them do the physical stuff.

I marched across the blacktop and diligently stared into the bank of mailboxes set into the brick wall. All were stuffed with envelopes. Morelli's was more stuffed than most. I crossed the breezeway and knocked on his door. No answer. Big surprise. I knocked again and waited. Nothing. I walked around to the back of the building and counted off windows. Four to Morelli and four to the apartment behind his. Morelli had his shades down, but I crept close and peeked in anyway, trying to see between the edge of the shade and the interior wall. If the shades suddenly rolled up and a face peered out, I'd wet my pants on the spot. Fortunately, the shades didn't roll up, and unfortunately, I couldn't see anything beyond them. I went back to the breezeway and tried the three remaining apartments. Two were no answers. The third was occupied by an elderly woman who had lived there for six years and had never seen Morelli. Dead end.

I went back to my car and sat there trying to think what to do next. There was no activity on the grounds—no televisions blaring from open windows, no children riding bikes, no dogs being rude on the lawn. Not the sort of place that drew families, I thought. Not the sort of place neighbors would know neighbors.

A sporty car pulled into the lot and swung wide of me, parking in one of the front spaces. The driver sat at the wheel for a while, and I wondered if this was an assignation. Since I had nothing better to do, I waited to see what would happen. After five minutes, the driver's door opened, and a man got out and walked to the breezeway next to Morelli's.

I couldn't believe my eyes. The guy was Joe's cousin, Mooch Morelli. Mooch undoubtedly had a real name, but I couldn't recall it. As long as I'd known him, he'd been Mooch. He'd lived one street over from St. Francis Hospital when he was a kid.

Used to hang out with Joe all the time. I crossed my fingers and hoped old Mooch was retrieving something Joe had left with a neighbor. Or maybe Mooch was at this very moment jimmying a window to Joe's apartment. I was warming to the idea of Mooch doing breaking and entering when he popped out from behind the building, key in hand, and let himself in through Joe's front door.

I held tight, and ten minutes later Mooch reappeared carrying a black duffel bag, got into his car, and took off. I waited for him to leave the lot, then I pulled out after him. I kept a couple car lengths behind, driving white-knuckled with my heart drilling hard in my chest, dizzy with the promise of $10,000.

I followed Mooch to State Street and watched him pull into a private drive. I circled the block and parked several houses down. At one time this had been a fashionable neighborhood of huge stone houses and large, well-kept lawns. Back in the sixties, when block busting was a popular activity for liberals, one of the State Street homeowners sold out to a black family, and over the course of the next five years the entire white population panicked and left. Poorer families moved in, the houses deteriorated and were subdivided, yards were neglected, windows were boarded. But, as is often the case with a desirable location, the neighborhood was now in the process of being reclaimed.

Mooch exited the house after a few minutes.

When he left, he was alone and without the duffel bag. Oh boy. A lead. What were the chances Joe Morelli was sitting in the house with the duffel bag on his lap? I decided they were fair to middlin'. Probably worth looking into. Now I had two choices. I could call the police right off, or I could go investigate on my own. If I called the police and Morelli wasn't there I'd look like a dunce, and the police might not be so anxious to come out and help me the second time around. On the other hand, I really didn't want to investigate on my own. Not a good attitude for someone who has recently accepted a job as a fugitive apprehender, but there it was.

I stared at the house for a long time, hoping Morelli would come sauntering out and I wouldn't have to go sauntering in. I checked my watch and thought about food. So far all I'd had was a bottle of beer for breakfast. I looked back out at the house. If I got this over with I could hit the golden arches and squander the loose change in the bottom of my pocketbook on a burger. Motivation.

I sucked in some air, shoved my door open, and levered myself out of the car. Just do it, I thought. Don't make a big deal out of something simple. He probably isn't even in there.

I strode purposefully down the sidewalk, talking to myself as I walked. I reached the house and went in without hesitation. Mailboxes in the vestibule indicated there were eight apartments. All apartment doors opened off a common stairwell. All mailboxes had names affixed to them with the exception of apartment 201. None of those names were Morelli.

For lack of a better plan, I decided to go with the mystery door. Adrenaline tripped into my bloodstream as I turned to the stairs. By the time I reached the second-floor landing, my heart was pounding. Stage fright, I told myself. Perfectly normal. I took a few deep breaths and without benefit of brain managed to motor myself to the appropriate door. A hand was knocking on the door. Holy cow, it was my hand.

I sensed movement behind the door. Someone was inside, looking at me through the security peephole. Morelli? I knew it with a certainty. Air stuck in my lungs, and my pulse throbbed painfully in my throat. Why was I doing this? I was a buyer for cheap lingerie. What did I know about catching murderers?

Don't think of him as a murderer, I reasoned. Think of him as a macho jerk. Think of him as the man who led you astray and then wrote the details on the men's room wall at Mario's Sub Shop. I gnawed on my lip and sent a wobbly smile of hope and insecurity to the person behind the peephole, telling myself no macho jerk could resist coming to the aid of that much guileless stupidity.

Another moment passed, and I could almost hear him silently swearing, debating the wisdom of opening the door. I did a little finger wave at the peephole. It was tentative, nonthreatening. It told him I was a piece of fluff, and I knew he was there.

The bolt slid back, the door was yanked open, and I found myself face-to-face with Morelli.

His stance was passive-aggressive, his voice laced with impatience. "What?"

He was more solid than I'd remembered. More angry. His eyes were more remote, the line of his mouth more cynical. I'd come looking for a boy who might have killed out of passion. I suspected the man standing in front of me would kill with professional detachment.

I took a moment to steady my voice, to formulate the lie. "I'm looking for Joe Juniak. . . ."

"You got the wrong apartment. There's no Juniak here."

I feigned confusion. Forced a tight smile. "Sorry . . ." I took a step backward and was about to bolt down the stairs when recognition hit Morelli.

"Jesus Christ!" he said. "Stephanie Plum?"

I was familiar with the tone of voice and the sentiment behind it. My father used that same tone when he caught the Smullens' dog lifting its leg on his hydrangea bush. Fine by me, I told myself. Get it straight from the beginning there was no love lost between us. That made my job easier.

"Joseph Morelli," I said. "What a surprise."

His expression narrowed. "Yeah. Almost as surprising as when you nailed me with your father's car."

In the interest of avoiding confrontation, I felt compelled to explain. I didn't feel obliged to do it convincingly. "It was an accident. My foot slipped."

"That was no accident. You jumped the goddamn curb and followed me down the sidewalk. You could have killed me." He leaned beyond the doorjamb and looked the length of the hallway. "So what are you *really* doing here? You read about me in the papers and decide my life wasn't fucked up enough?"

My plan evaporated in a rush of pique. "I could care less about your fucked-up life," I snapped. "I'm working for my cousin Vinnie. You're in violation of your bond agreement."

Good going, Stephanie. Wonderful control.

He grinned. "Vinnie sent *you* to bring me in?"

"You think that's funny?"

"Yeah, I do. And I have to tell you, I really enjoy a good joke these days, because I haven't had much to laugh about lately."

I could appreciate his point of view. If I was looking at twenty years to life, I wouldn't be laughing either. "We need to talk."

"Talk fast. I'm in a hurry."

I figured I had about forty seconds to convince him to give himself up. Hit him with the heavy stuff right off, I thought. Appeal to his familial guilt. "What about your mother?"

"What about her?"

"She signed the bond agreement. She's going to

be responsible for $100,000. She'll have to mort-
gage her house. And what will she say to everyone,
that her son Joe was too cowardly to stand trial?"

The contours of his face hardened. "You're wasting your time. I have no intention of going back
into custody. They'll lock me up and throw away
the key, and in the process I stand an excellent
chance of getting dead. You know what happens to
cops in prison. It's not nice. And if you want to
know more of the ugly truth, you'd be the last person I'd let collect the bounty money. You're a lunatic. You ran me over with a goddamn Buick."

I'd been telling myself I didn't give a hoot about
Morelli and his opinion of me, but in all honesty,
his animosity hurt. Deep down inside, I'd wanted
him to hold a tender feeling for me. I wanted to ask
him why he'd never called after he'd seduced me
in the bakery. Instead, I yelled at him. "You deserved to get run over. And besides, I barely tapped
you. The only reason you broke your leg was because you panicked and tripped over your own
feet."

"You're lucky I didn't sue you."

"You're lucky I didn't put the car into reverse
and back over you three or four times."

Morelli rolled his eyes and threw his hands into
the air. "I gotta go. I'd love to stand around and try
to understand female logic. . . ."

"Female logic? Excuse me?"

Morelli turned from the door, shrugged into a

lightweight sports coat, and grabbed the black nylon duffel from the floor. "I've got to get out of here."

"Where are you going?"

He nudged me aside, shoved an ugly black gun under the waistband of his Levi's, locked his door, and pocketed the key. "None of your business."

"Listen," I said, following him down the stairs. "I may be new at this apprehension stuff, but I'm not stupid, and I'm not a quitter. I told Vinnie I'd bring you in and that's exactly what I intend to do. You can run if you want, but I'll track you down and find you, and I'll do whatever is necessary to apprehend you."

What a load of bull! I couldn't believe I was saying it. I'd been lucky to find him this first time, and the only way I was ever going to apprehend him was if I stumbled upon him already bound, gagged, and knocked unconscious. Even then, I wasn't sure how far I could drag him.

He left through a back entrance and headed for a late-model car parked close to the building. "Don't bother tracing the plate," he said. "The car is borrowed. I'll have a different one an hour from now. And don't waste your energy following me. I'll lose you. I guarantee it."

He dumped the duffel onto the front seat, started to get into the car, and stopped. He turned and straightened, hooked an elbow over the door frame, and for the first time since I'd popped up on his doorstep he took a few moments to actually look at me. The first rush of angry emotion was gone, and in its place was quiet assessment. This was the cop, I thought. The Morelli I didn't know. The grown-up Morelli, if such an animal existed. Or maybe it was just the old Morelli, looking for a new angle.

"I like the way you've let your hair go curly," he finally said. "Suits your personality. Lots of energy, not much control, sexy as hell."

"You know nothing about my personality."

"I know about the sexy as hell part."

I felt my face burn. "Tactless of you to remind me."

Morelli grinned. "You're right. And you could be right about the Buick business, too. I probably deserved to get run over."

"Was that an apology?"

"No. But you can hold the flashlight next time we play train."

IT WAS ALMOST ONE WHEN I RETURNED TO VIN-nie's office. I slouched in a chair by Connie's desk and tipped my head back to get maximum benefit from the air-conditioning.

"You been out jogging?" Connie asked. "I haven't seen that much sweat since Nixon."

"My car doesn't have air."

"Bummer. How's it going with Morelli? You get any leads?"

"That's why I'm here. I need help. This capturing

stuff isn't as easy as it sounds. I need to talk to someone who's an expert at this job."

"I know just the guy. Ranger. His full name is Ricardo Carlos Mañoso. Second generation Cuban-American. Was Special Forces. Works for Vinnie now. He makes apprehensions other agents only dream about. He gets a little creative sometimes, but hey, that's the way it is with a genius, right?"

"Creative?"

"Doesn't always play by the rules."

"Oh."

"Like Clint Eastwood in that Dirty Harry movie," Connie said. "You don't have a problem with Clint Eastwood, do you?"

She punched a number on her speed dial, connected with Ranger's pager, and left a call-back message. "Not to worry," she said, smiling. "This guy'll tell you everything you need to know."

An hour later, I sat across from Ranger Mañoso in a downtown café. His straight black hair was slicked back in a ponytail. His biceps looked like they'd been carved out of granite and buffed up with Armor All. He was around 5' 10" with a muscular neck and a don't-mess-with-me body. I placed him in his late twenties.

He leaned back and grinned. "Sooooo, Connie says I'm supposed to make you into a badass fugitive apprehension agent. She says you need to get the crash course. What's the rush?"

"You see the brown Nova at the curb?"

His eyes swiveled to the front window. "Uh huh."

"That's my car."

He gave an almost imperceptible nod. "So you need money. Anything else?"

"Personal reasons."

"Bond enforcement is dangerous business. Those personal reasons better be pretty fucking good."

"What are your reasons for doing this?"

He did a palms up gesture. "It's what I do best."

Good answer, I thought. More eloquent than mine. "Maybe someday I'll be good at this, too. Right now my motive is steady employment."

"Vinnie give you a skip?"

"Joseph Morelli."

He tipped his head back and laughed, and the sound boomed off the walls of the little sandwich shop. "Oh, man! Are you kidding me? You aren't gonna get that dude. This isn't some street punk you're going after. This guy's smart. And he's good. You know what I'm telling you?"

"Connie says *you're* good."

"There's me, and then there's you, and you aren't ever gonna be as good as me, Sweet Thing."

At the best of times my patience was lacking, and this wasn't nearly the best of times. "Let me make my position clear to you," I said, leaning forward. "I'm out of work. I've had my car repossessed, my refrigerator is empty, I'm going to get kicked out of my apartment, and my feet don't fit in these shoes. I haven't got a lot of energy to waste socializing. Are you going to help me or what?"

Mañoso grinned. "This is gonna be fun. This here's gonna be like Professor Higgins and Eliza Doolittle Does Trenton."

"What do I call you?" I asked him.

"My street name. Ranger."

He reached across the table and took the paperwork I'd brought. He scanned the bond agreement. "You do anything on this yet? You check out his apartment?"

"He wasn't there, but I got lucky and found him in an apartment on State Street. I got there just as he was leaving."

"And?"

"He left."

"Shit," Ranger said. "Didn't anybody tell you that you were supposed to stop him?"

"I asked him to come to the police station with me, but he said he didn't want to."

Another bark of laughter. "I don't suppose you've got a gun?"

"You think I should get one?"

"Might be a good idea," he said, still beaming. He finished reading the bond agreement. "Morelli offed a guy named Ziggy Kulesza. Used his personal piece to put a .45 hydroshock between Ziggy's eyes at close range." Ranger glanced up at me. "You know anything about guns?"

"I know I don't like them."

"A .45 hydroshock goes in nice and neat, but when it comes out it makes a hole the size of a potato. You end up with brains all over the place. Ziggy's head probably exploded like an egg in a microwave."

"Gee, I'm glad you shared that with me."

His smile lit up the room. "I figured you'd want to know." He tipped back in his chair and folded his arms across his chest. "You know any of the background on this case?"

"According to newspaper articles Morty Beyers clipped to the bond agreement, the shooting took place late at night a little over a month ago in an apartment building on Shaw. Morelli was off duty and had gone to visit Carmen Sanchez. Morelli claimed Carmen had called him concerning a police matter, that he'd responded, and that when he got to Carmen's apartment, Ziggy Kulesza answered the door and drew on him. Morelli claimed he shot Ziggy in self-defense.

"Carmen's neighbors told a different story. Several of them rushed into the hall at the sound of gunfire and found Morelli standing over Kulesza with a smoking gun. One of the tenants subdued Morelli until the police arrived. None of the tenants could remember seeing a gun in Ziggy's hand, and the immediate investigation didn't turn up any evidence that Ziggy had been armed.

"Morelli had placed a second man in Carmen's apartment at the time of the shooting, and three of the tenants remembered seeing an unfamiliar face, but the man apparently disappeared before the police came on the scene."

"And what about Carmen?" Ranger asked.

"No one could remember seeing Carmen. The last article was written a week after the shooting, and as of that date, Carmen still hadn't surfaced."

Ranger nodded. "You know anything else?"

"That's about it."

"The guy Morelli shot worked for Benito Ramirez. The name mean anything?"

"Ramirez is a boxer."

"More than a boxer. He's a fucking wonder. Heavyweight. The biggest thing to happen to Trenton since George shafted the Hessians. Trains in a gym on Stark Street. Ziggy used to stick to Ramirez like white on rice. Sometimes Ziggy'd do some sparring. Mostly Ramirez kept him on as a gofer and a bodyguard."

"There any word on the street about why Morelli shot Kulesza?"

Ranger gave me a slow stare. "None. But Morelli must have had a good reason. Morelli's a cool guy, and if a cop wants to pop someone, there are ways."

"Even cool cops make mistakes."

"Not like this, babe. Not Morelli."

"So what are you telling me?"

"I'm telling you to be careful."

All of a sudden I had a sick feeling in my stomach. This wasn't just some slick adventure I was embarking upon to make a fast buck. Catching Morelli would be difficult. And turning him back in to the court would feel mean. He wasn't my favorite person, but I didn't hate him enough to want to see him spend the rest of his life in prison.

"You still want to tag him?" Ranger asked.

I was silent.

"If you don't do it, someone else will," Ranger said. "That's something you got to learn. And you got no business making judgments. You just do your job, and bring the man in. Got to trust in the system."

"Do you trust in the system?"

"Beats the shit out of anarchy."

"There's a lot of money involved here. If you're so good, why didn't Vinnie give Morelli to you? Why did he originally give him to Morty Beyers?"

"Vinnie moves in mysterious ways."

"Anything else I should know about Morelli?"

"If you want your money, you better find your man fast. Rumor has it the judicial system is the least of his problems."

"Are you telling me there's a contract out on him?"

Ranger made a gun sign with his hand. "Bang."

"You sure about this rumor?"

He shrugged. "Just repeating what I heard."

"The plot thickens," I said to Ranger.

"Like I said before, you don't care about the plot. Your job is simple. Find the man, bring him in."

"Do you think I can do it?"

"No."

If he was trying to discourage me, that was the wrong answer. "Will you help me anyway?"

"Long as you don't tell nobody. Wouldn't want to tarnish my image by looking like a good guy."

I nodded. "Okay, where do I begin?"

"First thing we need to do is get you outfitted. And while we collect your hardware, I'm gonna tell you about the law."

"This isn't going to be expensive, is it?"

"My time and knowledge are coming to you free of charge because I like you, and I always wanted to be Professor Higgins, but handcuffs cost $40 a pair. You got plastic?"

I was all out of plastic. I'd hocked my few pieces of good jewelry and sold my living room sleep sofa to one of my neighbors to make my charge card payments. My major appliances had gone for the Nova. The only thing left was a small cache of emergency money which I'd steadfastly refused to touch. I'd been saving it to use on orthopedic reconstruction after the bill collectors broke my knees.

Well hell, it probably wasn't nearly enough money for new knees anyway. "I have a few dollars set aside," I said.

I DROPPED MY NEW BIG BLACK LEATHER SHOULDER bag on the floor by my chair and took my place at the dinner table. My mother and father and Grandma Mazur were already seated, waiting to hear to hear how it went with Vinnie.

"You're twelve minutes late," my mother said. "I was listening for sirens. You weren't in an accident, were you?"

"I was working."

"Already?" She turned to my father. "The first day on the job and your cousin has her working overtime. You should talk to him, Frank."

"It's not like that," I told her. "My hours are flexible."

"Your father worked at the post office for thirty years, and he never once came home late for dinner."

A sigh popped out before I could squelch it.

"So what's with the sigh?" my mother asked. "And the new pocketbook. When did you get the new pocketbook?"

"I got the pocketbook today. I need to carry some things around with me for this job. I had to get a bigger bag."

"What things do you need? I thought you were doing filing."

"I didn't get that job. I got another job."

"What job did you get?"

I poured ketchup on my meatloaf and barely restrained a second sigh. "Recovery agent," I said. "I've got a job as a recovery agent."

"A recovery agent," my mother repeated. "Frank, do you know what a recovery agent is?"

"Yeah," he said. "Bounty hunter."

My mother slapped her forehead and rolled her eyes. "Stephanie, Stephanie, Stephanie, what are you thinking of? This is no kind of work for a nice young lady."

"It's a legitimate, respectable job," I said. "It's like being a cop or a private investigator." Neither one of which I had ever considered to be especially respectable.

"But you don't know anything about this."

"It's simple," I said. "Vinnie gives me an FTA, and then I find him and escort him back to the police station."

"What's an FTA?" my mother wanted to know.

"It's a person who's Failed To Appear."

"Maybe I could be a bounty hunter," Grandma Mazur said. "I could use to earn some spending money. I could go after those FTAs with you."

"Jesus," my father said.

My mother ignored both of them. "You should learn to make slipcovers," she said to me. "There's always a need for slipcovers." She looked at my father. "Frank, don't you think she should learn to make slipcovers? Isn't that a good idea?"

I felt the muscles tense along my spine and made an effort to relax. Buck up, I told myself. This was good practice for tomorrow morning when I intended to visit Morelli's mother.

• • •

IN THE ORDER OF THE BURG, JOSEPH MORELLI'S
mother made my mother look like a second-rate
housewife. My mother was no slouch, but by burg
standards, Mrs. Morelli was a housewife of heroic
proportions. God himself couldn't get windows
cleaner, wash whiter, or make better ziti than Mrs.
Morelli. She never missed mass, she sold Amway
in her spare time, and she scared the beejeebers out
of me with her piercing black eyes. I didn't think
Mrs. Morelli was likely to snitch on her last born,
but she was on my quiz list anyway. No stone un-
turned.

Joe's father could have been bought for five
bucks and a six-pack, but his father was dead.

I'd opted for a professional image this morning,
dressing in a tailored beige linen suit, complete with
pantyhose and heels and tasteful pearl earrings. I
parked at the curb, climbed the porch stairs, and
knocked on the Morelli front door.

"Well," Momma Morelli said, standing behind
the screen, staring out at me with a degree of cen-
sure usually reserved for atheists and slackers.
"Look who's here on my porch, bright and early . . .
little miss bounty hunter." She boosted her chin up
an additional inch. "I heard all about you and your
new job, and I have nothing to say to you."

"I need to find Joe, Mrs. Morelli. He missed a
court appearance."

"I'm sure he had good reason."

Yeah. Like he's guilty as hell. "I tell you what, I'll leave my card, just in case. I got them made yesterday." I rooted through the big black bag, finding handcuffs, hair spray, flashlight, hairbrush—no cards. I tipped the bag to look inside, and my gun fell out onto the green indoor-outdoor carpeting.

"A gun," Mrs. Morelli said. "What is this world coming to? Does your mother know you're carrying a gun? I'm going to tell her. I'm going to call and tell her right now."

She sent me a look of utter disgust and slammed the front door shut.

I was thirty years old, and Mrs. Morelli was going to tell my mother on me. Only in the burg. I retrieved my gun, dumped it back into my purse, and found my cards. I stuck one of the cards between the screen and the molding. Then I drove the short distance back to my parents' house and used their phone to call my cousin Francie, who knew everything about everyone.

He's long gone, Francie had said. He's a smart guy and he's probably wearing a fake mustache by now. He was a cop. He has contacts. He knows how to get a new social security number and start over far away. Give it up, Francie had said. You'll never find him.

Intuition and desperation told me otherwise, so I called Eddie Gazarra, who was a Trenton cop and had been one of my very best friends since the day I was born. Not only was he a good friend, but he was married to my cousin, Shirley the Whiner. Why

Gazarra had married Shirley was beyond my comprehension, but they'd been married for eleven years so I suppose they had something going between them.

I didn't bother with chitchat when I got Gazarra. I went right to the heart of the matter, telling him about my job with Vinnie and asking what he knew about the Morelli shooting.

"I know it's nothing you want to get involved in," Gazarra said. "You want to work for Vinnie? Fine. Get him to give you some other case."

"Too late. I'm doing this one."

"This one has a real bad odor."

"Everything in New Jersey has a bad odor. It's one of the few things a person can count on."

Gazarra lowered his voice. "When a cop gets charged with murder, it's serious shit. Everybody gets touchy. And this murder was especially ugly because the physical evidence was so strong against Morelli. He was apprehended at the scene with the gun still warm in his hand. He claimed Ziggy was armed, but there was no weapon found, no bullet discharged into the opposite wall or floor or ceiling, no powder residue on Ziggy's hand or shirt. The grand jury had no choice but to indict Morelli. And then if things aren't bad enough . . . Morelli goes Failure To Appear. This is a black eye to the department and fucking embarrassing. You mention Morelli in the halls and everybody suddenly remembers they've got something to do. Nobody's going to be happy about you sticking your nose in this. You go after Morelli and you're gonna be swinging on a broken branch, high off the ground, all alone."

"If I bring him in, I get $10,000."

"Buy lottery tickets. Your chances will be better."

"It's my understanding that Morelli went to see Carmen Sanchez, but that Sanchez wasn't there when he arrived."

"Not only wasn't she on the scene, but she's disappeared off the face of the earth."

"Still?"

"Still. And don't think we haven't looked for her."

"What about the guy Morelli says was in the apartment with Ziggy. The mystery witness?"

"Vanished."

I felt my nose wrinkle in disbelief. "Do you think this is odd?"

"I think it's odder than odd."

"Maybe Morelli went bad."

I could feel Gazarra shrug over the phone line. "All I know is my cop intuition tells me something doesn't add up."

"You think Morelli'll join the Foreign Legion?"

"I think he'll stick around and work to improve his odds on longevity . . . or die trying."

I was relieved to hear my opinion reinforced. "You have any suggestions?"

"None you want to hear."

"Come on, Eddie. I need help."

Another sigh. "You're not going to find him hiding out with a relative or a friend. He's smarter than that. The only thing I can think of is to look for Carmen Sanchez and the guy Morelli said was in the apartment with Ziggy. If I was Morelli, I'd want to get those two missing persons, either to prove my innocence, or to make sure they couldn't prove my guilt. I haven't a clue how you do this. We can't find them and chances are you can't find them either."

I thanked Gazarra and hung up. Looking for the witnesses sounded like a good idea. I didn't necessarily care that it was an impossible mission. What I cared about was that if I started running down leads on Carmen Sanchez, I might be following the same route as Morelli and maybe our paths would cross again.

Where to begin? Carmen's apartment building. I could talk to her neighbors, maybe get a line on her friends and family. What else? Talk to the boxer, Benito Ramirez. If Ramirez and Ziggy were all that close, maybe Ramirez knew Carmen Sanchez. Maybe he even had some ideas about the missing witness.

I took a can of soda from the refrigerator and a box of Fig Newtons from the pantry, deciding to talk to Ramirez first.

THREE

STARK STREET STARTED DOWN BY THE RIVER, JUST north of the statehouse, and ran in a northeasterly direction. Crammed with small inner-city businesses, bars, crack houses, and cheerless three-story row houses, the street stretched close to a mile. Most of the row houses had been converted to apartments or rooms to let. Few were air-conditioned. All were overcrowded. When it was hot, residents spilled from the row houses onto the stoops and street corners, looking for air and action. At ten-thirty in the morning, the street was still relatively quiet.

I missed the gym first time around, rechecked the address from the page I'd torn out of my phone book, and doubled back, driving slowly, reading off street numbers. I caught the sign, Stark Street Gym, professionally lettered in black on a door window. Not much of an advertisement, but then I supposed they didn't need much. They weren't exactly in competition with Spa Lady. It took two additional blocks before I found a parking space.

I locked the Nova, hung my big black bag over my shoulder, and set out. I'd put the fiasco with Mrs. Morelli behind me, and felt pretty damn slick in my suit and heels, toting my bounty hunter hardware. Embarrassing as it was to admit, I was beginning to enjoy the role, thinking there was nothing like packing a pair of cuffs to put some spring into a woman's step.

The gym sat in the middle of its block, over A & K Auto Body. The bay doors to the auto body were open, and catcalls and kissy sounds drifted out to me when I crossed the cement apron. My New Jersey heritage weighed heavy, demanding I respond with a few demeaning comments of my own, but discretion being the better part of valor, I kept my mouth shut and hurried on by.

Across the street, a shadowy figure pulled back from a filthy third-floor window, the movement catching my attention. Someone had been watching me. Not surprising. I'd roared down the street not once, but twice. My muffler had fallen off first thing this morning, and my engine noise had rumbled off the Stark Street brick storefronts. This wasn't what you'd call an undercover operation.

The door to the gym opened onto a small foyer with steps leading up. The stairwell walls were institutional green, covered with spray-painted graffiti and twenty years' worth of hand smudges. The smell was bad, ripe with urine steaming on the lower steps, bonding with the musty aroma of stale male sweat and body odor. Upstairs, the warehouse-style second floor was no better.

A handful of men were working the free weights. The ring was empty. No one was at the bags. I figured everybody must be out jumping rope or stealing cars. It was the last flip thought I entertained. Activity faltered when I entered, and if I'd been uncomfortable on the street, it hardly counted at all to what I felt here. I'd expected a champion to be surrounded by an aura of professionalism. I hadn't anticipated the atmosphere to be charged with hostility and suspicion. I was clearly a street-ignorant white woman invading a black man's gym, and if the silent rebuke had been any more forceful I'd have been hurled backward, down the stairs like a victim of a poltergeist.

I took a wide stance (more to keep myself from falling over in fright than to impress the boys) and hitched up my shoulder bag. "I'm looking for Benito Ramirez."

A hulking mountain of muscle rose from a workout bench. "I'm Ramirez."

He was over 6' tall. His voice was silky, his lips curved into a dreamy smile. The overall effect was eerie, the voice and the smile at odds to the stealthy, calculating eyes.

I crossed the room and extended my hand. "Stephanie Plum."

"Benito Ramirez."

His grasp was too gentle, too lingering. More of a caress than a handshake and unpleasantly sensual. I stared into his hooded, close-set eyes and wondered about prizefighters. Until this moment, I'd assumed boxing was a sport of skill and aggression, directed toward winning the match, not necessarily toward maiming the opponent. Ramirez looked like he'd enjoy the kill. There was something about the density of his eyes, black holes where everything gets sucked in and nothing comes out, that suggested a hiding place for evil. And the smile, a little goofy, a little sick in its sweetness, hinting of insanity. I wondered if this was a contrived image, designed to spook opponents before the bell. Contrived or not, it was creepy as hell.

I made an attempt to free my hand, and his grip tightened.

"So, Stephanie Plum," he said in his velvet voice. "What can I do for you?"

As a buyer for E.E. Martin, I'd dealt with my share of slime. I'd learned how to assert myself and still be pleasant and professional. My face and voice told Ramirez I was friendly. My words were more to the point. "You can release my hand, so I can give you my card," I said.

His smile stayed fixed in place, more amiable and inquisitive now than crazy. I gave him my card and watched him read it.

"Fugitive apprehension agent," he said, obviously amused. "That's a big title for a little girl."

I'd never thought of myself as little until I'd stood alongside Ramirez. I'm 5' 7" and rawboned from the Mazurs' good Hungarian peasant stock. Perfectly constructed for laboring in the paprika fields, pulling plows, and dropping babies out like bird's eggs. I ran and periodically starved to keep the fat off, but I still weighed in at 130. Not heavy, but not dainty, either. "I'm looking for Joe Morelli. Have you seen him?"

Ramirez shook his head. "I don't know Joe Morelli. I only know he shot Ziggy." He looked around at the rest of the men. "Any of you seen that guy Morelli?"

No one responded.

"I've been told there was a witness to the shooting and that the witness has disappeared," I said. "Do you have any idea who that witness might be?"

Again, no response.

I pushed on. "How about Carmen Sanchez? Do you know Carmen? Did Ziggy ever speak of her?"

"You ask a lot of questions," Ramirez said.

We were standing close to the big old-fashioned windows in the front of the room, and for no reason other than instinct, I shifted my attention to the building across the street. Again, the shadowy figure

in the same third-floor window. A man, I thought.
I couldn't tell if he was black or white. Not that it
mattered.

Ramirez stroked my jacket sleeve. "Would you
like a Coke? We got a Coke machine here. I could
buy you a soda."

"Thanks for the offer, but I have a busy morning,
and I really should be moving along. If you spot
Morelli, I'd appreciate a call."

"Most girls think it's a treat for the champ to buy
them a soda."

Not this girl, I thought. This girl thought the
champ was possibly missing a few marbles. And
this girl didn't like the climate of the gym.

"I'd really love to stay and have a soda," I said,
"but I have an early lunch date." With a box of Fig
Newtons.

"It's not good to go rushing around. You should
stay and relax a little. Your date won't mind."

I shifted my weight, trying to inch away while I
enhanced the lie. "Actually, it's a business luncheon
with Sergeant Gazarra."

"I don't believe you," Ramirez said. His smile
had turned tight, and the civility had slipped from
his voice. "I think you're lying about lunch."

I felt tendrils of panic curl into my stomach, and
I cautioned myself not to overreact. Ramirez was
playing with me. Showing off in front of his friends.
Probably stung because I hadn't succumbed to his
charms. Now he had to save face.

I made a display of looking at my watch. "Sorry you feel that way, but I'm supposed to meet Gazarra in ten minutes. He's not going to be pleased if I'm late."

I took a step backward, and Ramirez grabbed me by the scruff of my neck, his fingers digging in with enough force to make me hunch involuntarily.

"You're not going anywhere, Stephanie Plum," he whispered. "The champ isn't done with you yet."

The silence in the gym was oppressive. No one moved. No one voiced an objection. I looked at each of the men and received only blank stares back. No one's going to help me, I thought, feeling the first licks of real fear.

I lowered my voice to match Ramirez's soft pitch. "I came here as a member of the law enforcement community. I came looking for information to help me with the recovery of Joe Morelli, and I gave you no reason to misinterpret my intentions. I'm conducting myself as a professional, and I expect you to respect that."

Ramirez dragged me closer. "Something you got to understand about the champ," he said. "First off, you don't tell the champ about respect. And second, you got to know the champ always gets what he wants." He gave me a shake. "You know what the champ wants right now? The champ wants you to be nice to him, baby. Real nice. Gotta make up for refusing him. Show him some respect." His gaze shifted to my breasts. "Maybe show him some fear. You afraid of me, bitch?"

Any woman with an IQ over twelve would be afraid of Benito Ramirez.

He giggled and all the little hairs on my arm stood straight out.

"You're scared now," he said in his whispery voice. "I can smell it. Pussy fear. Bet it making your pants wet. Maybe I should put my hand in your pants and find out."

I had a gun in my bag, and I'd use it if I had to, but not until all else had failed. Ten minutes of instruction hadn't made me a crack shot. That's okay, I told myself. I didn't want to kill anyone. I just wanted to back everyone up enough to get the hell out. I slid my hand over the leather bag until I felt the gun, hard and unyielding under my palm.

Reach in, get the gun, I thought. Take aim at Ramirez and look serious. Could I pull the trigger? I honestly didn't know. I had my doubts. I hoped I wouldn't have to take it that far.

"Let go of my neck," I said. "This is the last time I'm telling you."

"Nobody tell the champ what to do," he roared, his composure gone, his face twisted and ugly. For a split second the door swung open, and I caught a glimpse of the inner man—a glimpse of insanity, and of hellfires burning and hatred so strong it whipped my breath away.

He grabbed the front of my shirt, and over my scream, I heard the fabric tear.

In times of crisis, when a person reacts on instinct, that person does whatever is most comfortable. I did what any other American woman would do in a similar circumstance. I roundhoused Ramirez square on the side of his head with my purse. Between the gun and the beeper and the other assorted paraphernalia, the bag must have weighed at least ten pounds.

Ramirez staggered sideways, and I bolted for the stairs. I didn't get five feet before he jerked me back by my hair and flung me across the room like a rag doll. I lost footing and went facedown to the floor, my hands hitting first, skidding over unvarnished wood, my body following, the impact knocking the air from my lungs.

Ramirez straddled me, his butt on my back, his hand fisting in my hair, pulling savagely. I grabbed at my bag, but I was unable to get to the gun.

I heard the crack of a high-powered weapon, and the front windows shattered. More shots. Someone was emptying a clip into the gym. Men were running and shouting, looking for cover. Ramirez was among them. I was moving, too, crab style across the floor, my legs not able to support me. I reached the stairs, stood, and lunged for the railing. I missed the second step, too panicked to coordinate my movements, and half slid the rest of the way down to the cracked linoleum landing at street level. I dragged myself to my feet and staggered outside into the heat and blinding sunlight. My stockings were torn and my knees were bleeding. I was hanging on to the door handle, laboring to breathe when a hand clamped onto my upper arm. I jumped and yelped. It was Joe Morelli.

"For crissake," he said, yanking me forward. "Don't just stand here. Haul ass!"

I wasn't sure Ramirez cared enough about me to come charging down the stairs, but it seemed prudent not to hang around and find out, so I clattered after Morelli with my chest burning from oxygen depravation and my skirt hiked up to my crotch. Kathleen Turner would have made it look good on the big screen. I was something less than glamorous. My nose was running, and I think I was drooling. I was grunting in pain and sniveling from fear, making ugly animal sounds and inventive promises to God.

We turned at the corner, cut through an alley on the next block, and ran down a narrow one-lane road carved out between backyards. The road was lined with broken-down single-car wooden garages and overflowing bashed-in garbage cans.

Sirens sounded two blocks away. No doubt a couple of cruisers and an ambulance responding to the shooting. Hindsight told me I should have stayed close to the gym and conned the cops into helping me track down Morelli. Something to remember next time I'm almost raped and brutalized.

Morelli stopped abruptly and jerked me into an empty garage. The double doors were cocked open enough to slide through, not enough for a passerby to see inside. The floor was packed dirt, and the air was close, smelling metallic. I was struck by the irony of it. Here I was, after all these years, once again in a garage with Morelli. I could see the anger in his face, hardening his eyes, pinching at the corners of his mouth. He grabbed me by the front of my suit jacket and pinned me against the crude wooden wall. The impact knocked dust from the rafters and made my teeth clack together.

His voice was tight with barely controlled fury. "What the hell did you think you were doing walking into the gym like that?"

He punctuated the end of the question with another body slam, rattling more filth onto the two of us.

"Answer me!" he ordered.

The pain was all mental. I'd been stupid. And now, to add insult to injury, I was getting bullied by Morelli. It was almost as humiliating as getting rescued by him. "I was looking for you."

"Well congratulations, you found me. You also blew my cover, and I'm not happy about it."

"You were the shadow in the third-floor window, watching the gym from across the street."

Morelli didn't say anything. In the dark garage his eyes were dilated solid black.

I mentally cracked my knuckles. "And now I

guess there's only one thing left to do."

"I can hardly wait to hear this."

I shoved my hand into my shoulder bag, pulled out my revolver, and jabbed Morelli in the chest with it. "You're under arrest."

His eyes opened wide in astonishment. "You have a gun! Why didn't you use it on Ramirez? Jesus, you hit him with your pocketbook like some sissy girl. Why the hell didn't you use your damn gun?"

I felt color flooding into my cheeks. What could I say? The truth was worse than embarrassing. It was counterproductive. Admitting to Morelli that I'd been more afraid of my gun than I'd been of Ramirez wasn't going to do much to further my credibility as an apprehension agent.

It didn't take Morelli long to put it together. He made a disgusted sound, pushed the barrel aside, and took the gun from me. "If you aren't willing to use it, you shouldn't be carrying it. You have a permit to carry a concealed weapon?"

"Yes." And I was at least ten percent convinced it was legal.

"Where'd you get your permit?"

"Ranger got it for me."

"Ranger Mañoso? Christ, he probably made it in his cellar." He shook out the bullets and gave the gun back to me. "Find a new job. And stay away from Ramirez. He's nuts. He's been charged with rape on three separate occasions and been acquitted each time because the victim always disappears."

"I didn't know. . . ."

"There's a lot you don't know."

His attitude was beginning to piss me off. I was only too well aware that I had a lot to learn about apprehension. I didn't need Morelli's sarcastic superiority. "So what's your point."

"Get off my case. You want a career in law enforcement? Fine. Go for it. Just don't learn on me. I have enough problems without worrying about saving your ass."

"No one asked you to save my ass. I would have saved my own ass if you hadn't interfered."

"Honey, you couldn't find your ass with both hands."

My palms were skinned and burned like the devil. My scalp was sore. My knees throbbed. I wanted to go back to my apartment and stand in a hot shower for five or six hours until I felt clean and strong. I wanted to get away from Morelli and regroup. "I'm going home."

"Good idea," he said. "Where's your car?"

"Stark Street and Tyler."

He flattened himself at the side of the door and took a quick look out. "It's okay."

My knees had stiffened up, and the blood had dried and caked on what was left of my pantyhose. Limping seemed like an indulgent weakness not to be witnessed by the likes of Morelli, so I forged ahead, thinking ouch, ouch, ouch but not saying a word. When we got to the corner I realized he was walking me all the way to Stark. "I don't need an escort," I said. "I'll be fine."

He had his hand at my elbow, steering me forward. "Don't flatter yourself. I'm not nearly so concerned about your welfare as I am about getting you the hell out of my life. I want to make sure you leave. I want to see your tailpipe fading off into the sunset."

Good luck, I thought. My tailpipe was somewhere on Route 1, along with my muffler.

We reached Stark, and I faltered at the sight of my car. It had been parked on the street for less than an hour, and in that time it had been spray-painted from one end to the other. Mostly Day-Glo pink and green, and the predominant word on both sides was "pussy." I checked the plate and looked in the backseat for the box of Fig Newtons. Yep, this was my car.

One more indignity in a day filled with indignities. Did I care? Not a whole lot. I was numb. I was becoming immune to indignity. I searched through my bag for my keys, found them, and plugged them into the door.

Morelli rocked back on his heels, hands in his pockets, a grin beginning to creep to his lips. "Most people are content with pinstriping and a vanity plate."

"Eat dirt and die."

Morelli tipped his head back and laughed out

loud. His laughter was deep and rich and infectious, and if I hadn't been so distraught, I'd have laughed along with him. As it was, I jerked the car door open and rammed myself behind the wheel. I turned the key in the ignition, gave the dash a good hard smack, and left him choking in a cloud of exhaust and a blast of noise that had the potential to liquify his insides.

OFFICIALLY, I LIVED AT THE EASTERN BOUNDARY of the city of Trenton, but in actuality my neighborhood felt more like Hamilton Township than Trenton proper. My apartment building was an ugly dark red brick cube built before central air and thermal pane windows. Eighteen apartments in all, evenly distributed over three floors. By modern-day standards it wasn't a terrific apartment. It didn't come with a pool membership or have tennis courts attached. The elevator was unreliable. The bathroom was vintage Partridge family with mustard yellow amenities and French Provincial trim on the vanity. The kitchen appliances were a notch below generic.

The good part about the apartment was that it had been built with sturdy stuff. Sound didn't carry from apartment to apartment. The rooms were large and sunny. Ceilings were high. I lived on the second floor, and my windows overlooked the small private parking lot. The building predated the balcony boom, but I was lucky enough to have an old-fashioned black metal fire escape skirt my bedroom window. Perfect for drying pantyhose, quarantining houseplants with aphids, and just big enough for sitting out on sultry summer nights.

Most important of all, the ugly brick building wasn't part of a sprawling complex of other ugly brick buildings. It sat all by itself on a busy street of small businesses, and it bordered a neighborhood of modest frame houses. Very much like living in the burg . . . but better. My mother had a hard time stretching the umbilical this far, and the bakery was only one block away.

I parked in the lot and slunk into the back entrance. Since Morelli wasn't around, I didn't have to be brave, so I bitched and complained and limped all the way to my apartment. I showered, did the first-aid thing, and dressed in T-shirt and shorts. My knees were missing the top layer of skin and were bruised, already turning shades of magenta and midnight blue. My elbows were in pretty much the same condition. I felt like a kid who'd fallen off her bike. I could hear myself singing out "I can do it; I can do it," and then next thing I know, I'm lying on the ground, looking the fool, with two scraped knees.

I flopped onto my bed, spread-eagle on my back. This was my thinking position when things appeared to be futile. It had obvious advantages: I could nap while I waited for something brilliant to pop into my mind. I lay there for what seemed like a long time. Nothing brilliant had popped into my mind, and I was too agitated to sleep.

I couldn't stop reliving my experience with Ramirez. I'd never before been attacked by a man. Never even come close. The afternoon's assault had been a degrading, frightening experience, and now that the dust had settled, and calmer emotions prevailed, I felt violated and vulnerable.

I considered filing a report with the police, but immediately shelved it. Whining to Big Brother wasn't going to win any points for me as a rough, tough bounty hunter. I couldn't see Ranger instituting an assault charge.

I'd been lucky, I told myself. I'd gotten away with superficial injuries. Thanks to Morelli.

The latter admission dragged a groan from me. Being rescued by Morelli had been damned embarrassing. And grossly unjust. All things considered, I didn't think I was doing all that badly. I'd been on the case for less than forty-eight hours, and I'd found my man twice. True, I hadn't been able to bring him in, but I was in a learning process. No one expected a first-year engineering student to build the perfect bridge. I figured I deserved to be cut the same kind of slack.

I doubted the gun would ever be of any use to me. I couldn't imagine myself shooting Morelli. Possibly in the foot. But what were my chances of hitting a small moving target? Not good at all. Clearly, I needed a less lethal way of subduing my quarry. Maybe a defense spray would be more my style. Tomorrow morning I'd go back to Sunny's Gun Shop and add to my bag of dirty tricks.

My clock radio blinked 5:50 P.M. I looked at it dully, not immediately responding to the significance of the time, then horror ripped through me. My mother was expecting me for dinner again!

I sprang out of bed and raced to the phone. The phone was dead. I hadn't paid my bill. I grabbed the car keys from the kitchen counter and hurtled out the door.

FOUR

My mother was standing on the porch steps when I parked at the curb. She was waving her arms and shouting. I couldn't hear her over the roar of the engine, but I could read her lips. "SHUT IT OFF!" she was yelling. "SHUT IT OFF!"

"Sorry," I yelled back. "Broken muffler."

"You've got to do something. I could hear you coming four blocks away. You'll give old Mrs. Ciak heart palpitations." She squinted at the car. "Did you have it decorated?"

"It happened on Stark Street. Vandals." I pushed her into the hallway before she could read the words.

"Wow, nice knees," Grandma Mazur said, bending down to take a closer look at my ooze. "I was

watching some TV show last week, think it was
Oprah, and they had a bunch of women on with
knees like that. Said it was rug burn. Never figured
out what that meant."

"Christ," my father said from behind his paper.
He didn't need to say more. We all understood his
plight.

"It's not rug burn," I told Grandma Mazur. "I fell
on my roller blades." I wasn't worried about the lie.
I had a long history of calamitous mishaps.

I glanced at the dining room table. It was set with
the good lace tablecloth. Company. I counted the
plates. Five. I rolled my eyes heavenward. "Ma, you
didn't."

"I didn't what?"

The doorbell rang, and my worst fears were confirmed.

"It's company. It's no big deal," my mother said,
going to the door. "I guess I can invite company
into my own house if I want to."

"It's Bernie Kuntz," I said. "I can see him
through the hall window."

My mother stopped, hands on hips. "So, what's
wrong with Bernie Kuntz?"

"To begin with . . . he's a man."

"Okay, you had a bad experience. That don't
mean you should give up. Look at your sister Valerie. She's happily married for twelve years. She
has two beautiful girls."

"That's it. I'm leaving. I'm going out the back door."

"Pineapple upside-down cake," my mother said. "You'll miss dessert if you leave now. And don't think I'll save some for you."

My mother didn't mind playing dirty if she thought the cause was worthy. She knew she had me locked in with the pineapple cake. A Plum would suffer a lot of abuse for a good dessert.

Grandma Mazur glared out at Bernie. "Who are you?"

"I'm Bernie Kuntz."

"What do you want?"

I looked the length of the hall, and I could see Bernie shift uncomfortably on his feet.

"I've been invited for dinner," Bernie said.

Grandma Mazur still had the screen door shut. "Helen," she yelled over her shoulder, "there's a young man at the door. He says he's invited to dinner. Why didn't someone tell me about this? Look at this old dress I'm wearing. I can't entertain a man in this dress."

I'd known Bernie since he was five. I'd gone to grade school with Bernie. We ate lunch together in grades one through three, and I would forever associate him with peanut butter and jelly on Wonder bread. I'd lost touch with him in high school. I knew he'd gone to college, and that after college he'd gone to work selling appliances in his father's store.

He was medium height, with a medium build that had never lost its baby fat. He was all dressed up in shiny tassel loafers, dress slacks, and sports coat. So far as I could see, he hadn't changed much since sixth grade. He looked like he still couldn't add fractions, and the little metal pull on his zipper was sticking out, creating a tiny tent with his fly.

We took our seats at the table and concentrated on the business of eating.

"Bernie sells appliances," my mother said, passing the red cabbage. "He makes good money at it, too. He drives a Bonneville."

"A Bonneville. Imagine that," Grandma Mazur said.

My father kept his head bent over his chicken. He rooted for the Mets, he wore Fruit of the Loom underwear, and he drove a Buick. His loyalties were carved in stone, and he wasn't about to be impressed by some upstart of a toaster salesman who drove a Bonneville.

Bernie turned to me. "So what are you doing now?"

I fiddled with my fork. My day hadn't exactly been a success, and announcing to the world that I was a fugitive apprehension agent seemed presumptuous. "I sort of work for an insurance company," I told him.

"You mean like a claims adjuster?"

"More like collections."

"She's a bounty hunter!" Grandma Mazur announced. "She tracks down dirty rotten fugitives just like on television. She's got a gun and everything." She reached behind her to the sideboard, where I'd left my shoulder bag. "She's got a whole pocketbook full of paraphernalia," Grandma Mazur said, setting my bag on her lap. She pulled out the cuffs, the beeper, and a travel pack of tampons and set them on the table. "And here's her gun," she said proudly. "Isn't it a beauty?"

I have to admit it was a pretty cool gun. It had a stainless steel frame and carved wood grips. It was a Smith and Wesson 5-shot revolver, Model 60. A .38 Special. Easy to use, easy to carry, Ranger had said. And it had been much more reasonable than a semi-automatic, if you can call $400 reasonable.

"My God," my mother shouted, "put it away! Someone take the gun from her before she kills herself!"

The cylinder was open and clearly empty of rounds. I didn't know much about guns, but I knew this one couldn't go bang without bullets. "It's empty," I said. "There are no bullets in it."

Grandma Mazur had both hands wrapped around the gun with her finger on the trigger. She scrinched an eye closed and sighted on the china closet. "Ka-pow," she said. "Ka-pow, ka-pow, ka-pow."

My father was busy with the sausage dressing, studiously ignoring all of us.

"I don't like guns at the table," my mother said.

"And the dinner's getting cold. I'll have to reheat the gravy."

"This gun won't do you no good if you don't have bullets in it," Grandma Mazur said to me. "How're you gonna catch those killers without bullets in your gun?"

Bernie had been sitting openmouthed through all of this. "Killers?"

"She's after Joe Morelli," Grandma Mazur told him. "He's a bona fide killer and a bail dodger. He plugged Ziggy Kulesza right in the head."

"I knew Ziggy Kulesza," Bernie said. "I sold him a big-screen TV about a year ago. We don't sell many big screens. Too expensive."

"He buy anything else from you?" I asked. "Anything recent?"

"Nope. But I'd see him sometimes across the street at Sal's Butcher Shop. Ziggy seemed okay. Just a regular sort of person, you know?"

No one had been paying attention to Grandma Mazur. She was still playing with the gun, aiming and sighting, getting used to the heft of it. I realized there was a box of ammo beside the tampons. A scary thought skittered into my mind. "Grandma, you didn't load the gun, did you?"

"Well of course I loaded the gun," she said. "And I left the one hole empty like I saw on television. That way you can't shoot nothing by mistake." She cocked the gun to demonstrate the safety of her action. There was a loud bang, a flash erupted from the gun barrel, and the chicken carcass jumped on its plate.

"Holy mother of God!" my mother shrieked, leaping to her feet, knocking her chair over.

"Dang," Grandma said, "guess I left the wrong hole empty." She leaned forward to examine her handiwork. "Not bad for my first time with a gun. I shot that sucker right in the gumpy."

My father had a white-knuckle grip on his fork, and his face was cranberry red.

I scurried around the table and carefully took the gun from Grandma Mazur. I shook out the bullets and shoveled all my stuff back into my shoulder bag.

"Look at that broken plate," my mother said. "It was part of the set. How will I ever replace it?" She moved the plate, and we all stared in silence at the neat round hole in the tablecloth and the bullet embedded in the mahogany table.

Grandma Mazur was the first to speak. "That shooting gave me an appetite," she said. "Somebody pass me the potatoes."

ALL IN ALL, BERNIE KUNTZ HAD HANDLED THE evening pretty well. He hadn't wet his pants when Grandma Mazur shot off the chicken privates. He'd suffered through two helpings of my mother's dreaded brusels sprouts casserole. And he'd been tolerably nice to me, even though it was obvious we weren't destined to hit the sheets together and my family was nuts. His motives for geniality were clear. I was a woman lacking appliances. Romance is good for frittering away a few evening hours, but commissions will get you a vacation in Hawaii. Ours was a match made in heaven. He wanted to sell, and I wanted to buy, and I wasn't unhappy to accept his offer of a 10 percent discount. And, as a bonus for sitting through the evening, I'd learned something about Ziggy Kulesza. He bought his meat from Sal Bocha, a man better known for making book than slicing fillet.

I tucked this information away for future reference. It didn't seem significant now, but who knows what would turn out to be helpful.

I was at my table with a glass of iced tea and Morelli's file, and I was trying to put together a plan of action. I'd made a bowl of popcorn for Rex. The bowl was on the table by me, and Rex was in the bowl, his cheeks puffed out with popcorn, his eyes bright, his whiskers a blur of motion.

"Well Rex," I said, "what do you think? Do you think we'll be able to catch Morelli?"

Someone tapped on my front door, and both Rex and I sat perfectly still with our radar humming. I wasn't expecting anyone. Most of my neighbors were seniors. No one I was especially chummy with. No one I could imagine knocking on my door at nine-thirty at night. Mrs. Becker, maybe, on the third floor. Sometimes she forgot where she lived.

The tapping continued, and Rex and I swiveled our heads toward the door. It was a heavy metal fire door with a security peephole, a dead bolt, and a double-thick chain. When the weather was nice, I left my windows wide open all day and night, but I always kept my door locked. Hannibal and his elephants couldn't have gotten through my front door, but my windows were welcome to any idiot who could climb a fire escape.

I put the splatter screen to my fry pan over the popcorn bowl so Rex couldn't climb out and went to investigate. I had my hand on the doorknob when the tapping stopped. I looked through the peephole and saw nothing but blackness. Someone had a finger on my peephole. Not a good sign. "Who's there?" I called.

A whisper of laughter filtered through the door frame, and I jumped back. The laughter was followed by a single word. "Stephanie."

The voice was unmistakable. It was melodic and taunting. It was Ramirez.

"I've come to play with you, Stephanie," he sang. "You ready to play?"

I felt my knees go slack, felt irrational fear swell in my chest. "Go away or I'll call the police."

"You can't call *anyone*, bitch. You haven't got a phone. I know because I tried your number."

My parents have never been able to understand my need to be independent. They're convinced I live a frightened, lonely life, and no amount of talking can persuade them otherwise. In truth, I'm almost never frightened. Maybe sometimes by gross multifooted insects. In my opinion, the only good spider is a dead spider, and woman's rights aren't worth dick if they mean I can't ask a man to do my bug squashing. I don't worry about serial skinheads bashing down my door or crawling through my open window. For the most part, they prefer to work the neighborhoods closer to the train station. Muggings and carjackings are also at a minimum in my neighborhood and almost never result in death.

Until this moment, my only truly worrisome times had been those infrequent occasions when I woke up in the middle of the night fearful of invasion by mystical horrors . . . ghosts, bogeymen, vampire bats, extraterrestrials. Held prisoner by my imagination gone berserk, I'd lie in bed, barely breathing, waiting to levitate. I must admit, it would be a comfort not to have to wait alone although, aside from Bill Murray, what good would another mortal be in the face of a spook attack, anyway? Fortunately, I've never done a total head rotation, been beamed up, or had an Elvis visitation. And the closest I've come to an out-of-body experience was when Joe Morelli took his mouth to me fourteen years ago, behind the éclair case.

Ramirez's voice cut through the door. "Don't like having unfinished business with a woman, Stephanie Plum. Don't like when a woman run away from the champ."

He tried the doorknob, and for a gut-cramping moment my heart leapt to my throat. The door held, and my pulse dropped down to prestroke level.

I did some deep breathing and decided the best course of action was simply to ignore him. I didn't want to get into a shouting match. And I didn't want to make things worse than they already were. I shut and locked my living room windows and drew the drapes tight. I hurried to my bedroom and debated using the fire escape to go for help. It felt foolish, somehow, lending more weight to the threat than I was willing to concede. This is no big deal, I told myself. Nothing to worry about. I rolled my eyes. Nothing to worry about . . . only a criminally insane, two-hundred-and-fifty-pound man standing in my hall, calling me names.

I clapped a hand to my mouth to squelch a hysterical whine. Not to panic, I told myself. It wouldn't be long before my neighbors would begin to investigate, and Ramirez would be forced to leave.

I got my gun out of my pocketbook and went back to the door for another look. The peephole was uncovered, and the hallway seemed empty. I put my ear to the door and listened. Nothing. I slid the bolt and cracked the door, leaving my megachain firmly attached and my gun at the ready. No Ramirez in sight. I unhooked the chain and peeked out into the hall. Very peaceful. He was definitely gone.

A splot of some noxious substance sliding down

the front of my door caught my eye. I was pretty sure it wasn't tapioca. I gagged, closed the door, and locked and chained it. Wonderful. Two days on the job and a world-class psycho had just jerked off on my door.

Things like this had never happened to me when I'd worked for E.E. Martin. Once a street person had urinated on my foot, and every now and then a man would drop his pants in the train station, but these were things you expected when you worked in Newark. I'd learned not to take them personally. This business with Ramirez was a whole other matter. This was very scary.

I yelped when a window opened and closed above me. Mrs. Delgado letting her cat out for the night, I told myself. Get a grip. I needed to get my mind off Ramirez, so I busied myself finding hock-ables. There wasn't much left. A Walkman, an iron, pearl earrings from my wedding, a kitchen clock that looked like a chicken, a framed Ansel Adams poster, and two bean-pot table lamps. I hoped it was enough to pay my phone bill and get myself reconnected. I didn't want a repeat performance of being trapped in my apartment, not able to call for help.

I returned Rex to his cage, brushed my teeth, changed into a nightshirt, and crawled into bed with every light in the apartment blazing away.

THE FIRST THING I DID ON WAKING THE FOLLOWING morning was to check my peephole. Nothing seemed out of the ordinary, so I took a fast shower and dressed. Rex was sound asleep in his soup can after a tough night of running on his wheel. I gave him fresh water and filled his cup with the dreaded hamster nuggets. A cup of coffee would have tasted great. Unfortunately, there was no coffee in the house.

I went to my living room window and scoped out the parking lot for Ramirez, and returned to the door and doubled-checked the peephole. I slid the bolt and opened my door with the chain in place. I put my nose to the crack and sniffed. I didn't smell boxer, so I closed the door, unhooked the chain, and reopened the door. I looked out with my gun drawn. The hall was empty. I locked my door and crept down the hall. The elevator binged, the door droned open, and I almost shot old Mrs. Moyer. I apologized profusely, told her the gun wasn't real, and slunk off to the stairs, lugging the first load of junk out to the car.

By the time Emilio opened his pawnshop, I was in caffeine withdrawal. I haggled over the earrings, but my heart wasn't in it, and in the end I knew I'd gotten gypped. Not that I especially cared. I had what I needed. Money for a minor weapon, and the phone company, and enough change left over for a blueberry muffin and large coffee.

I took five minutes out to luxuriate over my breakfast, and then I hustled to the phone office. I stopped at a light and got hooted at by two guys in a pickup. From the hand gestures they were making I supposed they liked my paint job. I couldn't hear what they were saying because of the engine noise. Thank God for small favors.

I noticed a haze building around me and realized I was smoking. Not the benign white exhaust of condensation on a cold day. This smoke was thick and black, and in the absence of a tailpipe was billowing out from my underbelly. I gave the dash a hard shot with my fist to see if any of the gauges would work, and sure enough, the red oil light blinked on. I pulled into a gas station on the next corner, bought a can of 10-W-30, dumped it in the car, and checked the dip-stick. It was still low, so I added a second can.

Next stop, the phone company. Settling my account and arranging for service to be resumed were only slightly less complicated than getting a green card. Finally, I explained that my blind, senile grandmother was living with me between heart attacks and having a phone would possibly make the difference between life and death. I don't think the woman behind the counter believed me, but I think I got a few entertainment points, and I was promised someone would throw a switch later in the day. Good deal. If Ramirez came back, I'd be able to dial the cops. As a backup, I intended to get a quart of defense spray. I wasn't much good with a gun, but I was bitchin' with an aerosol can.

By the time I got to the gun store, the oil light was flickering again. I didn't see any smoke, so I concluded the gauge must be stuck. And who cared anyway, I wasn't squandering more money on oil. This car was just going to have to make do. When I collected my $10,000 bounty money, I'd buy it all the oil it wanted—then I'd push it off a bridge.

I'd always imagined gun store owners to be big and burly and to wear baseball caps that advertised motorcycle companies. I'd always imagined them with names like Bubba and Billy Bob. This gun store was run by a woman named Sunny. She was in her forties with skin tanned the color and texture of a good cigar, hair that had been bleached to canary yellow frizz, and a two-pack-a-day voice. She was wearing rhinestone earrings, skintight jeans, and she had little palm trees painted on her fingernails.

"Nice work," I said, alluding to her nails.

"Maura, at The Hair Palace, does them. She's a genius with nails, and she'll bikini wax you till you're bald as a billiard ball."

"I'll have to remember."

"Just ask for Maura. Tell her Sunny sent you. And what can I do for you today? Out of bullets already?"

"I need some defense spray."

"What kind of spray do you use?"

"There's more than one kind?"

"Goodness, yes. We carry a full line of self-defense sprays." She reached into the case next to her and pulled out several shrink-wrapped packages. "This is the original Mace. Then we have Peppergard, the environmentally safe alternative now used by many police departments. And, last but certainly not least, is Sure Guard, a genuine chemical weapon. This can drop a three-hundred-pound man in six seconds. Works on neurotransmitters. This stuff touches your skin and you're out cold. Doesn't matter if you're drunk or on drugs. One spray and it's all over."

"Sounds dangerous."

"You better believe it."

"Is it fatal? Does it leave permanent damage?"

"The only permanent damage to your victim is going to be the memory of a downright humiliating experience. Of course there'll be some initial paralysis, and when that wears off there's usually a lot of throwing up and a monster headache."

"I don't know. What if I accidentally spray myself?"

She grimaced. "Darlin', you should avoid spraying yourself."

"Sounds complicated."

"It's not complicated at all. It's as simple as putting your finger on the button. For goodness sakes, you're a professional now." She patted my hand. "Take the Sure Guard. You can't go wrong."

I didn't feel like a professional. I felt like an idiot. I'd criticized foreign governments for using chemical warfare, and here I was buying nerve gas from a woman who waxed off all her pubic hair.

"Sure Guard comes in several sizes," Sunny said. "I carry the seventeen-gram key-chain model. It has its own stainless steel quick-release loop, comes in an attractive leather case, and you get to choose from three decorator colors."

"Gee, three colors."

"You should try it out," Sunny told me. "Make sure you know how to use it."

I stepped outside, held my arm straight out, and sprayed. The wind shifted, and I ran inside and slammed the door.

"That wind can be sneaky," Sunny said. "Maybe you should go out the back way. You can exit through the gun range."

I did as she suggested, and when I reached the street, I rushed to my car and jumped inside lest any droplets of Sure Guard were hanging around, waiting to attack my neurotransmitters. I shoved my key into the ignition and tried hard not to panic over the fact that I had tear gas under 125 pounds of pressure per square inch, which in my mind spelled nerve bomb, dangling between my knees. The engine caught and the oil light came on again, looking very red and a little frantic. Fuck it. Take a number, I thought. On my list of problems to solve, oil wasn't even in the top ten.

I pulled into traffic and refused to check my rear-view mirror for telltale clouds of smoke. Carmen lived several blocks east of Stark Street. Not a great neighborhood, but not the worst, either. Her building was yellow brick and looked like it could do with a good scrubbing. Four stories. No elevator. Chipped tile in the small ground-floor foyer. Her apartment was on the second floor. I was sweating by the time I got to her door. The yellow crime-scene tape had been removed, but a padlock was in place. There were two other apartments on the second floor. I knocked on each door. No one home at the first. A Hispanic woman, Mrs. Santiago, somewhere in her late forties, early fifties answered the second. She had a baby on her hip. Her black hair was pulled neatly back from her round face. She wore a blue cotton housecoat and terrycloth bedroom slippers. A television droned from the dark interior of the apartment. I could see two small heads silhouetted against the screen. I introduced myself and gave her my card.

"I don't know what more I can tell you," she said. "This Carmen only lived here a short time. No one knew her. She was quiet. Kept to herself."

"Have you seen her since the shooting?"

"No."

"Do you know where she might be? Friends? Relatives?"

"I didn't know her. Nobody knew her. They tell me she worked in a bar . . . the Step In on Stark

Street. Maybe somebody knew her there."

"Were you home the night of the shooting?"

"Yes. It was late, and Carmen had the television on real loud. I never heard her play it so loud. Then someone was banging on Carmen's door. A man. Turned out he was a cop. I guess he had to bang because no one could hear him over the television. Then there was a gunshot. That's when I called the police. I called the police, and when I got back to my front door I could hear there was a big commotion in the hall, so I looked out."

"And?"

"And John Kuzack was there, and some others from the building. We take care of our own here. We aren't like some of those people who pretend not to hear things. That's why we have no drugs here. We never have this kind of trouble. John was standing over the cop when I looked out. John didn't know the man was a cop. John saw someone shot dead in Carmen's doorway, and this other man had a gun, so John took matters into his own hands."

"Then what happened?"

"It was real confusing. There were so many people in the hall."

"Was Carmen there?"

"I didn't see her. There were just so many people. Everybody wanting to know what happened, you know? People trying to help the dead man, but it was no use. He was dead."

"Supposedly there were two men in Carmen's apartment. Did you see the second man?"

"I guess so. There was a man I didn't know. Never saw before. Skinny, dark hair, dark skin, about thirty, funny face. Like it'd been hit with a frying pan. Real flat nose. That's why I noticed him."

"What happened to him?"

She shrugged. "Don't know. I guess he just left. Like Carmen."

"Maybe I should talk to John Kuzack."

"He's in 4B. He should be home. He's between jobs right now."

I thanked her and walked up two more flights of stairs, wondering what sort of person would be willing and able to disarm Morelli. I knocked at 4B and waited. I knocked again, loud enough to bruise my knuckles. The door was thrown open and my "what kind of person" question was answered. John Kuzack was 6' 4" tall, weighed about two hundred and forty pounds, had his graying hair pulled into a ponytail, and had a rattler tattooed onto his forehead. He was holding a *TV Guide* in one hand and a can of beer in the other. The sweet aroma of pot drifted out of his hazy apartment. Vietnam vet, I thought. Airborne.

"John Kuzack?"

He squinted down at me. "What can I do for you?"

"I'm trying to get a lead on Joe Morelli. I was

hoping you could tell me something about Carmen Sanchez."

"You a cop?"

"I work for Vincent Plum. He posted the bond on Morelli."

"I didn't know Carmen Sanchez real good," he said. "I'd seen her around. Said hello to her a couple times. She seemed nice enough. I was coming up the stairs when I heard the gunshot."

"Mrs. Santiago, on the second floor, said you subdued the gunman."

"Yeah. I didn't know he was a cop. All I knew was he'd shot someone, and he was still armed. There were a lot of people coming into the hall, and he was telling them all to stay away. I figured it wasn't a good situation, so I hit him with a six-pack. Knocked him out cold."

A six-pack? I almost laughed out loud. The police report had stated that Morelli had been hit with a blunt instrument. It hadn't said anything about a six-pack.

"That was very brave."

He grinned. "Hell, bravery didn't have anything to do with it. I was shitfaced."

"Do you know what happened to Carmen?"

"Nope. Guess she disappeared in the scuffle."

"And you haven't seen her since?"

"Nope."

"How about the missing male witness? Mrs. Santiago said there was a man with a flattened nose. . . ."

"I remember seeing him, but that's about it."

"Would you recognize him if you saw him again?"

"Probably."

"Do you think there's anyone else in the building who might know more about the missing man?"

"Edleman was the only other person who got a good look at the guy."

"Is Edleman a tenant here?"

"Edleman *was* a tenant here. He got hit by a car last week. Right in front of the building. Hit and run."

My stomach gave a nervous flutter. "You don't suppose Edleman's death ties in to the Kulesza murder, do you?"

"No way of knowing."

I thanked Kuzack for his time and took the stairs slowly, enjoying the buzz from his secondary smoke.

It was close to noon, and the day was heating up. I'd gone with a suit and heels this morning, trying to look respectable and trust inspiring. I'd left the windows rolled down when I'd parked in front of Carmen's building, half hoping someone would steal my car. No one had, so I slouched behind the wheel and finished off the Fig Newtons I'd filched from my mom's pantry. I hadn't found out a whole lot from Carmen's neighbors, but at least I hadn't been attacked or fallen down a flight of stairs.

Morelli's apartment was next on my list.

FIVE

I'D CALLED RANGER AND ASKED FOR HELP, SINCE I
was too chicken to do breaking and entering on my
own. When I pulled into the lot, Ranger was waiting. He was all in black. Sleeveless black T-shirt
and black fatigue-type pants. He was leaning against
a gleaming black Mercedes that had enough antennae on it to get to Mars. I parked several spaces
away so my exhaust wouldn't tarnish his finish.

"Your car?" I asked. As if anyone else could possibly belong to this car.

"Life's been good to me." His eyes slid to my
Nova. "Nice paint job," he said. "You been on Stark
Street?"

"Yes, and they stole my radio."

"Heh, heh, heh. Good of you to make a contribution to the less fortunate."

"I'm willing to contribute the entire car, but no one wants it."

"Just 'cause the dudes be crazy don't mean they be stupid." He nodded toward Morelli's apartment. "Doesn't seem like anyone's home, so we'll have to do the unguided tour."

"Is this illegal?"

"Hell no. We got the law, babe. Bounty hunters can do anything. We don't even need a search warrant." He buckled a black nylon webbed gun belt around his waist and shoved his 9 mm Glock into it. He clipped cuffs onto the gun belt and shrugged into the same loose black jacket he'd worn when I'd met him at the coffee shop. "I don't expect Morelli to be in there," he said, "but you never know. You always want to be prepared."

I supposed I should be taking similar precautions, but I couldn't see myself with a gun butt sticking out of my skirt waistband. It'd be an empty gesture anyway, since Morelli knew I didn't have the guts to shoot him.

Ranger and I crossed the lot and walked through the breezeway to Morelli's apartment. Ranger knocked on the door and waited a moment. "Anybody home?" he hollered. No one answered.

"Now what?" I asked. "You going to kick the door in?"

"No way. You could break your foot doing that macho shit."

"You're going to pick the lock, right? Use a credit card?"

Ranger shook his head. "You've been watching too much television." He took a key from his pocket and inserted it in the lock. "Got a key from the super while I was waiting for you."

Morelli's apartment consisted of living room, dining alcove, galley kitchen, bath, and bedroom. It was relatively clean and sparsely furnished. Small square oak table, four ladder-back chairs, comfortable overstuffed couch, coffee table, and one club chair. He had an expensive stereo system in the living room and a small TV in the bedroom.

Ranger and I searched through the kitchen, looking for an address book, riffling through bills carelessly heaped in front of the toaster oven.

It was easy to imagine Morelli at home in his apartment, tossing his keys onto the kitchen counter, kicking off his shoes, reading his mail. A wave of remorse washed over me when I realized Morelli would most likely never again be free to enjoy any of those simple rituals. He'd killed a man and in the process had effectively ended his own life as well. It was such a hideous waste. How could he have been so stupid? How could he have gotten himself into this godawful mess? How do these things happen to people?

"Nothing here," Ranger said. He punched the

playback button on Morelli's answering machine. "Hi, hotstuff," a female voice cooed. "This is Carlene. Give me a call back." Beep.

"Joseph Anthony Morelli, it's your mother. Are you there? Hello? Hello?" Beep.

Ranger turned the machine over and copied the security code and special message code. "You take these numbers and you can access his messages from an outside phone. Maybe something'll turn up."

We moved on to the bedroom, going through his drawers, leafing through books and magazines, studying the few photographs on his dresser. The photographs were family. Nothing useful. No pictures of Carmen. For the most part his drawers had been emptied. He'd taken all his socks and underwear. Too bad. I'd been sort of looking forward to seeing his underwear.

We ended up back in the kitchen.

"This place is clean," Ranger said. "You're not going to find anything to help you here. And I doubt he'll return. Looks to me like he took everything he needed." He lifted a set of keys from a small hook on the kitchen wall and dropped them into my hand. "Hang on to these. No sense bothering the super if you want to get in again."

We locked Morelli's apartment and slid the super's master key through a slot in his door. Ranger eased his body into the Mercedes, put on a pair of mirrored shades, powered back his sun roof, punched up a tape with a heavy bass, and rolled out of the parking lot like Batman.

I gave a resigned sigh and looked at my Nova. It was dripping oil onto the pavement. Two parking slots away Morelli's new red and gold Jeep Cherokee sat gleaming in the sunshine. I could feel the weight of his keys dangling from my finger. A house key and two car keys. I decided it wouldn't do any harm to take a closer look, so I opened the door to the Cherokee and peered inside. The car still smelled new. The instrument panel was dust-free, the rugs were freshly vacuumed and unstained, the red upholstery was smooth and perfect. The car had five on the floor, four-wheel drive, and enough horses to make a man proud. It was equipped with air-conditioning, an Alpine radio and tape deck, a two-way police radio, a cellular phone, and a CB scanner. It was a terrific car. And it belonged to Morelli. It didn't seem fair that a scofflaw like him should have such a great car and I should have such a piece of shit.

Probably as long as I had the car open, I should start it up for him, I thought. It wasn't good for a car to sit around and not get driven. Everybody knows that. I took a deep breath and cautiously maneuvered myself behind the wheel. I adjusted the seat and the rearview mirror. I put my hands to the wheel and tested the feel of it. I could catch Morelli if I had a car like this, I told myself. I was smart. I was tenacious. All I needed was a car. I wondered if I should drive it. Maybe simply running it wasn't enough. Maybe the car needed to go around the block. Better yet, maybe I should drive it for a day or two to really work the kinks out.

Okay, who was I trying to kid? I was contemplating stealing Morelli's car. Not steal, I reasoned. Commandeer. After all, I was a bounty hunter, and probably I could commandeer a car if an emergency situation arose. I glanced over at the Nova. Looked like an emergency to me.

There was an added advantage to snitching Morelli's car. I was pretty sure he wouldn't like it. And if he was pissed off enough, maybe he'd do something stupid and come after it.

I turned the key in the ignition and tried to ignore the fact that my heart was beating double-time. The secret to being a successful bounty hunter is being able to seize the moment, I told myself. Flexibility. Adaptation. Creative thought. All necessary attributes. And it didn't hurt to have balls.

I did some slow breathing so I wouldn't hyperventilate and crash my first stolen car. I had one more item on my day's itinerary. I needed to visit the Step In Bar and Grill, Carmen's last known place of employment. The Step In was located on lower Stark Street, two blocks from the gym. I debated going home to change into something more casual, but in the end decided to stick with the suit. No matter what I wore, I wasn't going to blend in with the bar regulars.

I found a parking space half a block away. I locked the car, and I walked the short distance to the bar only to discover the bar was closed. The door was padlocked. The windows were boarded. No explanation was given. I wasn't all that disappointed. After the incident in the gym, I hadn't been looking forward to breaking into another bastion of Stark Street manhood. I scurried back to the Cherokee and drove up and down Stark Street on the long shot that I might see Morelli. By the fifth pass it was getting old and my gas was low, so I gave it up. I checked the glove compartment for credit cards but found none. Swell. No gas. No money. No plastic.

If I was going to keep after Morelli I was going to need living expenses. I couldn't keep existing hand to mouth. Vinnie was the obvious answer to my problem. Vinnie was going to have to advance me some cash. I stopped for a light and took a moment to study Morelli's phone. I powered it up and his number blinked on. How convenient. I figured I'd go whole hog. Why stop at stealing Morelli's car? Might as well run his phone bill up, too.

I called Vinnie's office, and Connie answered.

"Is Vinnie in?" I asked.

"Yeah," she said. "He'll be here all afternoon."

"I'll be around in about ten minutes. I need to talk to him."

"Did you catch Morelli?"

"No, but I've confiscated his car."

"Has it got a sun roof?"

I rolled my eyes skyward. "No sun roof."

"Bummer," she said.

I hung up and turned down Southard, trying to decide on a reasonable advance. I needed enough money to get me through two weeks, and if I was going to use the car to catch Morelli I might want to invest in an alarm system. I couldn't watch the car around the clock, and I didn't want Morelli sneaking it out from under me while I slept, or took a pee, or went to the market.

I was pondering an appropriate figure when the phone rang, the soft "brrrrp" almost causing me to run up onto the curb. It was a weird sensation. Like getting caught eavesdropping, or lying, or sitting on the toilet and having the bathroom walls suddenly drop away. I had an irrational urge to pull off the road and run shrieking from the car.

I gingerly put the handset to my ear. "Hello?" There was a pause and a woman's voice came on the line. "I want to talk to Joseph Morelli."

Holy cow. It was Momma Morelli. As if I wasn't in deep enough do-do. "Joe isn't here right now."

"Who's this?"

"I'm a friend of Joe's. He asked me to run his car once in a while for him."

"That's a lie," she said. "I know who I'm talking to. I'm talking to Stephanie Plum. I know your voice when I hear it. What are you doing in my Joseph's car?"

No one can show disdain like Momma Morelli. If it had been an ordinary mother on the phone I might have explained or apologized, but Morelli's mother scared the hell out of me.

"What?" I shouted. "I can't hear you. What? What?"

I slammed the receiver down and flipped the off switch on the phone. "Good going," I said to myself. "Very adult. Very professional. Really quick thinking."

I parked on Hamilton and power walked half a block to Vinnie's. I was pumping myself up for the confrontation, getting my adrenaline going, raising my energy level. I barreled through the door like Wonder Woman, gave Connie a thumbs up, and went straight to Vinnie's office. The door was open. Vinnie was behind his desk, hunched over a racing sheet.

"Hey," I said. "How's it going?"

"Oh shit," Vinnie said. "Now what?"

That's what I like about my family. We're so close, so warm, so polite to each other. "I want an advance on my fee. I have expenses associated with the job."

"An advance? Are you kidding me? You're joking, right?"

"I'm not joking. I'm going to get $10,000 when I bring Morelli in. I want a $2,000 advance."

"When hell freezes over. And don't think you can pull more of that blackmail crap on me. You blab to my wife, and I'll be as good as dead. See if you can squeeze a job out of a dead man, smart-ass."

He had a point. "Okay, so blackmail won't work. How about greed? You give me the $2,000 now, and I won't take my full 10 percent."

"What if you don't get Morelli? You ever think of that?"

Only every waking minute of my life. "I'll get Morelli."

"Uh huh. Excuse me if I don't share your positive attitude. And remember I only agreed to this lunacy for a week. You've got four days left. If you haven't brought Morelli in by next Monday, I'm giving him to somebody else."

Connie came into the office. "What's the problem here? Stephanie needs money? Why don't you give her Clarence Sampson?"

"Who's Clarence Sampson?" I asked.

"He's one of our family of drunks. Usually, he's perfectly peaceful. Every now and then he does something stupid."

"Such as?"

"Such as try to drive with a 150-proof blood alcohol level. On this particular occasion he had the misfortune to total a police cruiser."

"He ran into a cruiser?"

"Not exactly," Connie said. "He was attempting to drive the cruiser. He ran into a liquor store on State Street."

"Do you have a picture of this guy?"

"I have a two-inch file with pictures spanning two decades. We've posted bail on Sampson so many times I know his social security number by heart."

I followed her to the outer office and waited while she sorted through a stack of manila folders.

"Most of our recovery agents work a bunch of cases simultaneously," Connie said. "It's more efficient that way." She handed me a dozen folders. "These are the FTAs Morty Beyers was handling for us. He's gonna be out for a while longer, so you might as well take a crack at them. Some are easier than others. Memorize the names and addresses and hook them up to the photographs. You never know when you'll get lucky. Last week Andy Zabotsky was standing in line for a bucket of fried chicken and recognized the guy in front of him as a skip. It was a good find, too. A dealer. We would have been out $30,000."

"I didn't know you posted bond for drug dealers," I said. "I always thought you did mostly low-key stuff."

"Drug dealers are good," Connie said. "They don't like to leave the area. They've got clients. They're making good money. If they skip you can usually count on them to resurface."

I tucked the files under my arm, promising to make copies and return the originals to Connie. The chicken story had been inspiring. If Andy Zabotsky could catch a crook in a chicken franchise, just think of my own personal potential. I ate that crappy food all the time. I even liked it. Maybe this bounty hunter business would work out. Once I became financially solvent, I could support myself by collecting people like Sampson and making an occasional fast-food bust.

I pushed through the front door and caught my breath at the sudden absence of air-conditioning. The day had gone from hot to blistering. The air was thick and muggy, the sky hazy. The sun prickled on exposed skin, and I looked up, shielding my eyes, half expecting to see the ozone hole gaping over me like a big cyclops eye shooting out lethal rays of radioactive whatever. I know the hole is supposedly hanging out over Antarctica, but it seemed logical to me that sooner or later it would slide on up to Jersey. Jersey produced urea formaldehyde and collected New York's garbage offshore. I thought it only fitting that it have the ozone hole as well.

I unlocked the Cherokee and swiveled behind the wheel. Sampson's recovery money wouldn't get me to Barbados, but it would put something in my refrigerator besides mold. Even more important, it would give me a chance to run through the motions of an apprehension. When Ranger had taken me to the police station to get my gun permit, he'd also explained the recovery procedure, but there was no substitute for hands-on experience.

I flipped the switch on the car phone and dialed Clarence Sampson's home number. No one answered. No work number had been given. The police report listed his address as 5077 Limeing Street. I wasn't familiar with Limeing Street, so I'd looked it up on a map and discovered Sampson lived two blocks over from Stark, down by the state buildings. I had Sampson's picture taped to the dash, and every few seconds I checked it against men on the street as I drove.

Connie had suggested I visit the bars on lower Stark. On my list of favorite things to do, spending happy hour at the Rainbow Room on the corner of Stark and Limeing fell just below cutting off both my thumbs with a dull knife. It seemed to me it would be just as effective and a lot less dangerous to sit locked up in the Cherokee and surveil the street. If Clarence Sampson was in one of the bars, sooner or later he'd have to come out.

It took several passes before I found a space I liked at the corner of Limeing and Stark. I had a good view of Stark, and I was also able to see half a block down Limeing. I was a little conspicuous in my suit, with all my whiteness and big shiny red car, but I wasn't nearly as conspicuous as I'd be sashaying into the Rainbow Room. I cracked the windows and slouched down in my seat, trying to get comfortable.

A kid with a lot of hair and $700 worth of gold around his neck stopped and looked in at me while his two friends stood nearby. "Hey babe," he said. "What you doin' here?"

"Waiting for someone," I said.

"Oh yeah? A fine babe like you shouldn't have to wait for no one."

One of his friends stepped up. He made sucking sounds and waggled his tongue at me. When he saw he had my attention he licked my window.

I rooted through my pocketbook until I found my gun and my neuro spray. I laid them both on the dash. People stopped and stared from time to time after that, but they didn't linger.

By five o'clock I was feeling antsy, and my rayon skirt had serious crotch wrinkles. I was looking for Clarence Sampson, but I was thinking about Joe Morelli. He was somewhere close by. I could feel it in the pit of my stomach. It was like a low-volt electric charge that hummed against the inside of my spine. In my mind I walked myself through the arrest. The easiest scenario would be for him not to see me at all, for me to come at him from behind and spray him. If that wasn't possible, I'd have to talk to him and wait for the right moment to go for the spray. Once he was on the ground and incapacitated, I could cuff him. After I got him cuffed I'd rest easier.

By six I'd done the mental arrest about forty-two times and was psyched. By six-thirty I was on the down side of the peak, and my left cheek had fallen asleep. I stretched as best I could and tried isometrics. I counted passing cars, mouthed the words to the national anthem, and slowly read the ingredients on a pack of gum I found in my pocketbook. At seven I called time to make sure Morelli's clock was right.

I was berating myself for being the wrong sex and the wrong color to operate effectively in over half the neighborhoods in Trenton when a man fitting Sampson's description reeled out of the Rainbow Room. I looked at the picture on the dash. I looked back at the man. I looked at the picture again. I was 90 percent sure it was Sampson. Big flabby body, mean little head, dark hair and beard, white Caucasian. Looked like Bluto. Had to be Sampson. Let's face it, how many bearded fat white men lived in this neighborhood?

I tucked the gun and the spray into my pocketbook, pulled away from the curb, and drove around two blocks so I could turn down Limeing and put myself between Sampson and his house. I double-parked and got out of the car. A group of teens stood talking on the corner, and two little girls sat on a nearby stoop with their Barbie dolls. Across the street a bedraggled couch, missing its cushions, had been set out on the sidewalk. The Limeing Street version of a porch swing. Two old men sat on the couch, wordlessly staring off into space, their lined faces inanimate.

Sampson was slowly weaving up the street, obviously in the glow. His smile was contagious. I smiled back at him. "Clarence Sampson?"

"Yep," he said. "That's me."

His words were thick, and he smelled stale, like clothes that had been forgotten for weeks in the hamper.

I extended my hand. "I'm Stephanie Plum. I represent your bonding company. You missed a court appearance, and we'd like you to reschedule."

Momentary confusion rippled across his brow, the information was processed, and he smiled again.

"I guess I forgot."

Not what you'd call a type A personality. I didn't think Sampson would ever have to worry about a stress-related heart attack. Sampson would most likely die from inertia.

More smiling on my part. "That's okay. Happens all the time. I have a car here. . . ." I waved in the direction of the Cherokee. "If it wouldn't be too much trouble I'll drive you to the station, and we can take care of the paperwork."

He looked beyond me to his house. "I don't know. . . ."

I looped arms with him and nudged him over. Just a friendly ole cowpoke herding a dumber'n cat-shit steer. Git along little doggie. "This won't take long." Three weeks, maybe.

I was oozing well-being and charm, pushing my breast into the side of his fleshy arm as added incentive. I rolled him around the car and opened the passenger side door. "I really appreciate this," I said.

He balked at the door. "All I have to do is set a new court date, right?"

"Yeah. Right." And then hang around in a cell until that court date pops up on the calendar. I had no sympathy for him. He could have killed someone driving while intoxicated.

I coaxed him in and fastened the seat belt. I ran around, jumped in the car, and revved the engine, afraid the light bulb would go on in his minuscule brain and he'd realize I was a recovery agent. I couldn't imagine what would happen when we got to the police station. One step at a time, I told myself. If he got violent I'd gas him . . . maybe.

My fears were premature. I hadn't driven a quarter mile before his eyes glazed over, and he fell asleep, slouched against the door like a giant slug. I said a fast prayer that he didn't wet himself, or throw up, or do any of the other gross involuntary bodily things drunks are prone to do.

Several blocks later I stopped for a light and glanced sideways at him. He was still asleep. So far so good.

A faded blue Econoline van caught my eye on the other side of the intersection. Three antennae. A lot of equipment for a junky old van, I thought. I squinted at the driver, shadowy behind tinted glass, and an eerie feeling crept along the nape of my neck. The light turned. Cars moved through the intersection. The van rolled by, and my heart jumped to my throat as I was treated to a view of Joe Morelli behind the wheel, gaping at me in astonishment. My first impulse was to shrink in size until I was no longer visible. In theory, I should have been pleased to have made contact, but the instant reality was hurling confusion. I was good at fantasizing Morelli's recovery. I wasn't so confident when it came to actually pulling it off. Brakes squealed behind me, and in my rearview mirror I saw the van jump the curb to complete a midblock U-turn.

I'd expected he'd come after me. I hadn't expected him to do it with such speed. The Jeep's doors were locked, but I pushed the lock button again anyway. The Sure Guard was nestled in my lap. The police station was less than a mile away. I debated giving Clarence the boot and going after Morelli. Morelli was, after all, my main objective.

I did a fast run-through of possible arrest attempts, and none of them turned out satisfactory. I didn't want Morelli to come at me while I was struggling with Clarence. And I didn't want to drop Morelli in the street. Not in this neighborhood. I wasn't sure I could control the outcome.

Morelli was five cars back when I stopped for a light. I saw the driver's door open, saw Morelli get out of the van, running toward me. I gripped the gas canister and prayed for the light to change. Morelli was almost on me when we all moved forward, and Morelli was forced to go back to the van.

Good old Clarence was still sound asleep, his head dropped forward, his mouth open and drooling, emitting soft snuffling sounds. I left-turned up North Clinton, and the phone chirped.

It was Morelli, and he didn't sound happy. "What the fuck do you think you're doing?" he yelled.

"I'm taking Mr. Sampson to the police station. You're more than welcome to follow us. It would make everything much easier for me."

A pretty ballsy reply, considering I was having an anxiety attack.

"THAT'S MY CAR YOU'RE DRIVING!"

"Mmmmm. Well, I've commandeered it."

"You've WHAT?"

I flipped the switch to shut the phone off before the conversation deteriorated to death threats. The van disappeared from sight two blocks from the station, and I continued on with my FTA still sleeping like a baby.

The Trenton police department houses itself in a cubelike three-story brick building representing the Practical Pig approach to municipal architecture. Clearly low on the funding food chain, Police Headquarters has been afforded few frills, which is just as well considering it is surrounded by ghetto, and the location almost certainly ensures annihilation should a riot of major proportions ever occur.

A chain-link fenced lot adjoins the building and provides parking for squad cars and vans, employees, cops, and beleaguered citizens.

Gritty row houses and small businesses, typical of the area, face off with the headquarters' front entrance—Jumbos Seafood, a bar with no visible name and ominous metal grating on the windows, a corner grocery advertising RC Cola, Lydia's Hat Designs, a used-furniture store with a motley collection of washing machines displayed on the sidewalk, and the Tabernacle Church.

I pulled into the lot, tapped the phone back on, dialed dispatch, and requested aid with the transfer of custody. I was instructed to proceed to the rear security door, where a uniform would be waiting for me. I proceeded to the designated door and backed into the driveway, placing Clarence close to the building. I didn't see my uniform, so I made another call. I was promptly told not to get my shorts in a knot. Easy for them to say—*they* knew what they were doing.

A few minutes later Crazy Carl Costanza poked his head out the door. I'd made Communion with Crazy Carl, among other things.

He squinted past Clarence. "Stephanie Plum?"

"Hey, Carl."

His face cracked into a grin. "They told me there was a pain in the ass out here."

"That would be me," I said.

"What's with sleeping beauty?"

"He's FTA."

Carl came in for a closer look. "Is he dead?"

"I don't think so."

"He smells dead."

I agreed. "He could use to be hosed down." I gave Clarence a shake and yelled in his ear. "Let's go. Time to wake up."

Clarence choked on some spit and opened his eyes. "Where am I?"

"Police station," I said. "Everybody out."

He stared at me in unfocused drunken stupidity, and sat as still and unyielding as a sandbag.

"Do something," I said to Costanza. "Get him out of here."

Costanza grabbed Clarence's arms, and I put my foot to Clarence's butt. We pushed and pulled, and inch by inch, got Sampson's big ugly blob of putrid flesh off the seat and onto the pavement.

"This is why I became a cop," Costanza said. "I couldn't resist the glamor of it all."

We maneuvered Clarence through the security door, cuffed him to a wooden bench, and handed him over to the docket lieutenant. I ran back outside and moved the Cherokee into a regulation parking space where it would be less visible to cops who might mistake it for a stolen car.

When I returned, Clarence had been stripped of his belt and shoelaces and personal property and looked forlorn and pathetic. He was my first capture, and I'd expected to feel satisfaction for my success, but now found it was difficult to get elated over someone else's misfortune.

I collected my body receipt, spent a few minutes

reminiscing with Crazy Carl, and headed for the lot. I'd hoped to leave before dark, but night had closed in early under a blanket of clouds. The sky was starless and moonless. Traffic was sporadic. Easier to spot a tail, I told myself, but I didn't believe it. I had minimal confidence in my ability to spot Morelli.

There was no sign of the van. That didn't mean much. Morelli could be driving whatever by now. I headed for Nottingham with one eye on the road and one on my rearview mirror. There was little doubt in my mind that Morelli was out there, but at least he was giving me the courtesy of not being obvious. That meant he took me moderately seriously. It was a cheery thought that prompted me to rise to the occasion with a plan. The plan was simple. Go home, park the Cherokee in the lot, wait in the bushes with my killer gas, and zap Morelli when he tried to reclaim his car.

SIX

THE FRONT OF MY APARTMENT BUILDING SAT FLUSH
with the sidewalk. Parking was in the rear. The lot
was minimally scenic, consisting of an asphalt rec-
tangle subdivided into parking spaces. We weren't
so sophisticated that we were assigned slots. Parking was dog-eat-dog, with all the really good places
designated handicapped. Three Dumpsters hunkered
at the entrance to the lot. One for general garbage.
Two for recyclables. Good for the environment.
Didn't do much for local aesthetics. The rear entrance had been improved by a strip of overgrown
azaleas that hugged the building and ran almost the
entire length of the lot. They were wonderful in the
spring when they were filled with pink flowers, and
they were magical in the winter when the super

strung them with little blinking lights. The rest of
the year they were better than nothing.

I chose a well-lighted slot in the middle of the
lot. Better to see Morelli when he came to retrieve
his property. Not to mention it was one of the few
places left. Most of the people in my building were
elderly and didn't like to drive after dark. By nine
o'clock the lot was full and TVs were going full
blast inside all the seniors' apartments.

I looked around to make sure there was no sign
of Morelli. Then I popped the hood and removed
the Cherokee's distributor cap. This was one of my
many New Jersey survival skills. Anyone who has
ever left their car in long-term parking at Newark
Airport knows how to remove the distributor cap.
It is virtually the only way of ensuring your car will
be there upon your return.

I figured when the Cherokee didn't start, Morelli'd stick his head under the hood, and that's
when I'd gas him. I scurried to the building and hid
myself behind the azaleas, feeling fairly slick.

I sat on the ground on a newspaper in deference
to my skirt. I'd have liked to change my clothes,
but I was afraid of missing Morelli if I dashed upstairs. Cedar chips had been spread in front of the
azaleas. Back where I sat the ground was hard-
packed dirt. When I was a kid I might have thought
this was cozy, but I wasn't a kid anymore, and I
noticed things kids didn't notice. Mostly that azaleas don't look all that good from the rear.

A big Chrysler pulled into the lot, and a white-haired man got out. I recognized him, but I didn't know his name. He slowly walked to the building entrance. He didn't seem alarmed or yell out "Help, there's a crazy woman hiding in the bushes," so I felt secure that I was well hidden.

I squinted at my watch in the dark. Nine forty-five. Waiting wasn't among my favorite pastimes. I was hungry and bored and uncomfortable. There are probably people who put waiting time to good use organizing thoughts, composing chore lists, sinking into constructive introspection. Waiting, for me, was sensory deprivation. A black hole. Down time.

I was still waiting at eleven o'clock. I was cranky, and I had to go to the bathroom. Somehow I managed to sit there for another hour and a half. I was reviewing my options, considering a new plan, when it started to rain. The drops were big and lazy, falling in slow motion, spattering on the azalea bushes, leaving their imprint on the hard-packed dirt where I sat, encouraging musty smells reminiscent of cobwebs and crawl spaces to rise up from the earth. I sat with my back pressed against the building and my legs drawn up to my chest. With the exception of an occasional renegade drop, I was untouched by the rain.

After a few minutes the tempo evened out, the drops grew small and consistent, and the wind picked up. Water pooled on the black macadam, catching clots of reflective light, and the rain beaded on the shiny red paint of the Cherokee.

It was a wonderful night to be in bed with a book, listening to the tic, tic, tic of drops on the window and fire escape. It was a lousy night to be crouched behind an azalea bush. The rain had taken to swirling with the wind, catching me in gusts, soaking into my shirt, plastering my hair to my face.

By one o'clock I was shivering and miserable, soaking wet, close to peeing in my pants. Not that it would matter. At five after one I abandoned the plan. Even if Morelli did show up, which I was beginning to doubt, I wasn't sure I was in good enough shape to make a capture. And I definitely didn't want him to see me with my hair like this.

I was about to leave when a car swung into the lot, parked in a space at the far perimeter, and killed its lights. A man got out of the car and quickly walked, head down, to the Cherokee. It wasn't Joe. It was Mooch again. I rested my forehead on my knees and closed my eyes. I'd been naive to think Joe would fall into my trap. The entire police force was after his ass. He wasn't going to barge into a setup like this. I sulked for a few seconds and then pushed it aside, vowing to be smarter next time. I should have put myself in Joe's place. Would I have exposed myself by personally coming after the car? No. Okay, so I was learning. Rule number one: don't underestimate the enemy. Rule number two: think like a felon.

Mooch opened the driver's door with a key and

slid behind the wheel. The starter churned but didn't catch. Mooch waited a few minutes and tried again. He got out and looked under the hood. I knew this wouldn't take long. It didn't take a genius to notice a missing distributor cap. Mooch pulled his head out from under the hood, slammed the hood down, kicked a tire, and said something colorful. He jogged back to his car and peeled out of the lot.

I slunk out of the shadows and trudged the short distance to the back entrance to my building. My skirt clung to my legs and water squished in my shoes. The night had been a bust, but it could have been worse. Joe could have sent his mother to get the car.

The lobby was empty, looking even bleaker than usual. I punched the elevator button and waited. Water dripped from the end of my nose and off the hem of my skirt, forming a small lake on the gray tile floor. Two side-by-side elevators serviced the building. No one, so far as I knew, had ever plummeted to their death or been skyrocketed out of the top of the elevator shaft in a runaway elevator, but chances of getting stuck between floors was excellent. Usually I used the stairs. Tonight, I decided to carry my masochistic stupidity to the max and take the elevator. The cage lurched into place, the doors gaped open, and I stepped in. I ascended to the second floor without incident and sloshed down the hall. I fumbled in my pocketbook for the key and was letting myself into my apartment when I remembered the distributor cap. I'd left it downstairs, behind the azaleas. I thought about retrieving it, but it was a short thought and of no consequence. No way was I going back downstairs.

I bolted the door behind me and peeled my clothes off while standing on the small patch of linoleum that served as my foyer. My shoes were ruined, and the seat of my skirt bore the imprint of yesterday's headlines. I left every stitch I'd worn in a sodden heap on the floor and went straight to the bathroom.

I adjusted the water, stepped into the tub, pulled the shower curtain closed, and let the hard spray beat down on me. The day hadn't been all bad, I told myself. I'd made a recovery. I was legitimate now. First thing in the morning I'd collect my money from Vinnie. I lathered up and rinsed off. I washed my hair. I turned the dial to shower massage and stood for a very long time, letting the tension ease from my body. Twice now Joe had used Mooch as his errand boy. Maybe I should be watching Mooch. Problem was I couldn't watch everyone at once.

I was distracted by a blur of color on the other side of the translucent, soap-slicked shower curtain. The blur moved and my heart momentarily stopped dead in my chest. Someone was in my bathroom. The shock was numbing. I stood statue still for a few beats without a thought in my head. Then I remembered Ramirez, and my stomach rolled. Ra-

mirez could have come back. He could have talked
the super into giving him a key, or he could have
come in through a window. God only knows what
Ramirez was capable of doing.

I'd brought my pocketbook into the bathroom,
but it was out of reach on the vanity counter.

The intruder crossed the room in two strides and
ripped the shower curtain off the rod with such
force the plastic loops at the top popped off and
scattered. I screamed and blindly threw the shampoo
bottle, cowering back against the wall tiles.

It wasn't Ramirez. It was Joe Morelli. He had the
curtain bunched in one hand; the other hand curled
into a fist. A welt was forming on his forehead
where the bottle had made contact. He was beyond
angry, and I wasn't so sure gender was going to
keep me from getting a broken nose. Fine with me.
I was spoiling for a fight. Who did this yodel think
he was, first scaring me half to death and then
wrecking my shower curtain.

"What the hell do you think you're doing?" I
shrieked. "Haven't you ever heard of a goddamn
doorbell? How did you get in here?"

"You left your bedroom window open."

"The screen was locked."

"Screens don't count."

"If you've ruined that screen I'll expect you to
pay for it. And what about this shower curtain?
Shower curtains don't grow on trees, you know."
I'd lowered the volume on my voice, but the pitch

was still a full octave higher than normal. In all honesty, I hadn't any idea what I was saying. My mind was racing down uncharted roads of fury and panic. I was furious that he'd violated my privacy, and I was panicked that I was naked.

Under the right circumstances naked is fine—taking showers, making love, being born. Standing naked and dripping wet in front of Joe Morelli, who was completely clothed, was the stuff nightmares are made of.

I shut the water off and grabbed at a towel, but Morelli slapped my hand away and threw the towel onto the floor behind him.

"Give me that towel," I demanded.

"Not until we've gotten a few things straightened out."

As a kid, Morelli'd been out of control. I'd reached the conclusion that as an adult Morelli had control in spades. The Italian temper was clear in his eyes, but the amount of violence displayed was tightly calculated. He was wearing a black rain-drenched T-shirt and jeans. When he twisted toward the towel rack I could see the gun stuck into his jeans at the small of his back.

It wasn't difficult to envision Morelli killing, but I found myself agreeing with Ranger and Eddie Gazarra—I couldn't see this grown-up Morelli being stupid and impulsive.

He had his hands on his hips. His hair was wet, curling on his forehead and over his ears. His mouth was hard and unsmiling. "Where's my distributor cap?"

When in doubt, always take the offensive. "If you don't get out of my bathroom this instant I'm going to start screaming."

"It's two o'clock in the morning, Stephanie. All your neighbors are sound asleep with their hearing aids on their nightstands. Scream away. No one's going to hear you."

I stood my ground and scowled at him. It was my best effort at defiance. I'd be damned if I was going to give him the satisfaction of looking vulnerable and embarrassed.

"I'm going to ask you one more time," he said. "Where's my distributor cap?"

"I don't know what you're talking about."

"Listen, Cupcake, I'll tear this place apart if I have to."

"I don't have the cap. The cap isn't here. And I'm not your cupcake."

"Why me?" he asked. "What did I do to deserve this?"

I raised an eyebrow.

Morelli sighed. "Yeah," he said. "I know." He took my pocketbook from the counter, turned it upside down, and let the contents fall to the floor. He picked the cuffs out of the mess and took a step forward. "Give me your wrist."

"Pervert."

"You wish." He flicked the cuff out and clicked it onto my right wrist.

I yanked my right arm back hard and kicked at him, but it was difficult to maneuver in the tub. He sidestepped my kick and locked the remaining steel bracelet onto the shower curtain rod. I gasped and froze, unable to believe what had just happened.

Morelli stepped back and looked at me, doing a slow whole-body scan. "You want to tell me where the cap is?"

I was incapable of speech, bereft of bravado. I could feel the flush of apprehension and embarrassment staining my cheeks, constricting my throat.

"Wonderful," Morelli said. "Do the silent thing. You can hang there forever for all I care."

He rummaged through the vanity drawers, emptied the wastebasket, and took the lid off the toilet tank. He stormed out of the bathroom without giving me so much as a backward glance. I could hear him methodically, professionally moving through my apartment, searching every square inch. Silverware clanked, drawers slammed, closet doors were wrenched open. There were sporadic patches of quiet, followed by mutterings.

I tried hanging my full weight on the bar, hoping to bend it, but the rod was industrial strength, built to endure.

At last Morelli appeared in the bathroom doorway.

"Well?" I snapped. "Now what?"

He indolently leaned against the frame. "Just came back to take another look." A grin surfaced at the corners of his mouth as his eyes locked halfway down my chest. "Cold?"

When I got loose I was going to track him down like a dog. I didn't care if he was innocent or guilty. And I didn't care if it took the rest of my life. I was going to get Morelli. "Go to hell."

The grin widened. "You're lucky I'm a gentleman. There are individuals out there who'd take advantage of a woman in your situation."

"Spare me."

He shifted off the doorjamb. "It's been a pleasure."

"Wait a minute! You're not leaving, are you?"

"Afraid so."

"What about me? What about the handcuffs?"

He debated his options for a moment. He stepped off into the kitchen and returned with the portable phone. "I'm going to lock the front door when I leave, so make sure whoever you call has a key."

"Nobody has a key!"

"I'm sure you'll think of something," Morelli said. "Call the police. Call the fire department. Call the fucking Marines."

"I'm naked!"

He smiled and winked and walked out the door.

I heard the front door to my apartment close and lock. I didn't expect an answer, but I felt compelled to call out to Morelli as a test. I waited a few moments, holding my breath, listening to the silence. Morelli seemed to be gone. My fingers curled tighter around the phone. God help the phone company if they'd reneged on their promise to resume my service. I climbed onto the edge of the tub to bring myself up to the height of my secured hand. I carefully extended the antenna, pushed the on button, and put my ear to the handset. The dial tone sang out loud and clear. I was so relieved I almost burst into tears.

Now I was faced with a new problem. Who to call? The police and the fire company were out. They'd roar into my parking lot with their lights flashing, and by the time they got to my door, forty senior citizens would be standing in my hall in their jammies, waiting to see what all the excitement was about, waiting for an explanation.

I'd come to realize there were certain peculiarities about the seniors in my building. They were vicious when it came to parking, and they had a fascination for emergencies that bordered on the ghoulish. At the first hint of a flashing light, every senior in my building had their nose pressed to the window glass.

I also could do without four or five of the city's finest leering at me chained naked to my shower curtain rod.

If I called my mother, I'd have to move out of state because she'd never let up. And besides, she'd send my father, and then my father would see me naked. Being naked and handcuffed in front of my father wasn't something I could visualize.

If I called my sister, she'd call my mother.

I'd hang here and rot before I'd call my ex-husband.

To make it even more complicated, whoever came to rescue me was either going to have to climb the fire escape or jimmy the front door. I could only come up with one name. I squeezed my eyes shut. "Shit." I was going to have to call Ranger. I took a deep breath and tapped out his number, praying I'd remembered it correctly.

It took only one ring for him to pick up. "Yo."

"Ranger?"

"Who wants to know?"

"Stephanie Plum. I have a problem."

There was a pause two beats long, and I could imagine him coming alert, sitting up in bed. "What's the problem?"

I rolled my eyes, only half believing I was making this phone call. "I'm handcuffed to my shower curtain rod, and I need someone to open the cuffs."

Another pause and he disconnected.

I redialed, punching the buttons so hard I almost broke a finger.

"Yo!" Ranger said, sounding good and pissed off.

"Don't hang up! This is serious, dammit. I'm trapped in my bathroom. My front door is locked and no one has a key."

"Why don't you call the cops? They love this rescue shit."

"Because I don't want to have to explain to the cops. And besides, I'm naked."

"Heh, heh, heh."

"It's not funny. Morelli broke into my apartment while I was in the shower, and the son of a bitch handcuffed me to the shower rod."

"You gotta like the guy."

"Are you going to help me, or what?"

"Where do you live?"

"The apartment building at the corner of St. James and Dunworth. Apartment 215. It's a rear apartment. Morelli got in by climbing the fire escape and going through the window. You can probably do the same."

I couldn't actually blame Morelli for cuffing me to the curtain rod. After all, I had sort of stolen his car. And I could understand that he needed to keep me out of the way while he searched my apartment. I might even be able to forgive him for destroying my shower curtain in a show of macho force, but he went too far when he left me hanging here naked. If he thought this would discourage me, he was wrong. This whole deal was now in the ballpark of doubledare, and childish as it might be, I was not going to walk away from the challenge. I'd get Morelli or die trying.

I'd been standing in the tub for what seemed like hours when I heard my front door open and close.

The steam from the shower had long ago dissipated and the air had turned cool. My hand was numb from being held overhead. I was exhausted and hungry and had the beginnings of a headache.

Ranger appeared in the bathroom doorway, and I was too relieved to be embarrassed. "I appreciate your coming out in the middle of the night," I said.

Ranger smiled. "Didn't want to miss seeing you chained up naked."

"The keys are in the mess on the floor."

He found the keys, pried the phone loose from my fingers, and unlocked the cuffs. "You and Morelli got something kinky going on?"

"Remember when you gave me his keys this afternoon?"

"Uh huh."

"I sort of borrowed his car."

"Borrowed?"

"Commandeered, actually. You know, about us having the law and all?"

"Uh huh."

"Well, I commandeered his car, and he found out."

Ranger smiled and handed me a towel. "He understand about commandeering?"

"Let's just say he wasn't pleased. Anyway, I parked the car in the lot out here and removed the distributor cap as a safety precaution."

"Bet that went over big."

I got out of the tub and had to squelch a scream

when I saw my reflection in the vanity mirror. My hair looked like it had taken 2,000 volts and been spray starched. "I need to install an alarm system in his car, but I haven't got the money."

Ranger laughed soft and low in his chest. "An alarm system. Morelli'll love that." He took a pen from the floor and wrote an address on a piece of toilet paper. "I know a garage that'll give you a price."

I padded past him into the bedroom and exchanged the towel for a long terrycloth robe. "I heard you come in through the door."

"Picked the lock. Didn't think it prudent to wake up the super." He looked over at my window. Rain was spattering on the dark pane, and a piece of torn screening draped over the sill. "I only do the Spiderman shit in nice weather."

"Morelli wrecked my screen."

"Guess he in a hurry."

"I've noticed you only talk ghetto half of the time."

"I'm multilingual," Ranger said.

I followed him to the door, feeling jealous, wishing I knew a second language.

MY SLEEP WAS DEEP AND DREAMLESS, AND I MIGHT have slept until November if it weren't for the relentless pounding on my front door. I squinted at my bedside clock. The display read 8:35. Used to be I loved company. Now I cringed when someone knocked on my door. My first fear was of Ramirez. My second was that the police had come to haul me away for auto theft.

I picked the Sure Guard off my night table, stuffed my arms into my robe, and dragged myself to the door. I closed one eye and looked through the peephole with the other. Eddie Gazarra looked back at me. He was in uniform, holding two Dunkin' Donuts bags. I opened the door and sniffed the air like a hound on a scent. "Yum," I breathed.

"Hello to you, too," Gazarra said, squeezing past me in the little hallway, heading for the dining room table. "Where's your furniture?"

"I'm remodeling."

"Uh huh."

We sat opposite each other, and I waited while he took two cardboard cups of coffee out of one of the bags. We uncapped the coffee, spread napkins, and dug into the donuts.

We were good enough friends that we didn't have to talk while we ate. We ate the Boston creams first. Then we divided up the remaining four jelly donuts. At two donuts down he still hadn't noticed my hair, and I was left to wonder what my hair usually looked like. He also hadn't said anything about the mess Morelli had created while searching my apartment, which gave me pause to consider my housekeeping habits.

He ate his third donut more slowly, sipping his

coffee, savoring his donut, sipping his coffee, savoring his donut. "I hear you made a recovery yesterday," he said between savors.

He was left with just his coffee. He eyed my donut, and I protectively drew it closer to my edge of the table.

"Don't suppose you'd want to share that," Gazarra said.

"Don't suppose I would," I replied. "How did you find out about my recovery?"

"Locker room talk. You're prime conversation these days. The boys have a pool going on when you'll get boinked by Morelli."

My heart contracted so hard I was afraid my eyeballs might pop out of my head. I stared at Gazarra for a full minute, waiting for my blood pressure to ease out of the red zone, imagining capillaries bursting throughout my body.

"How will they know when I'm boinked?" I asked through clenched teeth. "Maybe he's boinked me already. Maybe we do it twice a day."

"They figure you'll quit the case when you get boinked. The winning time is actually when you quit the case."

"You in the pool?"

"Nope. Morelli nailed you when you were in high school. I don't think you'd let a second boinking go to your head."

"How do you know about high school?"

"Everybody knows about high school."

"Jesus." I swallowed the last piece of my last donut and washed it down with coffee.

Eddie sighed as he watched all hope for a part of the donut disappear into my mouth. "Your cousin, the queen of nags, has me on a diet," he said. "For breakfast I got decaf coffee, half a cup of cardboard cereal in skim milk, and a half grapefruit."

"I take it that's not cop food."

"Suppose I got shot," Eddie said, "and all I had in me was decaf and half a grapefruit. You think that'd get me to the trauma unit?"

"Not like real coffee and donuts."

"Damn straight."

"That overhang on your gun belt is probably good for stopping bullets, too."

Eddie drained his coffee cup, snapped the lid back on, and dumped it into the empty bag. "You wouldn't've said that if you weren't still pissed at the boinking stuff."

I agreed. "It was cruel."

He took a napkin and expertly flicked powdered sugar off his blue shirt. One of the many skills he'd learned at the academy, I thought. He sat back, arms folded across his chest. He was 5' 10" and stocky. His features were eastern Slavic with flat pale blue eyes, white blond hair, and a stubby nose. When we were kids he lived two houses down from me. His parents still live there. All his life he'd wanted to be a cop. Now that he was a uniform he had no desire to go further. He enjoyed driving the car, responding to emergencies, being first on the scene. He was good at comforting people. Everyone liked him, with the possible exception of his wife.

"I've got some information for you," Eddie said. "I went to Pino's last night for a beer, and Gus Dembrowski was there. Gus is the PC working the Kulesza case."

"PC?"

"Plainclothesman."

This brought me up straight in my seat. "Did he tell you anything more about Morelli?"

"He confirmed that Sanchez was an informant. Dembrowski let it slip that Morelli had a card on her. Informants are kept secret. The controlling supervisor keeps all the cards in a locked file. I guess in this case it was released as necessary information to the investigation."

"So maybe this is more complicated than it would first appear. Maybe the killing tied in to something Morelli had been working on."

"Could be. Could also be that Morelli had romantic interests in Sanchez. I understand she was young and pretty. Very Latino."

"And she's still missing."

"Yeah. She's still missing. The department's traced back to relatives in Staten Island and nobody's seen her."

"I talked to her neighbors yesterday, and it turns out one of the tenants who remembered seeing Morelli's alleged witness has suffered sudden death."

"What kind of sudden death?"

"Hit and run in front of the building."

"Could have been an accident."

"I'd like to think so."

He glanced at his watch and stood. "I gotta go."

"One last thing, do you know Mooch Morelli?"

"I see him around."

"You know what he does or where he lives?"

"Works for public health. Some kind of inspector. Lives in Hamilton Township somewhere. Connie'll have cross-street reference books at the office. If he has a phone, you'll be able to get a street address."

"Thanks. And thanks for the donuts and coffee."

He paused in the hallway. "You need money?"

I shook my head. "I'm doing okay."

He gave me a hug and a kiss on the cheek, and he left.

I closed the door after him and felt tears pool behind my eyes. Sometimes friendship chokes me up. I padded back to the dining room, gathered together the bags and napkins, and carted them off to the kitchen wastebasket. This was the first opportunity I'd had to actually take stock of my apartment. Morelli'd obviously gone through it in a snit, venting his frustration by making the worst possible mess. Kitchen cupboards were open, contents partially strewn on the counter and floor, books had been knocked from the bookcase, the cushion had been removed from my one remaining chair, the bedroom was cluttered with clothes pulled from drawers. I replaced the cushion and put the kitchen in order, deciding the rest of the apartment could wait.

I showered and dressed in black spandex shorts and an oversized khaki T-shirt. My bounty hunter paraphernalia was still scattered over the bathroom floor. I stuffed it back into my black leather bag and slung the bag over my shoulder. I checked all the windows to make sure they were locked. This would become a morning and evening ritual. I hated living like a caged animal, but I didn't want any more surprise visitors. Locking my front door seemed more a matter of formality than security. Ranger had picked the lock with little difficulty. Of course, not everyone had Ranger's skills. Still, it wouldn't hurt to add another dead bolt to my collection of locking devices. First chance I got I'd talk to the super.

I said good-bye to Rex, dredged up some courage, and poked my head into the hall before venturing farther, making certain Ramirez hadn't suddenly appeared.

SEVEN

THE DISTRIBUTOR CAP WAS JUST WHERE I'D LEFT it, under a bush, tucked in close to the building. I put it back where it belonged and pulled out of the lot, heading for Hamilton. I found a spot in front of Vinnie's office and managed to wedge the Cherokee into it on the third try.

Connie was at her desk, peering into a hand mirror, picking clumps of dried goo off the tips of heavily mascaraed lashes.

She looked up when she saw me. "You ever use this lash lengthener stuff?" she asked. "Looks like it's laced with rat hairs."

I waved the police receipt at her. "I got Clarence."

She made a fist and jerked her elbow back hard. "Yes!"

"Vinnie here?"

"Had to go to the dentist. Having his incisors sharpened, I think." She pulled her master copy of the file and took my receipt. "We don't need Vinnie to do this. I can write you a check." She made a notation on the file cover, and placed the file in a bin on the far corner of her desk. She took a ledger-style checkbook from her middle drawer and wrote out a check. "How's it going with Morelli? You able to get a fix on him?"

"Not exactly a fix, but I know he's still in town."

"He's a serious babe," Connie said. "Saw him six months ago, before all this happened. He was ordering a quarter pound of provolone at the meat market, and I had all I could do to keep from sinking my teeth into his butt."

"Sounds carnivorous."

"Carnivorous ain't the half of it. That man is fine."

"He's also accused of murder."

Connie sighed. "Gonna be a lot of women in Trenton unhappy to see Morelli on ice."

I supposed that was true, but I didn't happen to be one of them. After last night, the thought of Morelli behind bars conjured only cozy feelings in my humiliated, vindictive heart. "You have a cross-street reference here?"

Connie swiveled to face the file cabinets. "It's the big book over the G drawer."

"You know anything about Mooch Morelli?" I asked while I looked up his name.

"Only that he married Shirley Gallo."

The only Morelli in Hamilton Township was listed at 617 Bergen Court. I checked it against the wall map behind Connie's desk. If I remembered the area correctly, it was a neighborhood of split-level houses that looked like they deserved my bathroom.

"You seen Shirley lately?" Connie asked. "She's big as a horse. Must have gained a hundred pounds since high school. I saw her at Margie Manusco's shower. She took up three folding chairs when she sat down, and she had her pocketbook filled with Ding Dongs. I guess they were for an emergency . . . like in case someone beat her to the potato salad."

"Shirley Gallo? Fat? She was a rail in high school."

"The Lord moves in mysterious ways," Connie said.

"Amen."

Burg Catholicism was a convenient religion. When the mind boggled, there was always God, waiting in the wings to take the rap.

Connie handed me the check and plucked at a clump of mascara hanging at the end of her left eyelash. "I'm telling you, it's fucking hard to be classy," she said.

THE GARAGE RANGER RECOMMENDED WAS IN A small light-industrial complex that had its backside rammed up against Route 1. The complex consisted of six concrete bunker-type buildings painted yellow, the color faded by time and highway exhaust. At the inception of the project, the complex architect had most likely envisioned grass and shrubs. The reality was hard-packed dirt littered with butts and Styrofoam cups and some spiky weeds. Each of the six buildings had its own paved drive and parking lot.

I slowly drove past Capital Printing and A. and J. Extrusions and stopped at the entrance to Al's Auto Body. Three bay doors had been set into the front of the building, but only one gaped open. Bashed-in, rusted cars in various stages of disassembly were crammed into the junkyard at the rear, and late-model fender-bended cars were parked adjacent to the third bay, in a chain-link fenced compound topped with razor wire.

I rolled into the lot and parked next to a black Toyota four-by-four that had been jacked up on wheels that were sized for a backhoe. I'd stopped at the bank on the way and deposited my recovery check. I knew exactly how much money I was willing to spend on an alarm system, and I wasn't willing to pay a penny more. Most likely the job couldn't be done for my price, but it wouldn't hurt to inquire.

I opened the car door and stepped outside into oppressive heat, breathing shallowly so I didn't suck in any more heavy metals than was necessary. The sun looked squalid this close to the highway, the pollution diluting the light, compressing the image. The sound of an air wrench carried out of the open bay.

I crossed the lot and squinted into the dim hell-hole of grease guns and oil filters and potentially rude men wearing Day-Glo orange jumpsuits. One of the men ambled over to me. He was wearing the cutoff and knotted thigh portion of a pair of queen-size pantyhose on his head. Undoubtedly it was a timesaver in case he wanted to rob a 7-Eleven on the way home. I told him I was looking for Al, and he told me I'd found him.

"I need an alarm system installed in my car. Ranger said you'd give me a good price."

"How you come to know Ranger?"

"We work together."

"That covers a lot of territory."

I wasn't sure what he meant by that, and probably I didn't want to know. "I'm a recovery agent."

"So you need an alarm system because you gonna be in bad neighborhoods?"

"Actually, I sort of stole a car, and I'm afraid the owner will try to get it back."

Laughter flickered behind his eyes. "Even better."

He walked to a bench at the back of the building and returned with a black plastic gadget about three inches square. "This is state-of-the-art security," he said. "Works on air pressure. Anytime there's a change in air pressure, from a window getting broken or a door opening, this mother'll like to bust your eardrum." He turned it faceup in his hand. "You push this button to set it. Then there's a twenty-second delay before it goes into effect. Gives you time to get out and close the door. There's another twenty-second delay after the door is opened, so you can punch in your code to disarm."

"How do I shut it off once the alarm is triggered?"

"A key." He dropped a small silver key in my hand. "I suggest you don't leave the key in the car. Defeats the purpose."

"It's smaller than I'd expected."

"Small but mighty. And the good news is it's cheap because it's easy to install. All you do is screw it onto your dash."

"How cheap?"

"Sixty dollars."

"Sold."

He pulled a screwdriver out of his back pocket. "Just show me where you want it."

"The red Jeep Cherokee, next to the monster

truck. I'd like you to put the alarm some place inconspicuous. I don't want to deface the dash."

Minutes later I was on my way to Stark Street, feeling pretty pleased with myself. I had an alarm that was not only reasonably priced, but easily removed should I want to install it in the car I intended to buy when I cashed Morelli in. I'd stopped at a 7-Eleven on the way and gotten myself a vanilla yogurt and a carton of orange juice for lunch. I was drinking and driving and slurping, and I was very comfortable in my air-conditioned splendor. I had an alarm, I had nerve gas, I had a yogurt. What more could anyone want?

I parked directly across from the gym, guzzled the remaining orange juice, set the alarm, took my shoulder bag and file photos of Morelli, and locked up. I was waving the red flag at the bull. The only way I could possibly be more obvious was to plaster a sign to the windshield saying, "Here it is! Try and get it!"

Street activity was sluggish in the afternoon heat. Two hookers stood at the corner, looking like they were waiting for a bus, except buses didn't run down Stark Street. The women were standing there, obviously bored and disgusted, I suppose because nobody was buying at this time of day. They wore cheap plastic flip-flops, stretchy tank tops, and tight-fitting knit shorts. Their hair had been chopped short and cleverly straightened to boar-bristle quality. I wasn't sure exactly how prostitutes determined price, but if men bought hookers by the pound, these two would be doing okay.

They went into combat mode as I approached: Hands on hips, lower lips protruding, eyes opened so wide they bulged out like duck eggs.

"Hey girl," one of the lovelies called out. "What you think you doing here? This here's our corner, you dig?"

It would appear there was a fine line between being a babe from the burg and looking like a hooker.

"I'm looking for a friend. Joe Morelli." I showed them his picture. "Either of you see him around?"

"What you want with this Morelli?"

"It's personal."

"I bet."

"You know him?"

She shifted her weight. No small task. "Maybe."

"Actually, we were more than friends."

"How much more?"

"The son of a bitch got me pregnant."

"You don't look pregnant."

"Give me a month."

"There's things you can do."

"Yeah," I said, "and number one is find Morelli. You know where he is?"

"Nuh uh."

"You know someone named Carmen Sanchez? She worked at the Step In."

"She get you pregnant, too?"

"Thought Morelli might be with her."

"Carmen's disappeared," one of the hookers said. "Happens to women on Stark Street. Environmental hazard."

"You want to elaborate on that?"

"She want to keep her mouth shut, is what she want to do," the other woman said. "We don't know about any of that shit. And we don't got time to stand here talking to you. We got work to do."

I looked up and down the street. Couldn't see any work in sight, so I assumed I was getting the old heave-ho. I asked their names and was told Lula and Jackie. I gave each of them my card and told them I'd appreciate a call if they saw Morelli or Sanchez. I'd have asked about the missing male witness, but what would I say? Excuse me, have you seen a man with a face like a frying pan?

I went door-to-door after that, talking to people sitting out on stoops, questioning storekeepers. By four I had a sunburned nose to show for my efforts and not much more. I'd started on the north side of Stark Street and had worked two blocks west. Then I'd crossed the street and inched my way back. I'd slunk past the garage and the gym. I also bypassed the bars. They might be my best source, but they felt dangerous to me and beyond my abilities. Probably I was being unnecessarily cautious, probably the bars were filled with perfectly nice people who could give a rat's ass about my existence. Truth is, I wasn't used to being a minority, and I felt like a black man looking up white women's skirts in a WASP suburb of Birmingham.

I covered the south side of the next two and a half blocks and recrossed to the north side. Most of the buildings on this side were residential, and as the day progressed more and more people had drifted outdoors, so that the going was slow now as I moved down the street back to my car.

Fortunately, the Cherokee was still at the curb, and unfortunately, Morelli was nowhere to be seen. I diligently avoided looking up at the gym windows. If Ramirez was watching me, I'd prefer not to acknowledge him. I'd pulled my hair up into a lopsided ponytail, and the back of my neck felt scratchy. I supposed I was burned there too. I wasn't very diligent with sunscreen. Mostly, I counted on the pollution to filter out the cancer rays.

A woman came hurrying across the street to me. She was solidly built and conservatively dressed, with her black hair pulled back into a bun at the nape of her neck.

"Excuse me," she said. "Are you Stephanie Plum?"

"Yes."

"Mr. Alpha would like to speak to you," she said. "His office is just across the street."

I didn't know anyone named Alpha, and I wasn't eager to hover in the shadow of Benito Ramirez, but the woman reeked of Catholic respectability, so I took a chance and followed after her. We entered the building next to the gym. It was an average Stark Street row house. Narrow, three stories, sooty exterior, dark, grimy windows. We hurried up a flight of stairs to a small landing. Three doors opened off the landing. One door was ajar, and I felt air-conditioning spilling out into the hallway.

"This way," the woman said, leading me into a cramped reception room dwarfed by a green leather couch and large scarred blond wood desk. A shopworn end table held dog-eared copies of boxing magazines, and pictures of boxers covered walls that cried out for fresh paint.

She ushered me into an inner office and shut the door behind me. The inner office was a lot like the reception room with the exception of two windows looking down at the street. The man behind the desk stood when I entered. He was wearing pleated dress slacks and a short-sleeved shirt open at the neck. His face was lined and had a good start on jowls. His stocky body still showed muscle, but age had added love handles to his waist and streaks of gunmetal gray to his slicked-back black hair. I placed him in his late fifties and decided his life hadn't been all roses.

He leaned forward and extended his hand. "Jimmy Alpha. I manage Benito Ramirez."

I nodded, not sure how to respond. My first reaction was to shriek, but that would probably be unprofessional.

He motioned me to a folding chair placed slightly

to the side of his desk. "I heard you were back on the street, and I wanted to take this opportunity to apologize. I know what happened in the gym between you and Benito. I tried to call you, but your phone was disconnected."

His apology stirred fresh anger. "Ramirez's behavior was unprovoked and inexcusable."

Alpha looked genuinely embarrassed. "I never thought I'd have problems like this," he said. "All I ever wanted was to have a top boxer, and now I got one, and it's giving me ulcers." He took an economy-sized bottle of Mylanta from his top drawer. "See this? I buy this stuff by the case." He unscrewed the cap and chugged some. He put his fist to his sternum and sighed. "I'm sorry. I'm genuinely sorry for what happened to you in the gym."

"There's no reason for you to apologize. It's not your problem."

"I wish that was true. Unfortunately, it *is* my problem." He screwed the cap back on, returned the bottle to the drawer, and leaned forward, arms resting on his desk. "You work for Vinnie."

"Yes."

"I know Vinnie from way back. Vinnie's a character."

He smiled, and I figured somewhere in his travels he must have heard about the duck.

He sobered himself, fixed his eyes on his thumbs, and sagged a little in his seat. "Sometimes I don't know what to do with Benito. He's not a bad kid.

He just doesn't know a lot of stuff. All he knows is boxing. All this success is hard on a man like Benito, who comes from nowhere."

He looked up to see if I was buying. I made a derisive sound, and he acknowledged my disgust.

"I'm not excusing him," he said, his face a study in bitterness. "Benito does things that are wrong. I don't have any influence on him these days. He's full of himself. And he's got himself surrounded by guys who only got brains in their boxing gloves."

"That gym was filled with able-bodied men who did nothing to help me."

"I talked to them about it. Was a time when women were respected, but now nothing's respected. Drive-by killings, drugs . . ." He went quiet and sank into his own thoughts.

I remembered what Morelli had told me about Ramirez and previous rape charges. Alpha was either sticking his head in the sand or else he was actively engaged in cleaning up the mess made by the golden goose. I was putting money on the sand theory.

I stared at him in stony silence, feeling too isolated in his second-floor ghetto office to honestly vent my thoughts, feeling too angry to attempt polite murmurings.

"If Benito bothers you again, you let me know right away," Alpha said. "I don't like when this kind of stuff happens."

"He came to my apartment the night before last

and tried to get in. He was abusive in the hall, and he made a mess on my door. If it happens again, I'm filing charges."

Alpha was visibly shaken. "Nobody told me. He didn't hurt anybody, did he?"

"No one was hurt."

Alpha took a card from the top of his desk and scribbled a number on it. "This is my home phone," he said, handing me the card. "You have any more trouble, you call me right away. If he damaged your door I'll make good on it."

"The door's okay. Just keep him away from me."

Alpha pressed his lips together and nodded.

"I don't suppose you know anything about Carmen Sanchez?"

"Only what I read in the papers."

I TURNED LEFT AT STATE STREET AND PUSHED MY way into rush-hour traffic. The light changed, and we all inched forward. I had enough money left to buy a few groceries, so I bypassed my apartment and drove an extra quarter mile down the road to Super-Fresh.

It occurred to me while I was standing at the checkout that Morelli had to be getting food from somewhere or someone. Did he scuttle around Super-Fresh wearing a Groucho Marx mustache and glasses with a fake nose attached? And where was he living? Maybe he was living in the blue van. I'd assumed he'd dumped it after being spotted, but maybe not. Maybe it was too convenient. Maybe it was his command headquarters with a cache of canned goods. And I thought it was possible he had monitoring equipment in the van. He'd been across the street, spying on Ramirez, so maybe he was listening as well.

I hadn't seen the van on Stark Street. I hadn't been actively looking for it, but I wouldn't have passed it by, either. I didn't know a whole lot about electronic surveillance, but I knew the surveillor had to be fairly close to the surveillee. Something to think about. Maybe I could find Morelli by looking for the van.

I was forced to park at the rear of my lot, and did so harboring a few testy thoughts about handicapped old people who took all the best parking slots. I gripped three plastic grocery bags in each hand, plus a six-pack. I eased the Cherokee's door closed with my knee. I could feel my arms stretching against the weight, the bags clumsily banging around my knees as I walked, reminding me of a joke I'd once heard having to do with elephant testicles.

I took the elevator, wobbled the short distance down the hall, and set my bags on the carpet while I felt around for my key. I opened the door, switched on the light, shuttled my groceries into the kitchen, and returned to lock my front door. I did the grocery unpacking bit, sorting out cupboard stuff from refrigerator stuff. It felt good to have a little cache of food again. It was my heritage to hoard. Housewives in the burg were always prepared for disaster, stockpiling toilet paper and cans of creamed corn in case the blizzard of aughty-aught should ever repeat itself.

Even Rex was excited by the activity, watching from his cage with his little pink hamster feet pressed against the glass.

"Better days are coming, Rex," I said, giving him an apple slice. "From here on in it's all apples and broccoli."

I'd gotten a city map at the supermarket, and I spread it out on my table while I picked at dinner. Tomorrow I'd be methodical about searching for the blue van. I'd check the area surrounding the gym, and I'd also check out Ramirez's home address. I hauled out my phone book and looked up Ramirez. Twenty-three were listed. Three had B as the first initial. There were two Benitos. I dialed the first Benito and a woman answered on the fourth ring. I could hear a baby crying in the background.

"Does Benito Ramirez, the boxer, live there?" I asked.

The reply came in Spanish and didn't sound friendly. I apologized for disturbing her and hung up. The second Benito answered his own phone and was definitely not the Ramirez I was looking for. The three Bs were also dead ends. It didn't seem worthwhile to call the remaining eighteen numbers.

In a way I was relieved not to have found him. I don't know what I would have said. Nothing, I suppose. I was looking for an address, not a conversation. And the truth is the very thought of Ramirez sent a chill to my heart. I could stake out the gym and try to follow Ramirez when he left for the day, but the big red Cherokee wasn't exactly inconspicuous. Eddie might be able to help me. Cops had ways of getting addresses. Who else did I know who had access to addresses? Marilyn Truro worked for the DMV. If I had a license plate number, she could probably pull an address. Or I could call the gym. Nah, that'd be too easy.

Well, what the hell, I thought. Give it a shot. I'd torn the page advertising the gym out of my phone book, so I dialed information. I thanked the operator and dialed the number. I told the man who answered the phone that I was supposed to meet Benito, but I'd lost his address.

"Sure," he said. "It's 320 Polk. Don't know the apartment number, but it's on the second floor. It's at the rear of the hall. Got his name on the door. Can't miss it."

"Thanks," I told him. "Really appreciate it."

I pushed the phone to the far corner of the table and turned to the map to place Polk. The map showed it to be three blocks from the gym, running parallel to Stark. I circled the address with yellow marker. Now I had two sites to search for the van. I'd park and go on foot if I had to, prowling through alleys and investigating garages. I'd do this first thing in the morning, and if nothing developed, I'd go back to the stack of FTAs Connie had given me and try to make some rent money doing nickel-and-dime cases.

I double-checked all my windows to make sure they were locked, then I drew all the curtains. I wanted to take a shower and go to bed early, and I didn't want any surprise visitors.

I straightened my apartment, trying not to notice the empty spaces where appliances had been, trying to ignore the phantom furniture indentations persisting in the living room carpet. Morelli's $10,000 recovery fee would go a long way toward restoring some semblance of normalcy to my life, but it was a stopgap measure. Probably I should still be applying for jobs.

Who was I kidding. I'd covered all the bases in my field.

I could stay with skip tracing, but it seemed risky at best. And at worst . . . I didn't even want to think about worst. Besides getting used to being threatened, hated, and possibly molested, wounded, or God forbid killed, I'd have to establish a self-employed mind-set. And I'd have to invest in martial arts coaching and learn some police techniques for subduing felons. I didn't want to turn myself into the Terminator, but I didn't want to continue to operate at my present Elmer Fudd level, either.

If I had a television I could watch reruns of *Cagney and Lacey*.

I remembered my plan to get another dead bolt installed and decided to visit Dillon Ruddick, the super. Dillon and I were buds, being that we were just about the only two people in the building who didn't think Metamucil was one of the four major food groups. Dillon moved his lips when he read the funnies, but put a tool in the man's hand and he was pure genius. He lived in the bowels of the building, in a carpeted efficiency that never saw the natural light of day. There was a constant background serenade as boilers and water heaters rumbled and water swished through pipes. Dillon said he liked it. Said he pretended it was the ocean.

"Hey Dillon," I said when he answered the door. "How's it going?"

"Going okay. Can't complain. What can I do for you?"

"I'm worried about crime, Dillon. I thought it would be a good idea to get another dead bolt put on my door."

"That's cool," he said. "A person can never be too careful. In fact, I just finished putting a dead bolt on Mrs. Luger's door. She said some big, huge guy was yelling in the halls, late at night, couple days ago. Said it scared the whatever out of her. Maybe you heard him, too. Mrs. Luger's just two doors down from you."

I resisted the urge to swallow and go "gulp." I knew the name of the big, huge guy.

"I'll try to get the lock on tomorrow," Dillon said. "In the meantime, how about a beer?"

"A beer would be good."

Dillon handed me a bottle and a can of mixed nuts. He boosted the sound back up on the TV, and we both plopped down on the couch.

I'D SET MY ALARM FOR EIGHT, BUT I WAS UP AT seven, anxious to find the van. I took a shower and spent some time on my hair, doing the blow-drying thing, adding some gel and some spray. When I was done I looked like Cher on a bad day. Still, Cher on a bad day wasn't all that bad. I was down to my last clean pair of spandex shorts. I tugged on a matching sports bra that doubled as a halter top and slid a big, loose, purple T-shirt with a large, droopy neck over my head. I laced up my hightop Reeboks, crunched down my white socks, and felt pretty cool.

I ate Frosted Flakes for breakfast. If they were good enough for Tony the Tiger, they were good enough for me. I swallowed down a multivitamin, brushed my teeth, poked a couple of big gold hoops through my earlobes, applied glow-in-the-dark Cherry Red lipstick, and I was ready to go.

Cicadas droned their early warning of another scorcher day, and the blacktop steamed with what was left of morning dew. I pulled out of the lot into the steady stream of traffic on St. James. I had the map spread out on the seat next to me, plus a steno pad I'd begun to use for phone numbers, addresses, and miscellaneous bits of information relating to the job.

Ramirez's apartment building was set in the middle of the block, its identity lost in a crush of four-story walk-ups built cheek by jowl for the working poor. Most likely the building had originally held immigrant laborers—Irish, Italian, Polish hopefuls barged up the Delaware to work in Trenton's factories. It was difficult to tell who lived here now. There were no old men loitering on front stoops, no children playing on the sidewalk. Two middle-aged Asian women stood waiting at a bus stop, their purses held tight against their chests, their faces expressionless. There were no vans in sight, and no place to hide one. No garages or alleys. If Morelli was keeping tabs on Ramirez, it would have to be from the rear or from an adjacent apartment.

I drove around the corner and found the single-lane service road that cut the block. There were no garages back here, either. An asphalt slab had been laid tight to the rear of Ramirez's building. Diagonal parking for six cars had been lined off on the slab. Only four cars were parked. Three old clunkers and a Silver Porsche with a license plate holder that had "The Champ" printed on it in gold. None of the cars was occupied.

Across the service road were more tenement-type

apartments. This would be a reasonable place for Morelli to watch or listen, I thought, but there was no sign of him.

I drove through the service road and circled the block, methodically enlarging the area until I'd covered all drivable streets for a nine-block square. The van didn't turn up.

I headed for Stark Street and repeated the procedure, looking for the van. There were garages and alleys here, so I parked the Cherokee and set out on foot. By twelve-thirty I'd snooped in enough broken-down, smelly garages to last me a lifetime. If I crossed my eyes I could see my nose peeling, my hair was sticking to the back of my sweaty neck, and I had bursitis from carrying my hulking shoulder bag.

By the time I got back to the Cherokee, my feet felt like they were on fire. I leaned against the car and checked to make sure my soles weren't melting. A block away I could see Lula and Jackie staking out their corner. I figured it wouldn't hurt to talk to them again.

"Still looking for Morelli?" Lula asked.

I shoved my dark glasses to the top of my head. "Have you seen him?"

"Nope. Haven't heard nothing about him, either. Man's keeping a low profile."

"How about his van?"

"Don't know nothing about a van. Lately, Morelli's been driving a red and gold Cherokee . . . like the one you're driving." Her eyes widened. "Sheee-it, that ain't Morelli's car, is it?"

"I sort of borrowed it."

Lula's face split in a grin. "Honey, you telling me you *stole* Morelli's car? Girl, he gonna kick your skinny white butt."

"Couple days ago I saw him driving a faded blue Econoline," I said. "It had antennae sticking out all over the place. You see anything like that cruise by?"

"We didn't see nothing," Jackie said.

I turned to Lula. "How about you, Lula? You see a blue van?"

"Tell me the truth now? You really pregnant?" Lula asked.

"No, but I could have been." Fourteen years ago.

"So what's going on here. What you really want with Morelli?"

"I work for his bondsman. Morelli is FTA."

"No shit? There any money in that?"

"Ten percent of the bond."

"I could do that," Lula said. "Maybe I should change my profession."

"Maybe you should stop talking and look like you want to give some before your old man beats the crap out of you," Jackie said.

I drove back to my apartment, ate some more Frosted Flakes, and called my mother.

"I made a nice big pot of stuffed cabbages," she said. "You should come for supper."

"Sounds good, but I have things to do."

"Like what? What's so important you can't take time to eat some stuffed cabbages?"

"Work."

"What kind of work? Are you still trying to find the Morelli boy?"

"Yeah."

"You should get a different job. I saw a sign at Clara's Beauty Salon they need a shampoo girl."

I could hear my Grandma Mazur yelling something in the background.

"Oh yeah," my mother said. "You had a phone call this morning from that boxer you went to see, Benito Ramirez. Your father was so excited. Such a nice young man. So polite."

"What did Ramirez want?"

"He said he'd been trying to get in touch with you, but your phone had been disconnected. I told him it was okay now."

I mentally banged my head against the wall. "Benito Ramirez is a sleaze. If he calls up again, don't talk to him."

"He was polite to me on the phone."

Yeah, I thought, the most courteous homicidal rapist in Trenton. And now he knew he could call me.

EIGHT

MY APARTMENT BUILDING WAS PRE-LAUNDRY room vintage, and the present owner felt no compulsion to add amenities. The nearest coin-op, Super Suds, was about a half mile away on Hamilton. Not a journey of insurmountable proportions, but a pain in the ass all the same.

I tucked the stack of FTAs I'd received from Connie into my pocketbook and slung my pocketbook over my shoulder. I lugged my laundry basket into the hall, locked my door, and hauled myself out to the car.

As far as laundromats went, Super Suds wasn't bad. There was parking in a small lot to the side of the building and a luncheonette next door where a person could get a tasty chicken salad sandwich if a person had cash on hand. I happened to be low on cash on hand, so I dumped my laundry into a machine, added detergent and quarters, and settled down to review my FTAs.

Lonnie Dodd was at the top of the stack and seemed like the easiest apprehension. He was twenty-two and lived in Hamilton Township. He'd been charged with auto theft. A first-time offender. I used the laundromat pay phone to call Connie to verify that Dodd was still outstanding.

"He's probably in his garage, changing his oil," she said. "Happens all the time. It's one of those man things. Hell, they say to themselves, nobody's gonna push me around. All I did was steal a few cars. What's the big fuckin' deal? So they don't show up for their court date."

I thanked Connie for her insight and returned to my chair. As soon as my laundry was done, I'd mosey on over to Dodd's place and see if I could find him.

I slid the files back into my pocketbook and transferred my clothes to the dryer. I sat down, looked out the big plate glass front window, and the blue van rolled by. I was so startled I froze, mouth open, eyes glazed, mind blank. Not what you would call a quick draw. The van disappeared down the street, and in the distance I could see the brake lights go on. Morelli was stopped in traffic.

Now I moved. Actually, I think I flew, because I don't remember my feet touching pavement. I peeled out of the lot, smoking rubber. I got to the corner and the alarm went off. In my haste I'd forgotten to punch in the code.

I could barely think for the noise. The key was on my key ring, and the key ring was attached to the key in the ignition. I slammed my foot on the brake, fishtailing to a stop in the middle of the road. I looked in the rearview mirror after the fact, relieved to find there were no cars behind me. I deactivated the alarm and took off again.

Several cars were between me and Morelli. He turned right, and I gripped the wheel tighter, creeping along, inventing colorful new expletives as I made my way to the intersection. By the time I turned he was gone. I slowly worked my way up and down the streets. I was ready to quit when I spotted the van parked in the back lot to Manni's Deli.

I stopped at the entrance to the lot and stared at the van, wondering what to do next. I had no way of knowing if Morelli was behind the wheel. He could be stretched out in back, taking a snooze, or he could be in Manni's ordering tuna on a kaiser to go. Probably I should park and investigate. If it turned out he wasn't in the van, I'd hide behind one of the cars and gas him when he came into range.

I pulled into a slot at the back of the lot, four cars down from the van, and cut the engine. I was about to reach for my bag when suddenly the driver's side door was ripped open, and I was yanked from behind the wheel. I stumbled forward, slamming into the wall of Morelli's chest.

"Looking for me?" he asked.

"You might as well give up," I told him, "because I never will."

The line of his mouth tightened. "Tell me about it. Suppose I lay down on the pavement and you run over me a few times with my own car . . . just for old times. Would you like that? Do you get your money dead or alive?"

"No reason to get testy about it. I have a job to do. It's nothing personal."

"Nothing personal? You've harassed my mother, stolen my car, and now you're telling people I've gotten you pregnant! In my opinion, getting someone pregnant is pretty fucking personal! Jesus, isn't it enough I'm accused of murder? What are you, the bounty hunter from hell?"

"You're overwrought."

"I'm beyond overwrought. I'm resigned. Everyone has a cross to bear . . . you're mine. I give up. Take the car. I don't care anymore. All I ask is that you try not to get too many dings on the door and you change the oil when the red light goes on." His eyes flicked to the car interior. "You're not making phone calls, are you?"

"No. Of course not."

"Phone calls are expensive."

"Not to worry."

"Shit," he said. "My life is shit."

"Probably this is just a phase."

His expression softened. "I like this outfit you're wearing." He hooked a finger around the wide neck of my T-shirt and looked inside at the black spandex sports bra. "Very sexy."

A flash of heat shot through my stomach. I told myself it was anger, but I suspect carnal panic would be closer to the truth. I smacked his hand away. "Don't be rude."

"Well hell, I've made you pregnant, remember? One more little intimacy shouldn't bother you." He moved closer. "I like the lipstick, too. Cherry red. Very tempting."

He lowered his mouth and kissed me.

I know I should have kneed him in the groin, but the kiss was delicious. Joe Morelli still knew how to kiss. It had started out slow and tender in the beginning, and it had ended up hot and deep. He pulled back and smiled, and I knew I'd been had.

"Gotcha," he said.

"Dick breath."

He reached around me and removed the keys from the ignition. "I don't want you following."

"Furthest thought from my mind."

"Yeah, well I'm going to slow you down a little, anyway." He walked to the deli's Dumpster and pitched the keys inside. "Happy hunting," he said, heading for the van. "Make sure you wipe your feet before you get in my car."

"Wait a minute," I yelled after him. "I have some

questions. I want to know about the murder. I want to know about Carmen Sanchez. And is it true there's a contract out on you?"

He hitched himself up into the van and drove out of the lot.

The Dumpster was industrial-sized. Five feet high, five feet wide, and six feet long. I stood on tiptoe and peered over the side. It was one-quarter full and smelled like dead dog. I couldn't see the keys.

A lesser woman would have burst into tears. A smarter woman would have had an extra set of keys. I dragged a wooden crate to the side of the Dumpster and stood on it for a better look. Most of the garbage was bagged. Some of the bags had split on impact, spewing out half-eaten subs, globs of potato salad, coffee grounds, grill grease, unrecognizable slop, and heads of lettuce turning to primordial ooze.

I was reminded of road kill. Ashes to ashes . . . mayo to its various components. Doesn't matter whether it's cats or cole slaw, death is not attractive.

I did a rundown of everyone I knew, but I couldn't think of anyone dumb enough to climb into the Dumpster for me. Okay, I told myself, now or never. I swung my leg up and over the side and hung there for a moment, gathering courage. I lowered myself slowly, upper lip curled. If I smelled even the *hint* of rat breath, I was out of there.

Cans rolled underfoot, giving way to soft,

squishy gunk. I felt myself slide and hooked a hand onto the Dumpster rim, cracking my elbow against the side in the process. I swore and blinked back tears.

I found a plastic bread bag that was relatively clean and used it like a glove to carefully paw through the slop, moving cautiously, scared to death I'd fall face first into the artichoke and calf brains vinaigrette. The amount of discarded food was sobering, the wastefulness almost as revolting as the all-pervasive odor of rot that seared the inside of my nose and clung to the roof of my mouth.

After what seemed like an eternity I discovered the keys sunk into some yellow-brown glop. I didn't see any Pampers nearby, so I hoped the glop was mustard. I stuck my bagged hand in whatever-it-was and gagged.

I held my breath, tossed the keys over the edge onto the blacktop, and didn't waste any time following. I wiped off the keys as best I could with the bread bag. Most of the yellow stuff came off, rendering the keys good enough for emergency driving. I got out of my shoes by stepping on the heels, and I used the two-fingers sissy approach to peel my socks away. I inspected the rest of me. Aside from some Thousand Island dressing smeared on the front of my shirt, I seemed unscathed.

Newspapers had been stacked for recycling beside the Dumpster. I covered the driver's seat with the sports section, just in case I'd missed seeing some noxious substance stuck to my ass. I spread paper over the passenger-side floor mat and gingerly set my shoes and socks in the center.

I glanced at the remaining section of paper, and a headline jumped out at me. "Local Man Killed in Drive-by Shooting." Beneath the headline was a picture of John Kuzack. I'd seen him on Wednesday. Today was Friday. The paper in my hand was a day old. I read the story without breathing. Kuzack had been gunned down late Wednesday night in front of his apartment building. It went on to say how he'd been a hero in Nam, getting the purple heart, and how he was a colorful, well-liked neighborhood figure. As of press time, the police had no suspect and no motive.

I leaned against the Cherokee, trying to absorb the reality of John Kuzack's death. He'd been so big and alive when I'd spoken to him. And now he was dead. First Edleman, the hit and run, and now Kuzack. Of the three people who'd seen and remembered the missing witness, two were dead. I thought about Mrs. Santiago and her children and shivered.

I carefully folded the paper and slid it into the map pocket. When I got back to my apartment I'd call Gazarra and try to get some reassurance of Mrs. Santiago's safety.

I was beyond being able to smell myself, but I drove with the windows down as a precaution.

I parked in the laundromat lot and slipped in

barefoot to get my clothes. Only one other person was in the room, an elderly woman at the folding table on the far wall.

"Oh my goodness," she said, looking bewildered. "What is that smell?"

I felt my cheeks heat up. "Must be outside," I said. "Must have followed me in when I opened the door."

"It's *awful*!"

I sniffed, but I couldn't smell anything. My nose had shut down in self-defense. I glanced at my shirt. "Does it smell like Thousand Island dressing?"

She had a pillowcase pressed to her face. "I think I'm going to be sick."

I rammed my laundry into the basket and made my exit. Halfway home I stopped for a light and noticed my eyes were watering. Ominous, I thought. Fortunately, no one was afoot when I swung into the parking lot to my apartment building. The foyer and the elevator were both empty. So far so good. The elevator doors opened to the second floor and no one was about there, either. I breathed a sigh of relief, dragged my laundry to my door, slunk into my apartment, stripped off my clothes, and tied them up in a big black plastic garbage bag.

I jumped into the shower and lathered and scrubbed and shampooed thrice. I dressed in clean clothes and went across the hall to Mr. Wolesky as a test.

He opened the door and instantly clamped a hand

over his nose. "Whoa," he gasped. "What's that smell?"

"That's what I was wondering," I said. "It seems to be hanging in the hall here."

"Smells like dead dog."

I sighed. "Yeah. That was my first impression, too."

I retreated back to my apartment. I needed to rewash everything, and I'd run out of quarters. I was going to have to go home to do my laundry. I looked at my watch. It was almost six. I'd call my mother on the car phone and warn her I'd be there for dinner after all.

I parked in front of the house, and my mother appeared like magic, driven by some mysterious maternal instinct always to know when her daughter set foot on the curb.

"A new car," she said. "How nice. Where did you get it?"

I had the basket under one arm and the plastic trash bag under the other. "I borrowed it from a friend."

"Who?"

"You don't know him. Someone I went to school with."

"Well, you're lucky to have friends like that. You should bake him something. A cake."

I pushed past her, heading for the cellar stairs. "I brought my laundry. I hope you don't mind."

"Of course I don't mind. What's that smell? Is

that you? You smell like a garbage can."

"I accidentally dropped my keys in a Dumpster, and I had to climb in and get them out."

"I don't understand how these things happen to you. They don't happen to anyone else. Who else do you know dropped their keys in a Dumpster? No one, that's who. Only you would do such a thing."

Grandma Mazur came out of the kitchen. "I smell throw-up."

"It's Stephanie," my mother said. "She was in a Dumpster."

"What was she doing in a Dumpster? Was she looking for bodies? I saw a movie on TV where the mob splattered some guy's brains all over the place and then left him for rat food in a Dumpster."

"She was looking for her keys," my mother told Grandma Mazur. "It was an accident."

"Well that's disappointing," Grandma Mazur said. "I expected something better from her."

When we were done eating, I called Eddie Gazarra, put the second load of laundry in the washer, and hosed down my shoes and my keys. I sprayed the inside of the Jeep with Lysol and opened the windows wide. The alarm wasn't usable with the windows open, but I didn't think I was running much risk of the car being reclaimed from in front of my parents' house. I took a shower and dressed in clean clothes fresh from the dryer.

I was spooked over John Kuzack's death and not anxious to walk into a dark apartment, so I made a point of getting home early. I'd just locked the door behind me when the phone rang. The voice was muffled, so that I had to strain to hear, squinting at the handset as if that would help.

Fear is not a logical emotion. No one can physically hurt me on the phone, but I flinched all the same when I realized it was Ramirez.

I immediately hung up, and when the phone rang again I snapped the plug from the wall jack. I needed an answering machine to monitor my calls, but I couldn't afford to buy one until I made a recovery. First thing in the morning I was going to have to go after Lonnie Dodd.

I AWOKE TO THE STEADY DRUMMING OF RAIN ON my fire escape. Wonderful. Just what I needed to complicate my life further. I crawled out of bed and pulled the curtain aside, not pleased at the sight of an all-day soaker. The parking lot had slicked up, reflecting light from mysterious sources. The rest of the world was gunmetal gray, the cloud cover low and unending, the buildings robbed of color behind the rain.

I showered and dressed in jeans and a T-shirt, letting my hair dry on its own. No sense fussing when I was going to get drenched the instant I stepped out of the building. I did the breakfast thing, brushed my teeth, and applied a nice thick line of turquoise eyeliner to offset the gloom. I was wearing my Dumpster shoes in honor of the rain. I looked down and sniffed. Maybe I smelled a hint of boiled ham, but all things considered I didn't think that was so bad.

I did a pocketbook inventory, making sure I had all my goodies—cuffs, bludgeoning baton, flashlight, gun, extra ammo (not much good to me since I'd already forgotten how to load the gun—still, you never knew when you might need something heavy to throw at an escaping felon). I crammed Dodd's file in along with a collapsible umbrella and a package of peanut butter crackers for emergency snacking. I grabbed the ultracool black and purple Gore-Tex jacket I'd purchased when I was of the privileged working class, and I headed for the parking lot.

This was the sort of day to read comic books under a blanket tent and eat the icing from the middle of the Oreos. This was *not* the sort of day to chase down desperados. Unfortunately, I was hard up for money and couldn't be choosy about selecting desperado days.

Lonnie Dodd's address was listed as 2115 Barnes. I hauled my map out and looked up the coordinates. Hamilton Township is about three times the size of Trenton proper and roughly shaped like a wedge of pie that's suffered some nibbles. Barnes ran with its back pressed to the Conrail tracks just north of Yardville, the beginning of the lower third of the county.

I took Chambers to Broad and cut up on Apollo. Barnes struck off from Apollo. The sky had lightened marginally, and it was possible to read house numbers as I drove. The closer I got to 2115 the more depressed I became. Property value was dropping at a frightening rate. What had begun as a respectable blue-collar neighborhood with trim single-family bungalows on good-sized lots had deteriorated to neglected low-income to no-income housing.

Twenty-one fifteen was at the end of the street. The grass was overgrown and had gone to seed. A rusted bike and a washing machine with its top lid askew decorated the front yard. The house itself was a small cinder block rancher built on a slab. It looked to be more of an outbuilding than a home. Something intended for chickens or porkers. A sheet had been tacked haphazardly over the front picture window. Probably to afford the inhabitants privacy while they crushed cans of Bull's-Eye beer against their foreheads and plotted mayhem.

I told myself it was now or never. Rain pattered on the roof and sluiced down the windshield. I pumped myself up by applying fresh lipstick. There was no great surge of power, so I deepened the blue liner and added mascara and blush. I checked myself out in the rearview mirror. Wonder Woman, eat your heart out. Yeah, right. I studied Dodd's picture one last time. Didn't want to overwhelm the wrong man. I dropped my keys into my pocketbook, pulled my hood up, and got out of the car. I knocked on the door and caught myself secretly hoping no one was home. The rain and the neighborhood and the grim little house were giving me the creeps. If the second knock goes unanswered, I thought, I'll consider it the will of God that I'm not destined to catch Dodd, and I'll get the hell out of here.

No one answered on the second knock, but I'd heard a toilet flush, and I knew someone was in there. Damn. I gave the door a few good shots with my fist. "Open up," I yelled at the top of my voice. "Pizza delivery."

A skinny guy with dark, tangled shoulder-length hair answered the door. He was a couple inches taller than me. He was barefoot and shirtless, wearing a pair of filthy, low-slung jeans that were unsnapped and only half zipped. Beyond him I could see a trash-filled living room. The air drifting out was pungent with cat fumes.

"I didn't order no pizza," he said.

"Are you Lonnie Dodd?"

"Yeah. What's with the pizza delivery shit?"

"It was a ploy to get you to answer your door."

"A what?"

"I work for Vincent Plum, your bond agent. You missed your trial date, and Mr. Plum would like you to reschedule."

"Fuck that. I'm not rescheduling nothing."

The rain was running off my jacket in sheets, soaking my jeans and shoes. "It would only take a few minutes. I'd be happy to drive you."

"Plum doesn't have no limo service. Plum only hires two kinds of people ... women with big pointy tits and scumbag bounty hunters. Nothing personal, and it's hard to see with that raincoat on, but you don't look like you got big pointy tits. That leaves scumbag bounty hunter."

Without warning he reached out into the rain, grabbed my pocketbook off my shoulder, and tossed the contents onto the tan shag carpet behind him. The gun landed with a thunk.

"You could get into a lot of crap carrying concealed in this state," he said.

I narrowed my eyes. "Are you going to cooperate here?"

"What do you think?"

"I think if you're smart you'll get a shirt and some shoes and come downtown with me."

"Guess I'm not that smart."

"Fine. Then just give me my stuff, and I'll be more than happy to leave." Truer words were never spoken.

"I'm not giving you nothing. This here stuff looks like *my* stuff now."

I was debating kicking him in the nuts when he gave me a shove to the chest, knocking me backward off the small cement pad. I came down hard on my ass in the mud.

"Take a hike," he said, "or I'll shoot you with your own fucking gun."

The door slammed shut and the bolt clicked into place. I got up and wiped my hands on my jacket. I couldn't believe I'd just stood there flat-footed and let him take my shoulder bag. What had I been thinking?

I'd been thinking about Clarence Sampson and not about Lonnie Dodd. Lonnie Dodd wasn't a fat drunk. I should have approached him with a much more defensive posture. I should have stood farther back, out of his reach. And I should have had my defense spray in my hand, not in my pocketbook.

I had a lot to learn as a bounty hunter. I lacked skills, but even more problematic, I lacked attitude. Ranger had tried to tell me, but it hadn't taken hold. Never let your guard down, he'd said. When you walk the street, you have to see everything, every second. You let your mind wander, and you could be dead. When you go after your FTA, always be prepared for the worst.

It had seemed overly dramatic at the time. Looking at it in retrospect, it had been good advice.

I stomped back to the Jeep and stood there fuming, swearing at myself and Dodd and E.E. Martin. I threw in a few choice thoughts about Ramirez and Morelli and kicked a tire.

"Now what?" I yelled in the rain. "Now what are you going to do, girl genius?"

Well, I sure as hell wasn't going to leave without Lonnie Dodd shackled and stuffed into my backseat. As I saw it, I needed help, and I had two choices.

The police or Ranger. If I called the police I might be in trouble with the gun. It'd have to be Ranger.

I closed my eyes. I really didn't want to call Ranger. I'd wanted to do this myself. I'd wanted to show everyone I was capable.

"Pride goeth before the fall," I said. I wasn't sure exactly what that meant, but it felt right.

I took a deep groaning breath, shucked the muddy, dripping-wet raincoat, slid behind the wheel, and called Ranger.

"Yo," he said.

"I have a problem."

"Are you naked?"

"No, I'm not naked."

"Too bad."

"I have an FTA cornered in his house, but I'm not having any luck making an apprehension."

"You want to be more specific about the not having any luck part."

"He took my pocketbook and kicked me out of the house."

Pause. "I don't suppose you managed to keep your gun."

"Don't suppose I did. On the bright side, the gun wasn't loaded."

"You have ammo in your pocketbook?"

"I might have had a few loose bullets rolling around."

"Where are you now?"

"In front of the house, in the Jeep."

"And you want me to come over there and persuade your FTA to behave."

"Yeah."

"Good thing for you I'm into this Henry Higgins shit. What's the address?"

I gave him the address and hung up feeling disgusted with myself. I'd virtually armed my FTA, and now I was sending Ranger in to clean up the mess I'd made of things. I was going to have to get smarter faster. I was going to learn how to load the damn gun, and I was going to learn how to shoot it. I might not ever have the guts to shoot Joe Morelli, but I was pretty sure I could shoot Lonnie Dodd.

I watched the clock on the dash, waiting for Ranger, anxious to resolve this unfinished business. Ten minutes passed before his Mercedes appeared at the end of the street, gliding through the rain, sleek and sinister, water not daring to adhere to the paint finish.

We simultaneously got out of our cars. He wore a black baseball cap, tight black jeans, and a black T-shirt. He strapped on his black nylon gun belt and holster, the gun held tight to his leg by a black Velcro strap. At first glance he'd pass for a SWAT cop. He shrugged into a Kevlar vest. "What's the FTA's name?"

"Lonnie Dodd."

"You got a photo?"

I ran to the Jeep, pulled out Dodd's picture, and gave it to Ranger.

"What'd he do?" Ranger wanted to know.

"Auto theft. First-time offender."

"He alone?"

"As far as I know. I can't guarantee it."

"This house have a back door?"

"Don't know."

"Let's find out."

We took a direct route to the back, cutting through the tall grass, keeping our eyes on the front door, watching the windows for movement. I hadn't bothered with my jacket. It seemed like an unnecessary encumbrance at this point. My energies were directed at catching Dodd. I was soaked to the skin, and it was liberating to know I couldn't get any wetter. The backyard was similar to the front: tall grass, a rusted swing set, two garbage cans overflowing with garbage, their dented lids lying on the ground nearby. A back door opened to the yard.

Ranger pulled me close to the building, out of window sight. "You stay here and watch the back door. I'm going in the front. I don't want you to be a hero. You see anybody run for the train tracks, you keep out of their way. Got that?"

Water dripped from the tip of my nose. "Sorry to put you through this."

"This is partly my fault. I haven't been taking you serious enough. If you're really going to do this job, you're going to need somebody to help you

with the takedown. And we need to spend some
time talking about apprehension techniques."

"I need a partner."

"Yeah. You need a partner."

He moved off, rounding the house, his footsteps
muffled by the rain. I held my breath, straining to
hear, catching his knock on the door, hearing him
identify himself.

There was obviously a reply from within, but it
was lost to me. What followed after that was a blur
of sound and action on fast forward. Warnings from
Ranger that he was coming in, the door crashing
open, a lot of shouting. A single report from a gun.

The back door banged open and Lonnie Dodd
charged out, heading not for the tracks, but for the
next house down. He was still clad only in jeans.
He was running blind in the rain, clearly panicked.
I was partially hidden by a shed, and he ran right
by me without a sideways glance. I could see the
silver glint of a gun stuck in his waistband.
Wouldn't you know it? On top of every other insult,
now the creep was making off with my gun. Four
hundred dollars shot to hell, and just when I'd decided to learn how to use the damn thing.

No way was I going to let this happen. I yelled
for Ranger and took off after Dodd. Dodd wasn't
that far in front of me, and I had the advantage of
shoes. He was sliding in the rain-slicked grass, stepping on God-knows-what. He went down to one
knee, and I bodyslammed into the back of him,

knocking us both to the ground. He hit with an "unh!" thanks to 125 pounds of angry female landing on top of him. Well okay, maybe 127, but not an ounce more, I swear.

He was laboring to breathe, and I grabbed the gun, not from any defensive instinct, but out of sheer possessiveness. It was *my* gun, dammit. I scrambled to my feet and pointed the .38 in Dodd's direction, holding it with both hands to minimize the shaking. It never occurred to me to check for bullets. "Don't move!" I yelled. "Don't fucking move or I'll shoot."

Ranger appeared in my peripheral vision. He put his knee to the small of Dodd's back, snapped cuffs on him, and jerked him to his feet.

"The sonofabitch shot me," Ranger said. "Do you believe this shit? A lousy car thief shot me." He shoved Dodd ahead of him toward the road. "I'm wearing a fucking Kevlar vest. You think he could shoot me in the vest? No way. He's such a lousy shot, he's so chicken-shit scared, he shoots me in my fucking leg."

I looked down at Ranger's leg and almost keeled over.

"Run ahead and call the police," Ranger said. "And call Al at the body shop to come get my car."

"You sure you're going to be okay?"

"Flesh wound, babe. Nothing to worry about."

I made the calls, retrieved my pocketbook and assorted goods from Dodd's house, and waited with

Ranger. We had Dodd trussed up like a Christmas goose, facedown in the mud. Ranger and I sat on the curb in the rain. He didn't seem concerned about the seriousness of his wound. He said he'd had worse, but I could see the pain wearing him down, pinching his face.

I wrapped my arms tight around myself and clamped my teeth together to keep them from chattering. Outwardly, I was keeping a stiff upper lip, trying to be as stoic as Ranger, trying to be confidently supportive. Inside, I was shaking so bad I could feel my heart shivering in my chest.

NINE

THE COPS CAME FIRST, THEN THE PARAMEDICS, then Al. We gave preliminary statements, Ranger was trundled off to the hospital, and I followed the squad car to the station.

It was close to five by the time I reached Vinnie's office. I asked Connie to write out separate checks. Fifty dollars to me. The remainder to Ranger. I wouldn't have taken any money at all, but I really needed to screen my calls, and this was the only way I could buy an answering machine.

I dearly wanted to go home, take a shower, change into clean, dry clothes, and have a decent meal. I knew once I got settled in, I wasn't going to want to go out again, so I detoured to Kuntz Appliances before heading back to my apartment.

Bernie was using a small roller device to paste price stickers onto a carton of alarm clocks. He looked up when I walked in the door.

"I need an answering machine," I told him. "Something under fifty dollars."

My shirt and my jeans were relatively dry by now, but my shoes still leaked water when I walked. Everywhere I stood, amoebalike puddles formed around me.

Bernie politely pretended not to notice. He shifted into salesman mode and showed me two models of answering machines, both in my price range. I asked which he recommended and followed his advice.

"MasterCard?" he asked.

"I just got a fifty-dollar check from Vinnie. Can I sign it over to you?"

"Sure," he said. "That'd be okay."

From where I was standing I could look out the front window, across the street, into Sal's Meat Market. There wasn't much to see—a shadowy display window with the name lettered in black and gold and the single glass door with the red and white OPEN sign affixed by a small suction cup halfway up. I imagined Bernie spending hours peering out his window, numbly staring at Sal's door.

"You said Ziggy Kulesza shopped at Sal's?"

"Yeah. Of course, there's all kinds of shopping you can do at Sal's."

"So I hear. What kind of shopping do you think Ziggy was doing?"

"Hard to say, but I didn't notice him coming out with bags of pork chops."

I tucked my answering machine under my shirt and ran to my car. I took a last wondering look at Sal's, and I pulled away.

Traffic was slow in the rain, and I found myself mesmerized by the beat and the swish of the wiper and the smear of red brake lights appearing in front of me. I was driving on autopilot, reviewing the day, worrying about Ranger. It's one thing to see someone shot on television. It's quite another to see the destruction firsthand. Ranger kept saying it wasn't a bad wound, but it was bad enough for me. I owned a gun, and I was going to learn how to use it correctly, but I'd lost some of my earlier enthusiasm for pumping lead into a body.

I turned into my lot and found a spot close to the building. I set the alarm and dragged myself out of the car and up the stairs. I left my shoes in the foyer and put the answering machine and my pocketbook on the kitchen counter. I cracked open a beer and called the hospital to check on Ranger. I was told he'd been treated and released. That was good news.

I stuffed myself full of Ritz crackers and peanut butter, washed them down with a second beer, and staggered into my bedroom. I peeled my damp clothes away, half expecting to see that I'd started to mildew. I didn't check everywhere, but the body parts I saw looked mold-free. Hot dog. What luck. I dropped a T-shirt-type nightgown over my head, hiked up a clean pair of undies, and crashed into bed.

I woke with my heart racing and not knowing why. The cobwebs parted, and I realized the phone was ringing. I fumbled for the receiver and stared stupidly at the bedside clock. Two o'clock. Someone must have died, I thought. My Grandma Mazur or my Aunt Sophie. Or maybe my father passed a kidney stone.

I answered breathless, expecting the worst. "Hello."

There was silence on the other end. I heard labored breathing, scuffling noises, and then someone moaned. A woman's voice carried from a distance. "No," she begged. "Oh God, no." A terrible scream split the air, jolting the phone from my ear, and I broke out in a cold sweat as I realized what I was hearing. I slammed the receiver down and switched on my bedside light.

I got out of bed on shaky legs and stumbled to the kitchen. I hooked up the answering machine and set it to answer on one ring. My recording said to leave a message. That was it. I didn't give my name. I went to the bathroom and brushed my teeth and returned to bed.

The phone rang, and I heard the machine snap on. I sat up and listened. The caller crooned to me, half song, half whisper. "Stephanie," he chanted. "Stephanie."

My hand instinctively went to my mouth. It was a reflex action designed to control a scream in primal man, but the scream had been bred out of me. What was left was a quick intake of air. Part gasp, part sob.

"You shouldn't have hung up, bitch," he said. "You missed the best part. You gotta know what the champ can do, so you can look forward to it."

I ran to the kitchen, but before I could disconnect the machine, the woman came on the line. She sounded young. Her words were barely audible, thick with tears and trembling with the effort of speech. "It was g-g-good," she said. Her voice broke. "Oh God help me, I'm hurt. I'm hurt something awful."

The connection was severed, and I immediately called the police. I explained the tape and told them it was originating with Ramirez. I gave them Ramirez's home address. I gave them my number if they wanted to institute a call trace. I hung up and padded around the apartment, triple-checking locked doors and windows, thankful that I'd had the dead bolt installed.

The phone rang, and the machine answered. No one came on the line, but I could feel the vibrations of evil and insanity pulsing in the silence. He was out there, listening, savoring the contact, trying to get a bead on my fear. Far off, almost too faint to discern, I heard a woman softly crying. I ripped the phone plug out of the wall jack, splintering the little plastic clip, and then I threw up in the sink. Thank God for garbage disposals.

I AWOKE AT DAYBREAK, RELIEVED TO HAVE THE night behind me. The rain had stopped. It was too early for bird chatter. There were no cars traveling St. James. It was as if the world was holding its breath, waiting for the sun to burst upon the horizon.

The phone call replayed in my mind. I didn't need the recorder to remember the message. The good, sensible Stephanie wanted to file for a restraining order. Stephanie the neophyte bounty hunter was still worried about credibility and respect. I could hardly go running to the police every time I was threatened and then expect them to accept me as an equal. I was on record for requesting help for the abused woman on my tape. I thought about it for a while, and I decided to leave it at that for now.

Later in the day I'd give Jimmy Alpha a call.

I'd intended to ask Ranger to take me to the firing range, but since he was recovering from the gunshot wound I would have to lay the burden on Eddie Gazarra. I glanced at the clock again. Gazarra should be at work. I dialed the station and left a message for a call back.

I dressed in T-shirt and shorts and laced up my running shoes. Running isn't one of my favorite activities, but it was time to get serious about the job, and keeping in shape seemed like part of it.

"Go for it," I said by way of a pep talk.

I trotted down the hall, the stairs, through the front door. I heaved a large sigh of resignation and pushed off on my three-mile route, mapped out with great care to avoid hills and bakeries.

I slogged through the first mile, and then it got really bad. I'm not one of those people who find their stride. My body was not designed to run. My body was designed to sit in an expensive car and drive. I was sweating and breathing hard when I turned the corner and saw my building half a block away. So near and yet so far. I sprinted the last piece as best I could. I came to a ragged stop at the door and bent at the waist, waiting for my vision to clear, feeling so fucking healthy I could hardly stand myself.

Eddie Gazarra pulled up to the curb in a patrol car. "I got your message," he said. "Jesus, you look like shit."

"I've been running."

"Maybe you should check with a doctor."

"It's my fair skin. It flushes easily. Did you hear about Ranger?"

"Only every detail. You're a real hot topic. I even know what you were wearing when you came in with Dodd. I take it your T-shirt was real wet. I mean *real* wet."

"When you first started out as a cop, were you afraid of your gun?"

"I've been around guns most of my life. I had an air rifle when I was a kid, and I used to go hunting with my dad and my Uncle Walt. I guess guns were always just another piece of hardware to me."

"If I decide to keep working for Vinnie, you think it's necessary for me to carry a gun?"

"It depends what kind of cases you take. If you're just doing skip tracing, no. If you're going after crazies, yes. Do you have a gun?"

"Smith and Wesson .38. Ranger gave me about ten minutes of instruction on it, but I don't feel comfortable. Would you be willing to baby-sit me while I do some target practice?"

"You're serious about this, aren't you?"

"There's no other way to be."

He nodded. "I heard about your phone call last night."

"Anything come of it?"

"Dispatch sent someone out, but by the time they got there Ramirez was alone. Said he didn't call you. Nothing came in from the woman, but you can register a harassment charge."

"I'll think about it."

I waved him off and huffed and puffed my way up the stairs. I let myself into my apartment, dug out an auxiliary phone cord, put a new tape in the answering machine, and took a shower. It was Sunday. Vinnie had given me a week, and the week was up. I didn't care. Vinnie could give the file to someone else, but he couldn't stop me from dogging Morelli. If someone else bagged him before I did, that was the breaks, but until that happened I intended to keep at it.

Gazarra had agreed to meet me at the pistol range behind Sunny's Gun Shop when he got off work at four o'clock. That left me with a whole day of snooping. I started out by driving past Morelli's mother's house, his cousin's house, and various other relatives' houses. I circled the parking lot to his apartment, noting that the Nova was still where I'd left it. I cruised up and down Stark Street and Polk. I didn't see the van or anything else that might indicate Morelli's presence.

I drove by the front of Carmen's building, and then I went around back. The service road cutting the block was narrow and badly maintained, pocked with holes. There was no tenant parking back here. The single rear door opened onto the service road. Across the way, asphalt-shingled row houses also butted up to the road.

I parked as close to the apartment building as possible, leaving barely enough room for a car to squeeze by me. I got out and looked up, trying to place Carmen's second-floor apartment, surprised to see two boarded and fire-blackened windows. The windows belonged to the Santiago apartment.

The street-level back door was propped open, and the acrid odor of smoke and charred wood hung in the air. I heard the sweep of a broom and realized someone was working in the narrow corridor that led to the front foyer.

A trickle of sooty water tumbled over the sill, and a dark-skinned, mustached man looked out at me. He cut his eyes to my car, and jerked his head in the direction of the road. "No parking here."

I gave him my card. "I'm looking for Joe Morelli. He's in violation of his bond agreement."

"Last I saw him he was flat on his back, out cold."

"Did you see him get hit?"

"No. I didn't get there until after the police. My apartment's in the cellar. Sound doesn't carry good."

I looked up at the damaged windows. "What happened?"

"Fire in the Santiago apartment. Happened on Friday. I guess if you wanted to be picky you'd say it happened Saturday. Was about two in the morning. Thank God no one was home. Mrs. Santiago was at her daughter's. She was baby-sitting. Usually the kids come here, but on Friday she went to their place."

"Anybody know how it started?"

"Could have started a million ways. Not everything's up to code in a building like this. Not that this building's so bad compared to some others, but it's not new, you know what I mean?"

I shaded my eyes and took one last look and wondered how hard it'd be to lob a firebomb through Mrs. Santiago's bedroom window. Probably not hard, I decided. And, at two in the morning, in an apartment this size, a fire started in a bedroom would be a bitch. If Santiago had been home, she'd have been toast. There were no balconies and no fire escapes. All of these apartments had only one way out—through the front door. Although it didn't seem as though Carmen and the missing witness had left through the front door.

I turned and stared into the dark windows of the row houses across the way and decided it wouldn't hurt to question the residents. I got back into the Cherokee and drove around the block, finding a parking place one street over. I rapped on doors and asked questions and showed pictures. The responses were all similar. No, they didn't recognize Morelli's picture, and no, they hadn't seen anything unusual from their back windows on the night of the murder or the fire.

I tried the row house directly across from Carmen's apartment and found myself face-to-face with a stooped old man wielding a baseball bat. He was beady-eyed and hooked-nosed and had ears that probably kept him indoors when the wind was blowing.

"Batting practice?" I asked.

"Can't be too careful," he said.

I identified myself and asked if he'd seen Morelli.

"Nope. Never seen him. And I got better things to do than to look out my damn windows. Couldn't've seen anything anyway on the night of the murder. It was dark. How the hell was I supposed to see anything?"

"There are streetlights back there," I said. "It looks to me like it would be pretty well lit."

"The lights were out that night. I told this to the cops that come around. The damn lights are always out. Kids shoot them out. I know they were out because I looked to see what all the noise was about. I could hardly hear my TV what with all the noise from the cop cars and the trucks.

"The first time I looked out it was because of the motor running on one of them refrigerator trucks . . . like from a food store. Damn thing was parked right behind my house. I tell you the neighborhood's going to hell. People got no consideration. They park trucks and delivery cars here in the alley all the time while they do personal visits. Shouldn't be allowed."

I nodded in vague affirmation, thinking it was a good thing I owned a gun because if I ever got this crotchety I'd want to kill myself.

He took my nod as encouragement and kept going. "Then the next truck to come along was a police wagon about the same size as the refrigerator truck, and they left their motor running too. These guys must have gas to burn."

"So then you didn't really see anything suspicious?"

"Was too damn dark, I'm telling you. King Kong could have been climbing up that wall and nobody would've seen."

I thanked him for his help and walked back to the Jeep. It was close to noon, and the air was crackling hot. I drove to my Cousin Roonie's bar, snagged an ice-cold six-pack, and headed for Stark Street.

Lula and Jackie were hawking wares on the corner, just like always. They were sweating and swaying in the heat, yelling out intimate pet names and graphic suggestions to potential customers. I parked close by, set the six-pack on the hood, and popped one open.

Lula eyed the beer. "You tryin' to lure us away from our corner, girl?"

I grinned. I sort of liked them. "Thought you might be thirsty."

"Sheeit. Thirsty ain't the half of it." Lula sauntered over, took a beer, and chugged some. "Don't know why I'm wasting my time standing out. Nobody want to fuck in this weather."

Jackie followed. "You shouldn't be doing that," she warned Lula. "Your old man gonna get mad."

"Hunh," Lula said. "I suppose I care. Dumbass

prick pimp. Don't see *him* standing out here in the sun, do you?"

"So what's the word on Morelli?" I asked. "Anything happening?"

"Haven't seen him," Lula said. "Haven't seen the van neither."

"You hear anything about Carmen?"

"Like what?"

"Like is she around somewhere?"

Lula was wearing a halter top with a lot of boob hanging out. She rolled the cold can of beer across her chest. I figured it was wasted effort. She'd need a keg to cool off a chest that size.

"Don't hear nothing about Carmen."

An ugly thought flashed through my mind. "Carmen ever spend time with Ramirez?"

"Sooner or later everybody spend time with Ramirez."

"You ever spend time with him?"

"Not me. He like to do his magic on skinny pussy."

"Suppose he wanted to do his magic on you? Would you go with him?"

"Honey, nobody refuses Ramirez nothing."

"I hear he abuses women."

"Lots of men abuse women," Jackie said. "Sometimes men get in a mood."

"Sometimes they're sick," I said. "Sometimes they're freaks. I hear Ramirez is a freak."

Lula looked down the street to the gym, her eyes

locked on the second-story windows. "Yeah," she said softly. "He's a freak. He scares me. I had a friend go with Ramirez, and he cut her bad."

"Cut her? With a knife?"

"No," she said. "With a beer bottle. Broke the neck and then used it to . . . you know, do the deed."

I felt my head go light, and time stood still for a moment. "How do you know it was Ramirez?"

"People know."

"People don't know nothing," Jackie said. "People shouldn't be talking. Somebody gonna hear, and you be in for it. Be all your own fault, too, 'cause you know better'n to go shootin' your mouth. I'm not staying here and being party to this. Nuh unh. Not me. I'm going back to my corner. You know what's good for you, you'll come too."

"I know what's good for me I wouldn't be standing out here at all, would I?" Lula said, moving off.

"Be careful," I called after her.

"Big woman like me don't gotta be careful," she said. "I just stomp on them weird-ass motherfuckers. Nobody mess with Lula."

I stashed the rest of the beer in the car, slid behind the wheel, and locked the doors. I started the engine and turned the air on full blast, positioning all the vents so the cold hit me in the face. "Come on, Stephanie," I said. "Get a grip." But I couldn't get a grip. My heart was racing, and my throat was closed tight with grief for a woman I didn't even know, a woman who must have suffered terribly. I wanted to get as far away from Stark Street as was humanly possible and never come back. I didn't want to know about these things, didn't want the terror of it creeping into my consciousness at unguarded moments. I hung onto the wheel and looked down the street at the second-floor gym and was rocked with rage and horror that Ramirez hadn't been punished, and that he was free to mutilate and terrorize other women.

I lunged out of the car, slammed the door closed, and stalked across the street to Alpha's office building, taking the stairs two at a time. I barreled past his secretary and threw the door to Alpha's inner office open with enough force to make it crash against the wall.

Alpha jumped in his chair.

I leaned palms down on his desk top and got right in his face. "I got a phone call last night from your fighter. He was brutalizing some young woman, and he was trying to terrorize me with her suffering. I know all about his previous rape charges, and I know about his fondness for sexual mutilation. I don't know how he's managed to escape prosecution this far, but I'm here to tell you his luck has run out. Either you stop him, or else I'll stop him. I'll go to the police. I'll go to the press. I'll go to the fight commissioner."

"Don't do that. I'll take care of it. I swear, I'll take care of it. I'll get him into counseling."

"Today!"

"Yeah. Today. I promise, I'll get him some help."

I didn't believe it for a second, but I'd said my piece, so I left in the same whirlwind of bad temper that I'd entered. I forced myself to breathe deep on the stairs and cross the street with a calmness I didn't feel. I pulled out of the parking space and very slowly, very carefully drove away.

It was still early in the day, but I'd lost my energy for the hunt. My car headed home of its own volition, and next thing I knew I was in my parking lot. I locked up, climbed the stairs to my apartment, flopped down on the bed, and assumed my thinking position.

I woke up at three and felt better. While I was sleeping, my mind had obviously been hard at work finding secluded repositories for my latest collection of depressing thoughts. They were still with me, but they were no longer forcefully pressing against my forehead.

I made myself a peanut butter and jelly sandwich, gave a bite of it to Rex, and scarfed the rest down while I accessed Morelli's messages.

A photo studio had called with an offer of a free eight by ten if Morelli came in for a sitting. Someone wanted to sell him light bulbs, and Carlene called with an indecent suggestion, did some heavy panting, and either had a hell of an orgasm or else stepped on her cat's tail. Unfortunately, she also ran the tape out, so there were no more messages. It was just as well. I couldn't have managed listening to much more.

I was straightening the kitchen when the phone rang and the machine picked it up.

"Are you listening, Stephanie? Are you home? I saw you talking to Lula and Jackie today. Saw you drinking beer with them. I didn't like that, Stephanie. Made me feel bad. Made me feel like you liked them better than me. Made me angry because you don't want what the champ want to give you.

"Maybe I'll give you a present, Stephanie. Maybe I'll deliver it to your door when you're sleeping. Would you like that? All women like presents. 'Specially the kind of presents the champ gives. Gonna be a surprise, Stephanie. Gonna be just for you."

With that promise ringing in my ears I made sure my gun and my bullets were in my pocketbook, and I took off for Sunny's. I got there at four and waited in the lot until Eddie showed up at four-fifteen.

He was out of uniform, and he had his off-duty .38 clipped to his waist.

"Where's your gun?" he asked.

I patted my pocketbook.

"That's considered carrying concealed. It's a serious offense in New Jersey."

"I have a permit."

"Let me see it."

I pulled the permit out of my wallet.

"This is a permit to own, not to carry," Eddie said.

"Ranger told me it was multipurpose."

"Ranger gonna come visit you when you're making license plates?"

"Sometimes I think he stretches the limits of the law a trifle. Are you going to arrest me?"

"No, but it's going to cost you."

"Dozen donuts?"

"Dozen donuts is what it takes to fix a parking ticket. This is worth a six-pack and a pizza."

It was necessary to go through the gun shop to get to the rifle range. Eddie paid the range fee and bought a box of shells. I did the same. The range was directly behind the gun shop and consisted of a room the size of a small bowling alley. Seven booths were partitioned off, each booth with a chest-high shelf. Beyond the booths was known as downrange. Standard targets of ungendered humans cut off at the knees, with bull's-eye rings radiating out from the heart, were hung on pulleys. Range etiquette was never to point the gun at the guy standing next to you.

"Okay," Gazarra said, "let's start at the beginning. You have a Smith and Wesson .38 Special. It's a 5-shot revolver, which puts it into the category of small gun. You're using hydroshock bullets to cause maximum pain and suffering. This little doohickey here gets pushed forward with your thumb, the cylinder releases, and you can load your gun. A bullet is a round. Load a round in each chamber and click the cylinder closed. Never leave your trigger finger resting on the trigger. It's a natural reflex to squeeze when surprised, and you could end up blowing a hole in your foot. Stretch your trigger finger straight toward the barrel until you're ready to shoot. We're going to use the most basic stance today. Feet shoulder-width apart, weight on the balls of your feet, hold the gun in both hands, left thumb over right thumb, arms straight. Look at the target, bring the gun up and sight. The front sight is a post. The rear sight is a notch. Line the sights up on the desired spot on the target and fire.

"This revolver is double action. You can fire by pulling the trigger or by cocking the hammer and then pulling the trigger." He'd been demonstrating while he talked, doing everything but firing the gun. He released the cylinder, spilled the bullets out onto the shelf, laid the gun on the shelf, and stepped back. "Any questions?"

"No. Not yet."

He handed me a pair of ear protectors. "Go for it."

My first shot was single action, and I hit the bull's-eye. I shot several more rounds single action, and then switched over to double action. This was more difficult to control, but I did pretty well.

After a half hour, I'd used up all my ammo, and I was shooting erratically from muscle fatigue. Usually when I go to the gym I spend most of my time working abdominals and legs because that's where my fat goes. If I was going to be any good at shooting, I was going to have to get more upper body strength.

Eddie pulled my target in. "Damn fair shooting, Tex."

"I'm better at single action."

"That's 'cause you're a girl."

"You don't want to say stuff like that when I've got a gun in my hand."

I bought a box of shells before I left. I dropped the shells in my pocketbook along with my gun. I was driving a stolen car. Worrying about carrying concealed at this point seemed like overkill.

"So do I get my pizza now?" Eddie wanted to know.

"What about Shirley?"

"Shirley's at a baby shower."

"The kids?"

"Mother-in-law."

"What about your diet?"

"You trying to get out of buying this pizza?"

"I've only got twelve dollars and thirty-three cents distinguishing me from the bag lady at the train station."

"Okay, I'll buy the pizza."

"Good. I need to talk. I have problems."

Ten minutes later, we met at Pino's Pizzeria. There were several Italian restaurants in the burg, but Pino's was the place to get pizza. I was told at night cockroaches as big as barn cats came out to raid the kitchen, but the pizza was first rate—crust that was crisp and puffy, homemade sauce, and enough grease from the pepperoni to run down your arm and drip off your elbow. There was a bar and a family room. Late at night the bar was filled with off-duty cops trying to wind down before they went home. At this time of the day the bar was filled with men waiting for takeout.

We got a table in the family room and asked for a pitcher while we waited for the pizza. There was a shaker of crushed hot pepper in the middle of the table, and another shaker of Parmesan. The tablecloth was red-and-white checked plastic. The walls were paneled and lacquered to a shiny gloss and decorated with framed photos of famous Italians and a few non-Italian locals. Frank Sinatra and Benito Ramirez were the dominant celebs.

"So what's the problem?" Eddie wanted to know.

"Two problems. Number one. Joe Morelli. I've run into him four times since I've taken on this assignment, and I've never once come close to making an apprehension."

"Are you afraid of him?"

"No. But I am afraid to use my gun."

"Then do it the ladies' way. Spray him and cuff him."

Easier said than done, I thought. It's hard to spray a man when he has his tongue down your throat. "That was my plan, too, but he always moves faster than I do."

"You want my advice? Forget Morelli. You're a beginner, and he's a pro. He has years of experience behind him. He was a smart cop, and he's probably even better at being a felon."

"Forgetting Morelli isn't an option. I'd like you to run a couple car checks for me." I wrote the van's license number on a napkin and gave it to him. "See if you can find out who owns this. I'd also like to know if Carmen Sanchez owns a car. And if she does own a car, has it been impounded?"

I drank some beer and slouched back, enjoying the cold air and the buzz of conversation around me. Every table was filled now, and there was a knot of people waiting at the door. No one wanted to cook when it got this hot.

"So what's the second problem?" Eddie asked.

"If I tell you, you have to promise not to get overwrought."

"Christ, you're pregnant."

I stared at him, nonplussed. "Why would you think that?"

His expression was sheepish. "I don't know. It just popped out. It's what Shirley always says to me."

Gazarra had four kids. The oldest was nine. The youngest was a year. They were all boys, and they were all monsters.

"Well, I'm not pregnant. It's Ramirez." I gave him the full story on Ramirez.

"You should have filed a report on him," Gazarra said. "Why didn't you call the police when you got roughed up in the gym?"

"Would Ranger have filed a report if he got roughed up?"

"You're not Ranger."

"That's true, but you see my point?"

"Why are you telling me this?"

"I guess if I suddenly disappear, I want you to know where to start looking."

"Jesus. If you think he's that dangerous, you should get a restraining order."

"I don't have a lot of confidence in a restraining order. Besides, what am I going to tell the judge . . . that Ramirez threatened to send me a present? Look around you. What do you see?"

Eddie sighed. "Pictures of Ramirez, side by side with the Pope and Frank Sinatra."

"I'm sure I'll be fine," I said. "I just needed to tell someone."

"If you have any more problems I want you to call me right away."

I nodded.

"When you're home alone, make sure your gun is loaded and accessible. Could you use it on Ramirez if you had to?"

"I don't know. I think so."

"Scheduling got screwed up, and I'm working

days again. I want you to meet me at Sunny's every day at four-thirty. I'll buy the ammo and pay the range fee. The only way to feel comfortable with a gun is to use it."

TEN

I WAS HOME BY NINE, AND FOR LACK OF SOMETHING better to do, I decided to clean my apartment. There were no messages on my machine and no suspicious packages on my doorstep. I gave Rex new bedding, vacuumed the carpet, scrubbed the bathroom, and polished the few pieces of furniture I had left. This brought me up to ten. I checked one last time to make sure everything was locked, took a shower, and went to bed.

I awoke at seven feeling elated. I'd slept like a brick. My machine was still gloriously message free. Birds were warbling, the sun was shining, and I could see my reflection in my toaster. I pulled on shorts and shirt and started coffee brewing. I opened the living room curtains and gasped at the magnificence of the day. The sky was a brilliant blue, the air was still washed clean from the rain, and I had an overwhelming desire to belt out something from *The Sound of Music*. I sang, "The hills are aliiiiive with the sound of muuusic," but then I didn't know any more words.

I twirled myself into my bedroom and threw the curtain open with a flourish. I froze at the sight of Lula tied to my fire escape. She hung there like a big rag doll, her arms crooked over the railing at an unnatural angle, her head slumped forward onto her chest. Her legs were splayed so that she seemed to be sitting. She was naked and blood-smeared, the blood caked in her hair and clotted on her legs. A sheet had been draped behind her to hide her from view of the parking lot.

I shouted her name and clawed at the lock, my heart hammering so hard in my chest that my vision blurred. I heaved the window open and half fell onto the fire escape, reaching out for her, tugging ineffectually at her bindings.

Lula didn't move, didn't utter a sound, and I couldn't collect myself enough to tell if she was breathing. "You're going to be okay," I cried, my voice sounding hoarse, my throat closed tight, my lungs burning. "I'm going to get help." And under my breath I sobbed, "Don't be dead. God, Lula, don't be dead."

I floundered back through the window to call for an ambulance, caught my foot on the sill, and crashed to the floor. There was no pain, only panic as I scrambled on hands and knees to the phone. I couldn't remember the emergency number. My mind had shut down in the face of hysteria, leaving me to cope helplessly with the confusion and denial accompanying sudden and unexpected tragedy.

I punched 0 and told the operator Lula was hurt on my fire escape. I had a flashback of Jackie Kennedy crawling over the car seat to get help for her dead husband, and I burst into tears, crying for Lula and Jackie and for myself, all victims of violence.

I clattered through the cutlery drawer, looking for my paring knife, finally finding it in the dish drainer. I had no idea how long Lula had been tied to the railing, but I couldn't bear her hanging there seconds longer.

I ran back with the knife and sawed at the ropes until they were severed, and Lula collapsed into my arms. She was almost twice my size, but somehow I dragged her inert, bloodied body through the window. My instincts were to hide and protect. Stephanie Plum, mother cat. I heard the sirens wailing from far away, getting closer and closer, and then the police were pounding on my door. I don't remember letting them in, but obviously I did. A uniformed cop took me aside, into the kitchen, and sat me down on a chair. A medic followed.

"What happened?" the cop asked.

"I found her on the fire escape," I said. "I opened the curtains and there she was." My teeth were chattering, and my heart was still racing in my chest. I gulped in air. "She was tied to keep her up, and I cut her down and dragged her through the window."

I could hear the medics shouting to bring the stretcher. There was the sound of my bed being shoved aside to make room. I was afraid to ask if Lula was alive. I sucked in more air and clenched my hands in my lap until my knuckles turned white and my nails dug into the fleshy part of my palm.

"Does Lula live here?" the cop wanted to know.

"No. I live here. I don't know where Lula lives. I don't even know her last name."

The phone rang and I automatically reached out to answer.

The caller's voice whispered from the handset. "Did you get my present, Stephanie?"

It was as if the earth suddenly stopped rotating. There was a moment of feeling off balance, and then everything snapped into focus. I pushed the record button on the machine and turned up the volume so everyone could hear.

"What present are you talking about?" I asked.

"You know what present. I saw you find her. Saw you drag her back through the window. I've been watching you. I could have come and got you last night when you were asleep, but I wanted you to see Lula. I wanted you to see what I can do to a woman, so you know what to expect. I want you to think about it, bitch. I want you to think about how it's going to hurt, and how you're going to beg."

"You like to hurt women?" I asked, control beginning to return.

"Sometimes women need to be hurt."

I decided to take a winger. "How about Carmen Sanchez? Did you hurt her?"

"Not as good as I'm going to hurt you. I have special things planned for you."

"No time like the present," I said, and I was shocked to realize that I meant it. There was no bravado in the statement. I was in the grip of cold, hard, sphincter-cramping fury.

"The cops are there now, bitch. I'm not coming when the cops are there. I'm going to get you when you're alone and you're not expecting me. I'm going to make sure we have lots of time together."

The connection was broken.

"Jesus Christ," the uniform said. "He's crazy."

"Do you know who that was?"

"I'm afraid to guess."

I popped the tape out of the machine, and wrote my name and the date on the label. My hand was shaking so badly the writing was barely readable.

A handheld radio crackled from the living room. I could hear the murmur of voices in my bedroom. The voices were less frantic, and the rhythm of activity had become more orderly. I looked at myself and realized I was covered with Lula's blood. It had soaked into my shirt and shorts, and it was coagulating on my hands and the bottoms of my bare feet.

The phone was tacky with blood smears, as was the floor and the counter.

The cop and the medic exchanged glances. "Maybe you should get that blood washed off," the medic said. "How about we get you into the shower real fast."

I looked in at Lula on my way to the bathroom. They were getting ready to move her out. She was strapped to the stretcher, covered with a sheet and blanket. She was hooked up to an IV. "How is she?" I asked.

A squad member tugged the stretcher forward. "Alive," he said.

The medics were gone when I got out of the shower. Two uniformed cops had stayed, and the one who'd talked to me in the kitchen was conferring with a PC in the living room, the two of them going over notes. I dressed quickly and left my hair to dry on its own. I was anxious to make my statement and be done with it. I wanted to get to the hospital to see about Lula.

The PC's name was Dorsey. I'd seen him before. Probably at Pino's. He was medium height, medium build, and looked to be in his late forties. He was in shirtsleeves and slacks and penny loafers. I could see my recorder tape tucked into his shirt pocket. Exhibit A. I told him about the incident in the gym, omitting Morelli's name, leaving Dorsey to think the identity of my rescuer was unknown. If the police wanted to believe Morelli'd left town, that was fine with me. I still had hopes of bringing him in and collecting my money.

Dorsey took a lot of notes and looked knowingly at the patrolman. He didn't seem surprised. I suppose if you're a cop long enough, nothing surprises you.

When they left I shut off the coffeemaker, closed and locked the bedroom window, grabbed my pocketbook, and squared my shoulders to what I knew awaited me in the hall. I was going to have to make my way past Mrs. Orbach, Mr. Grossman, Mrs. Feinsmith, Mr. Wolesky, and who knows how many others. They would want to know the details, and I wasn't up to imparting details.

I put my head down, shouted apologies, and went straight for the stairs, knowing that would slow them. I bolted out of the building and ran to the Cherokee.

I took St. James to Olden and cut across Trenton to Stark. It would have been easier to go straight to St. Francis Hospital, but I wanted to get Jackie. I barreled down Stark and passed the gym without a sideways glance. As far as I was concerned, Ramirez was finished. If he slipped through the loopholes of the law on this one, I'd get him myself. I'd cut off his dick with a carving knife if I had to.

Jackie was just coming out of the Corner Bar, where I imagined she'd had breakfast. I screeched to a stop and half hung out the door. "Get in!" I yelled to Jackie.

"What's this about?"

"Lula's in the hospital. Ramirez got to her."

"Oh God," she wailed. "I was so afraid. I knew something was wrong. How bad is it?"

"I honestly don't know. I found her on my fire escape just now. Ramirez had left her tied there as a message to me. She's unconscious."

"I was there when he come for her. She didn't want to go, but you don't say no to Benito Ramirez. Her old man would've beat her bloody."

"Yeah. Well, she's been beaten bloody anyway."

I found a parking place on Hamilton one block from the emergency entrance. I set the alarm, and Jackie and I took off at a trot. She had about two hundred pounds on the hoof, and she wasn't even breathing hard when we pushed through the double glass doors. I guess humping all day keeps you in shape.

"A woman named Lula was just brought in by ambulance," I told the clerk.

The clerk looked at me, and then she looked at Jackie. Jackie was dressed in poison green shorts with half her ass hanging out, matching rubber sandals, and a hot pink tank top. "Are you family?" she asked Jackie.

"Lula don't got any family here."

"We need someone to fill out forms."

"I guess I could do that," she said.

When we were done with the forms, we were told to sit and wait. We did this in silence, aimlessly thumbing through torn magazines, watching with inhuman detachment as one tragedy after another rolled down the hall. After a half hour I asked about Lula and was told she was in X ray. How long would she be in X ray? I asked. The clerk didn't know. It would be a while, but then a doctor would come out to talk to us. I reported this to Jackie.

"Hunh," she said. "I bet."

I was a quart down on caffeine, so I left Jackie to wait and went in search of the cafeteria. I was told to follow the footprints on the floor, and darned if they didn't bring me to food. I loaded a take-out carton with pastries, two large coffees, and added two oranges just in case Jackie and I felt the need to be healthy. I thought it was unlikely, but I figured it was like wearing clean panties in case of a car crash. It never hurt to be prepared.

An hour later, we saw the doctor.

He looked at me, and he looked at Jackie. Jackie hiked up her top and tugged at her shorts. It was a futile gesture.

"Are you family?" he asked Jackie.

"I guess so," Jackie said. "What's the word?"

"The prognosis is guarded but hopeful. She's lost a lot of blood, and she's suffered some head trauma. She has multiple wounds that need suturing. She's being taken to surgery. It will probably be a while before she's brought to her room. You might want to go out and come back in an hour or two."

"I'm not going nowhere," Jackie said.

Two hours dragged by without further information. We'd eaten all the pastries and were forced to eat the oranges.

"Don't like this," Jackie said. "Don't like being cooped up in institutions. Whole fucking place smells like canned green beans."

"Spend much time in institutions, have you?"

"My share."

She didn't seem inclined to elaborate, and I didn't actually want to know anyway. I fidgeted in my chair, looked around the room, and spotted Dorsey talking to the clerk. He was nodding, getting answers to questions. The clerk pointed to Jackie and me, and Dorsey ambled over.

"How's Lula?" he asked. "Any news?"

"She's in surgery."

He settled himself into the seat next to me. "We haven't been able to pick up Ramirez yet. You have any idea where he might be? He say anything interesting before you started recording?"

"He said he was watching me pull Lula through the window. And he knew the police were in my apartment. He must have been close."

"Probably on a car phone."

I agreed.

"Here's my card." He wrote a number on the back. "This is my home phone. You see Ramirez, or you get another call, get in touch right away."

"It'll be hard for him to hide," I said. "He's a local celebrity. He's easy to recognize."

Dorsey returned his pen to an inside jacket pocket, and I got a glimpse of his hip holster. "There are a lot of people in this city who'll go out of their way to hide and protect Benito Ramirez. We've been this route with him before."

"Yes, but you've never had a tape."

"True. The tape might make a difference."

"Won't make no difference," Jackie said when Dorsey left. "Ramirez do what he want. Nobody cares about him beating on a whore."

"We care," I said to Jackie. "We can stop him. We can get Lula to testify against him."

"Hunh," Jackie said. "You don't know much."

It was three before we were allowed to see Lula. She hadn't regained consciousness and was in ICU. Our visit was restricted to ten minutes each. I squeezed her hand and promised her she'd be okay. When my time was up, I told Jackie I had an appointment I needed to keep. She said she was staying until Lula opened her eyes.

I got to Sunny's a half hour before Gazarra. I paid my fee, bought a box of shells, and went back to the range. I shot a few with the hammer pulled back, and then settled in for serious practice. I envisioned Ramirez in front of the target. I aimed for his heart, his balls, his nose.

Gazarra came on the range at four-thirty. He dropped a new box of shells on my loading table and took the booth next to me. By the time I was done with both boxes I was pleasantly relaxed and feeling comfortable with my gun. I loaded five rounds and slid the gun back into my bag. I tapped Gazarra on the shoulder and motioned that I was done.

He holstered his Glock and followed me out. We waited until we were in the parking lot to talk.

"I heard the call come in," he said. "Sorry I couldn't get to you. I was in the middle of something. I saw Dorsey at the station. He said you were cool. Said you switched on the recorder when Ramirez came on the line."

"You should have seen me five minutes before. I couldn't remember 911."

"I don't suppose you'd consider taking a vacation?"

"It's crossed my mind."

"You got your gun in your pocketbook?"

"Hell no, that would be breaking the law."

Gazarra sighed. "Just don't let anyone see it, okay? And call me if you get spooked. You're welcome to stay with Shirley and me for as long as you want."

"I appreciate it."

"I checked on the plate number you gave me. The plates belong to a vehicle seized for a parking violation, impounded, and never retrieved."

"I saw Morelli driving said vehicle."

"He probably borrowed it."

We both smiled at the thought of Morelli driving a vehicle stolen from the impound yard.

"What about Carmen Sanchez? Does she have a car?"

Gazarra dug a piece of paper out of his pocket. "This is the make and her license number. It hasn't been impounded.

"You want me to follow you home? Make sure your apartment's safe?"

"Not necessary. Half the building's population is probably still camped out in my hall."

What I really dreaded was facing the blood. I was going to have to walk into my apartment and face the grisly aftermath of Ramirez's handiwork. Lula's blood would still be on the phone, the walls, the countertops, and the floor. If the sight of that blood triggered a renewed rush of hysteria, I wanted to deal with it alone, in my own way.

I parked in the lot and slipped into the building unnoticed. Good timing, I thought. The halls were clear. Everyone was eating dinner. I had my defense spray in my hand and my gun wedged under my waistband. I turned the key in the lock and felt my stomach lurch. Just get it over with, I told myself. Barge right in, check under the bed for rapists, pull on some rubber gloves, and clean up the mess.

I took a tentative step into my foyer, and realized someone was in my apartment. Someone was cooking in the kitchen, making cozy cooking sounds, clanking pots and running water. Under the clanking I could hear food sizzling in a frying pan.

"Hello," I called, gun now in hand, barely able

to hear myself over the pounding of my heart. "Who's here?"

Morelli sauntered out of the kitchen. "Just me. Put the gun away. We need to talk."

"Jesus! You are so fucking arrogant. Did it ever occur to you I might shoot you with this gun?"

"No. It never occurred to me."

"I've been practicing. I'm a pretty good shot."

He moved behind me, closed and locked the door. "Yeah, I'll bet you're hell on wheels blasting the shit out of those paper men."

"What are you doing in my apartment?"

"I'm cooking dinner." He went back to his sautéing. "Rumor has it you've had a tough day."

My mind was spinning. I'd been racking my brain, trying to find Morelli, and here he was in my apartment. He even had his back turned to me. I could shoot him in the butt.

"You don't want to shoot an unarmed man," he said, reading my thoughts. "The state of New Jersey frowns on that sort of thing. Take it from someone who knows."

All right, so I wouldn't shoot him. I'd zap him with the Sure Guard. His neurotransmitters wouldn't know what hit them.

Morelli added some fresh sliced mushrooms to the pan and continued to cook, sending heavenly food smells wafting my way. He was stirring red and green peppers, onions, and mushrooms, and my killer instincts were weakening in direct proportion to the amount of saliva pooling in my mouth.

I found myself rationalizing a decision to hold off on the spray, telling myself I needed to hear him out, but the ugly truth was my motives weren't nearly so worthy. I was hungry and depressed, and I was a lot more frightened of Ramirez than I was of Joe Morelli. In fact, I suppose in a bizarre way, I felt safe with Morelli in my apartment.

One crisis at a time, I decided. Have some dinner. Gas him for dessert.

He turned and looked at me. "You want to talk about it?"

"Ramirez almost killed Lula and hung her on my fire escape."

"Ramirez is like a fungus that feeds on fear. You ever see him in the ring? His fans love him because he goes the distance unless the referee calls the fight. He plays with his opponent. Loves to draw blood. Loves to punish. And all the time he's punishing, he's talking to his victim in that soothing voice of his, telling them how much worse it's going to get, telling them he'll only stop when they beg to get knocked out. He's like that with women. Likes to see them squirm in fear and pain. Likes to leave his mark."

I dumped my pocketbook on the counter. "I know. He's very large on mutilation and begging. In fact, you might say he's obsessed with it."

Morelli turned the heat down. "I'm trying to scare you, but I don't think it's working."

"I'm all scared out. I don't have any more scare left in me. Maybe tomorrow." I looked around and realized someone had cleaned up the blood. "Did you scrub the kitchen?"

"The kitchen and the bedroom. You're going to have to have your carpet professionally cleaned."

"Thank you. I wasn't looking forward to seeing more blood today."

"Was it bad?"

"Yeah. Her face is battered almost beyond recognition, and she was bleeding . . . everywhere." My voice broke and hitched in my throat. I looked down at the floor. "Shit."

"I have wine in the refrigerator. Why don't you trade in that gun for a couple glasses?"

"Why are you being nice to me?"

"I need you."

"Oh boy."

"Not that way."

"I wasn't thinking 'that way.' All I said was oh boy. What are you making?"

"Steak. I put it in when you pulled into the parking lot." He poured the wine and gave me a glass. "You're living a little Spartan here."

"I lost my job and couldn't get another. I sold off my furniture to keep going."

"That's when you decided to work for Vinnie?"

"I didn't have a lot of options."

"So you're after me for the money. It's nothing personal."

"In the beginning it wasn't."

He was moving around my kitchen like he'd lived there all his life, setting plates on the counter, pulling a bowl of salad from the refrigerator. It should have seemed invasive and pushy, but it was actually very comfortable.

He flipped a rib steak onto each plate, covered them with the peppers and onions, and added a foil-wrapped baked potato. He set out salad dressing, sour cream, and steak sauce, shut the broiler off, and wiped his hands on a kitchen towel. "Why is it personal now?"

"You chained me to the shower rod! Then you made me go rooting around in a Dumpster to get my keys! Every time I catch up to you, you do everything possible to humiliate me."

"They weren't your keys. They were *my* keys." He took a sip of wine, and our eyes locked. "You stole my car."

"I had a plan."

"You were going to snag me when I came after my car?"

"Something like that."

He carried his plate to the table. "I hear Macy's has openings for make-over ladies."

"You sound like my mother."

Morelli grinned and dug into his steak.

The day had been exhausting, and the wine and good food were mellowing me out. We were eating at the table, sitting across from each other, absorbed in the meal like an old married couple. I cleaned my plate and pushed back in my chair. "What do you need from me?"

"Cooperation. And in return for that cooperation, I'll see to it that you collect your bounty money."

"You've got my attention."

"Carmen Sanchez was an informant. One night I'm sitting home watching television, and I get a call from her asking for help. She says she's been raped and beaten. She says she needs money, and she needs a safe place to stay, and in return she's going to give me something big.

"When I get to her apartment Ziggy Kulesza answers the door, and Carmen is nowhere in sight. Another guy, better known as the missing witness, comes out of the bedroom, recognizes me from who-knows-where, and panics. 'This guy's a cop,' he yells to Ziggy. 'I can't believe you opened the door to a goddamn cop.'

"Ziggy draws a gun on me. I return fire and shoot him almost point-blank. Next thing I know, I'm staring at the ceiling. The second guy is gone. Carmen's gone. Ziggy's gun is gone."

"How could he have missed you at such close range? And if he missed you, where'd the bullet go?"

"The only explanation I can come up with is that the gun misfired."

"And now you want to find Carmen so Carmen can back up your story."

"I don't think Carmen's going to be backing up anyone's story. My guess is she was beaten up by Ramirez, and Ziggy and his pal were sent to finish the job. Ziggy did all Ramirez's dirty work.

"When you're out on the street like I am, you hear things. Ramirez likes to punish women. Sometimes women last seen in his company are known to disappear. I think he gets carried away and kills them, or maybe he hurts them so bad he has to send someone to finish the job to keep things quiet. Then the body vanishes. No body. No crime. I think Carmen was dead in the bedroom when I arrived. That's why Ziggy freaked."

"There's only one door," I said, "and no one saw her leave . . . dead or alive."

"There's a window in the bedroom that overlooks the service road."

"You think Carmen was pitched out the window?"

Morelli took his plate into the kitchen and started coffee brewing. "I'm looking for the guy who recognized me. Ziggy dropped the gun when he hit the floor. I saw it skitter to the side. When I got hit from behind, Ziggy's partner must have taken the gun, slipped off into the bedroom, dumped Carmen out the window, and followed her."

"I've been back there. It's a long drop if you're not dead."

Morelli shrugged. "Maybe he was able to slide through the crowd hovering over Ziggy and me.

Then he went out the back door, collected Carmen, and drove off."

"I want to hear the part about me getting the $10,000."

"You help me prove I shot Kulesza in self-defense, and I'll let you bring me in."

"I can hardly wait to hear how I'm going to do this."

"The only link I have to the missing witness is Ramirez. I've been watching him, but nothing's come of it. Unfortunately, my movements are getting restricted. I've called in just about every favor I had out there. Lately, I've been spending more hours hiding than looking. I feel like I'm running out of time and ideas.

"You're the one person no one would suspect of helping me," Morelli said.

"Why would I want to help you? Why don't I just use the opportunity to turn you in?"

"Because I'm innocent."

"That's your problem, not mine." It was a hard-ass answer and not entirely the truth. The truth was, I'd actually started to feel kind of soft on Morelli.

"Then let's up the ante for you. While you're helping me find my witness, I'll be protecting you from Ramirez."

I almost said I didn't need protection, but that was absurd. I needed all the protection I could get. "What happens when Dorsey picks up Ramirez and I no longer need your protection?"

"Ramirez will be out on bail and twice as hungry He has some powerful friends."

"And how are you going to protect me?"

"I'm going to guard your body, Sweet Cakes."

"You're not sleeping in my apartment."

"I'll sleep in the van. Tomorrow I'll wire you up for sound."

"What about tonight?"

"It's your decision," he said. "Probably you'll be okay. My guess is Ramirez wants to play with you a while. This is like a fight for him. He's going to want to go all ten rounds."

I agreed. Ramirez could have come crashing through my bedroom window any time he wanted, but he chose to wait.

"Even if I wanted to help you, I wouldn't know where to begin," I said. "What could I do that you haven't already done? Maybe the witness is in Argentina."

"The witness isn't in Argentina. He's out there killing people. He's killing everyone who can place him at the scene. He's killed two people from Carmen's apartment building and failed in his attempt to murder a third. I'm also on his list, but he can't find me while I'm in hiding, and if I go public to draw him out, the police will get me."

The light bulb went on. "You're going to use me as bait. You're going to dangle me in front of Ramirez and expect me to extract information from him while he's coaching me on his torture techniques. Jesus, Morelli, I know you're pissed because I scored you with the Buick, but don't you think this is carrying revenge too far?"

"It's not revenge. The truth is . . . I like you." His mouth softened into a seductive smile. "If circumstances were different, I might even try to right some past wrongs."

"Oh boy."

"I can see when this is all over, we're going to have to do something about that streak of cynicism you've acquired."

"You're asking me to put my life on the line to help save your ass."

"Your life is already on the line. You're being stalked by a very large man who rapes and mutilates women. If we can find my witness, we can link him to Ramirez and, hopefully, put them both away for the rest of their unnatural lives."

He had a point.

"I'll put a bug in your foyer and bedroom," Morelli said, "and I'll be able to hear throughout your apartment, with the exception of the bathroom. If you close the bathroom door, I probably won't be able to hear. When you go out we'll hide a wire under your shirt, and I'll follow at a distance."

I took a deep breath. "And you'll let me collect the finder's fee on you when we get the missing witness?"

"Absolutely."

"You said Carmen was an informant. What sort of stuff was she informing about?"

"She sold whatever scraps came her way. Mostly low-level drug stuff and names of posse members. I don't know what she had for me when she called. I never got it."

"Posse members?"

"Jamaican gang members. Striker is the parent posse, based in Philly. It's got its finger in every drug deal in Trenton. Striker makes the mob look like a bunch of pussies. They're bringing in shit faster than they can sell it, and we can't figure out how they get it here. We had twelve deaths from heroin overdose this summer. The stuff is so available the dealers aren't bothering to cut it down to the standard."

"You think Carmen had information on Striker?"

Morelli stared at me for a few beats. "No," he finally said. "I think she had something to tell me about Ramirez. She probably picked something up while she was with him."

ELEVEN

MY PHONE RANG AT SEVEN A.M. THE MACHINE GOT
it, and I recognized Morelli's voice. "Rise and
shine, Badass," he said. "I'll be at your door in ten
minutes to install equipment. Put the coffeepot on."

I started the coffee, brushed my teeth, and pulled
on running shorts and a shirt. Morelli arrived five
minutes early, carrying a toolbox. His short-sleeved
shirt had an official-looking patch on the pocket that
suggested he worked for Long's Service.

"What's Long's Service?" I asked.

"It's anything you want it to be."

"Ah hah," I said. "A disguise."

He tossed his shades onto my kitchen counter and
headed for the coffee. "People don't notice repair-
men. They remember the color of the uniform and

that's it. And if you do it right, a uniform'll get you into almost any building."

I poured myself coffee and dialed the hospital for a progress report on Lula. I was told she was in stable condition and had been moved out of ICU.

"You need to talk to her," Morelli said. "Make sure she presses charges. They picked Ramirez up last night and questioned him for aggravated sexual assault. He's out already. Released on his own recognizance."

He put his coffee down, opened the toolbox, and took out a small screwdriver and two plates for covering electrical outlets. "These look like ordinary wall plugs," he said, "but they have listening devices built in. I like to use them because they don't require battery replacement. They run off your wires. They're very dependable."

He took the plate off my hall outlet and clamped off wires, working with rubber-tipped pliers. "I have the ability to listen and record from the van. If Ramirez breaks in, or if he shows up at your door, you're going to have to go with your instincts. If you think you can engage him in conversation and pull information out of him without endangering yourself, you should give it a shot."

He finished up in the foyer and moved on to the bedroom, repeating the procedure. "Two things you need to remember. If you play the radio, I can't hear what's going on up here. And if I have to break in, it's most likely going to be through your bedroom window. So leave your curtains closed to give me some cover."

"You think it'll come to that?"

"I hope not. Try to get Ramirez to talk on the phone. And remember to record." He put the screwdriver back in the box and took out a roll of surgical tape and a small plastic case about the size of a pack of gum. "This is a miniature body transmitter. It's got two nine-volt lithium batteries in it, which gives you fifteen hours of usable operating time. It has an external electret microphone, it weighs seven ounces, and it costs about $1200. Don't lose it and don't wear it in the shower."

"Maybe Ramirez will be on good behavior now that he's been charged with assault."

"I'm not sure Ramirez knows good from bad."

"What's the plan for the day?"

"I thought we'd put you back on Stark Street. Now that you don't have to worry about driving *me* crazy, you can concentrate on driving Ramirez crazy. Push him into making another move."

"Gosh, Stark Street. My favorite place. What am I supposed to do there?"

"Stroll around and look sexy, ask annoying questions, in general get on everyone's nerves. All those things that come naturally to you."

"You know Jimmy Alpha?"

"Everybody knows Jimmy Alpha."

"What do you think of him?"

"Mixed feelings. He's always been an okay guy

in my dealings with him. And I used to think he was a great manager. He did all the right things for Ramirez. Got him the right fights. Got him good trainers." Morelli topped his coffee. "Guys like Jimmy Alpha spend their whole life hoping to get someone the caliber of Ramirez. Most of them never even come close. Managing Ramirez is like holding the winning ticket to the million-dollar lottery . . . only better because Ramirez will keep paying off. Ramirez is a gold mine. Unfortunately, Ramirez is also fucking nuts, and Alpha is caught between a rock and a hard spot."

"That was my opinion, too. I guess holding that winning ticket would tempt a person to turn a blind eye to some of Ramirez's personality faults."

"Especially now when they're just starting to make big money. Alpha supported Ramirez for years while he was just a punk kid. Now Ramirez has the title and has signed a contract for televised fights. He's literally worth millions to Alpha in future payoffs."

"So your opinion of Alpha is tarnished."

"I think Alpha is criminally irresponsible." He looked at his watch. "Ramirez does road work first thing in the morning, then he eats breakfast at the luncheonette across from the gym. After breakfast he works out and usually he stays at it until four."

"That's a lot of training."

"It's all half-assed. If he had to fight anybody decent he'd be in trouble. His last two opponents have been handpicked losers. He has a fight in three weeks with another bum. After that he'll start to get serious for his fight with Lionel Reesey."

"You know a lot about boxing."

"Boxing is the ultimate sport. Man against man. Primal combat. It's like sex . . . puts you in touch with the beast."

I made a strangled sound in the back of my throat.

He selected an orange from the bowl of fruit on the counter. "You're just pissed off because you can't remember the last time you saw the beast."

"I see the beast plenty, thank you."

"Honey, you don't see the beast at all. I've been asking around. You have no social life."

I gave him a stiff middle finger. "Oh yeah, well social life this."

Morelli grinned. "You're damn cute when you act stupid. Any time you want me to unleash the beast, you just let me know."

That did it. I was going to gas him. I might not turn him in, but I'd enjoy watching him pass out and throw up.

"I have to split," Morelli said. "One of your neighbors saw me come in. I wouldn't want to soil your reputation by staying too long. You should come onto Stark Street around noon and strut around for an hour or two. Wear your transmitter. I'll be watching and listening."

I had the morning to kill, so I went out for a run.

It wasn't any easier, but at least Eddie Gazarra didn't show up and tell me I looked like death warmed over. I ate breakfast, took a long shower, and planned how I was going to spend my money after I bagged Morelli.

I dressed in strappy sandals, a tight black knit miniskirt, and a stretchy red top with a low scoop neck that showed as much cleavage as was possible, given my bra size. I did the mousse and the spray thing with my hair so that I had a lot of it. I lined my eyes in midnight blue, gunked them up with mascara, painted my mouth whore red, and hung the biggest, brassiest earrings I owned from my lobes. I lacquered my nails to match my lips and checked myself out in the mirror.

Damned if I didn't make a good slut.

It was eleven o'clock. A little early, but I wanted to get this strutting around over with so I could visit Lula. After Lula I figured I'd do some shooting and then go home and wait for my phone to ring.

I parked a block from the gym and started down the street with my pocketbook hung from my shoulder and my hand wrapped around the Sure Guard. I'd discovered that the transmitter showed under the stretchy top, so I had it snug inside my bikini underpants. Eat your heart out, Morelli.

The van was parked almost directly across from the gym. Jackie stood between me and the van. She looked even more sullen than usual.

"How's Lula?" I asked. "Have you seen her today?"

"They don't have no visiting hours in the morning. I don't got time to see her anyway. I gotta earn a living, you know."

"The hospital said her condition was stable."

"Yeah. They got her in a regular room. She gotta stay there awhile on account of she's still bleeding inside, but I think she'll be okay."

"She have a safe place to stay when she gets out?"

"Ain't no place gonna be safe for Lula to stay when she gets out unless she get smart. She gonna be telling the police some white motherfucker cut her."

I glanced down the street at the van and felt Morelli's telepathic grunt of exasperation. "Someone's got to stop Ramirez."

"Ain't gonna be Lula," Jackie said. "What kind of witness you think she gonna make, anyway? You think people gonna believe a whore? They gonna say she got what she deserved and probably her old man beat her and leave her for you to see. Maybe they say you been doing some whoring and not paying the price and this be a lesson to you."

"Have you seen Ramirez today? Is he in the gym?"

"Don't know. These eyes don't see Ramirez. He the invisible man far as I'm concerned."

I'd expected as much from Jackie. And she was

probably right about Lula on the witness stand. Ramirez would hire the best defense lawyer in the state, and he wouldn't even have to work up a sweat to discredit Lula.

I moved on down the street. Has anyone seen Carmen Sanchez? I asked. Is it true she was seen with Benito Ramirez the night Ziggy Kulesza was shot?

No one had seen her. No one knew anything about her and Ramirez.

I paraded around for another hour and capped the effort with a trip across the street to lay some grief at Jimmy Alpha's feet. I didn't barge into his office this time. I waited patiently while his secretary announced me.

He didn't seem surprised. Probably he'd been watching from his window. He had dark circles under his eyes, the kind a person gets from sleepless nights and problems with no solutions. I stood in front of his desk, and we stared at each other for a full minute without talking.

"You know about Lula?" I asked him.

Alpha nodded.

"He almost killed her, Jimmy. He cut her and beat her and left her tied to my fire escape. Then he called and asked me if I'd received his present and told me I could look forward to an even worse fate."

Alpha's head was nodding again. This time it was nodding "no" in denial. "I talked to him," Alpha said. "Benito admits he spent some time with Lula, and maybe he got a little rough, but he said that was it. He said someone must have got to her after him. He says someone's trying to make him look bad."

"I talked to him on the phone. I know what I heard. I have it on tape."

"He swears it wasn't him."

"And you believe him?"

"I know he goes a little crazy with women. Got this tough-guy macho attitude. Got this thing about being disrespected. But I can't see him hanging a woman on a fire escape. I can't see him making that phone call. I know he's not Einstein, but I just can't see him being that dumb."

"He's not dumb, Jimmy. He's sick. He's done terrible things."

He ran his hand through his hair. "I don't know. Maybe you're right. Look, do me a favor and stay away from Stark Street for a while. The cops are going to investigate what happened to Lula. Whatever they find . . . I'm going to have to live with. In the meantime, I've got to get Benito ready to fight. He's going up against Tommy Clark in three weeks. Clark isn't much of a threat, but you have to take these things seriously all the same. The fans buy a ticket, they deserve a fight. I'm afraid Benito sees you, he gets all stirred up, you know? It's hard enough to get him to train. . . ."

It was about forty degrees in his office, but Alpha

had dark stains under his armpits. If I was in his place I'd be sweating, too. He was watching his dream turn into a nightmare, and he didn't have the guts to face up.

I told him I had a job to do and couldn't stay away from Stark Street. I let myself out and walked down the single flight of stairs. I sat on the bottom step and talked to my crotch. "Damn," I said. "That was fucking depressing."

Across the street, Morelli was listening in his van. I couldn't imagine what he was thinking.

MORELLI KNOCKED ON MY DOOR AT TEN-THIRTY that night. He had a six-pack and a pizza and a portable TV tucked under his arm. He was out of uniform, back to wearing jeans and a navy T-shirt.

"Another day in that van, and I might be glad to go to jail," he said.

"Is that a Pino's pizza?"

"Is there any other kind?"

"How'd you get it?"

"Pino delivers to felons." He looked around. "Where's your cable hookup?"

"In the living room."

He plugged the TV in, set the pizza and the beer on the floor, and hit the remote. "You get any phone calls?"

"Nothing."

He opened a beer. "It's early yet. Ramirez does his best work at night."

"I talked to Lula. She's not going to testify."

"Big surprise."

I sat on the floor next to the pizza box. "Did you hear the conversation with Jimmy Alpha?"

"Yeah, I heard it. What the hell kind of outfit were you supposed to be wearing?"

"It was my slut outfit. I wanted to speed things up."

"Christ, you had guys running their cars up on the curb. And where did you hide the mike? It wasn't under that top. I'd have seen Scotch tape under that top."

"I stuck it in my underpants."

"Dang," Morelli said. "When I get it back I'm going to have it bronzed."

I popped open a beer and helped myself to a piece of pizza. "What do you make of Alpha? You think he could be pushed into testifying against Ramirez?"

Morelli flipped through the channels, clicked onto a ballgame, and watched it for a few seconds. "Depends how much he knows. If he's got his head deep in the sand, he's not going to have hard facts. Dorsey paid him a visit after you left, and he got less than you did."

"You have Alpha's office bugged?"

"No. Bar talk at Pino's."

There was one piece of pizza left. We both eye-balled it.

"It'll go straight to your hips," Morelli said.

He was right, but I took it anyway.

I kicked him out a little after one and dragged myself to bed. I slept through the night, and in the morning there were no messages on my machine. I was about to start coffee when the car alarm went off in the lot below. I grabbed my keys and ran from my apartment, taking the steps three at a time. The driver's door was open when I got to the Jeep. The alarm was wailing away. I deactivated and reset the alarm, locked the car, and returned to my apartment.

Morelli was in the kitchen, and I could tell the effort to stay calm was jacking his blood pressure into the red zone.

"I didn't want anyone to steal your car," I said. "So I had an alarm installed."

"It wasn't 'anyone' you were worried about. It was *me*. You had a goddamn alarm installed in my goddamn car so I couldn't snatch it out from under you!"

"It worked, too. What were you doing in our car?"

"It's not *our* car. It's *my* car. I'm *allowing* you to drive it. I was going to get some breakfast."

"Why didn't you take the van?"

"Because I wanted to drive my car. I swear, when this mess gets cleared up, I'm moving to Alaska. I don't care what sort of sacrifice I have to make, I'm putting miles between us, because if I stay I'll strangle you, and they'll get me for murder one."

"Jesus, Morelli, you sound like you have PMS. You have to learn to lighten up a little. It's just a car alarm. You should be thanking me. I had it installed with my own money."

"Well shit, what was I thinking of?"

"You're under a lot of strain lately."

There was a knock on the door, and we both jumped.

Morelli beat me to the peephole. He stepped back several paces and pulled me with him. "It's Morty Beyers," he said.

There was another knock on the door.

"He can't have you," I said. "You're mine, and I'm not sharing."

Morelli grimaced. "I'll be under the bed if you need me."

I went to the door and took a look for myself. I'd never seen Morty Beyers before, but this guy looked like he'd just had an appendectomy. He was close to forty, overweight, ashen-faced, and he was stooped over, holding his stomach. His sandy hair was thin, combed over the top of his balding dome, and slick with sweat.

I opened the door to him.

"Morty Beyers," he said, extending his hand. "You must be Stephanie Plum."

"Aren't you supposed to be in the hospital?"

"An exploded appendix only gets you a couple

hours' stay. I'm back to work. They tell me I'm good as new."

He didn't look good as new. He looked like he had met Vampira on the stairs. "Your stomach still hurt?"

"Only when I straighten up."

"What can I do for you?"

"Vinnie said you had my FTAs. I thought now that I was feeling okay . . ."

"You want the paperwork back."

"Yeah. Listen, I'm sorry it didn't work out for you."

"It wasn't a complete bust. I brought two of them in."

He nodded. "Didn't have any luck with Morelli?"

"None at all."

"I know this sounds weird, but I could've sworn I saw his car in your parking lot."

"I stole it. I thought maybe I could flush him out by making him come after his car."

"You stole it? No shit? Jesus, that's great." He was leaning against the wall with his hand pressed to his groin.

"You want to sit down for a minute? You want some water?"

"Nah, I'm fine. I gotta get to work. I just wanted the pictures and stuff."

I ran to the kitchen, gathered up the files, and rushed back to the door. "This is it."

"Great." He tucked the folders under an arm. "So are you gonna keep the car a while?"

"I'm not sure."

"If you spotted Morelli walking down the street, would you bring him in?"

"Yeah."

He smiled. "If I was you, I'd do the same thing. I wouldn't pack it in just because my week was up. Just between you and me, Vinnie would pay out to anyone brought Morelli back. Well, I'll be on my way. Thanks."

"Take care of yourself."

"Yeah. I'm gonna use the elevator."

I closed the door, slid the bolt home, and latched the security chain. When I turned around, Morelli was standing in the bedroom doorway. "Do you think he knew you were here?" I asked.

"If he knew I was here, he'd have his gun aimed at my forehead by now. Don't underestimate Beyers. He's not as stupid as he looks. And he's not nearly as nice as he'd like you to believe. He was a cop. Got kicked off the force for demanding favors from prostitutes of both genders. We used to call him Morty the Mole because he'd bury his doo-dah in whatever hole was available."

"I bet he and Vinnie get along just great."

I went to the window and stared down at the parking lot. Beyers was examining Morelli's car, peering into the windows. He tried the door handle and the trunk latch. He wrote something on the outside of a folder. He straightened slightly and looked around the lot. His attention caught on the van. He slowly walked over and pressed his nose against the windows in an attempt to see the interior; then he laboriously climbed on the front bumper and tried to see through the windshield. He stepped back and stared at the antennae. He stood to the rear and copied the tag. He turned and looked up at my building, and I jumped back from the window.

Five minutes later, there was another knock on my door.

"I was wondering about that van in your lot," Beyers said. "Have you noticed it?"

"The blue one with the antennae?"

"Yeah. Do you know the owner?"

"No, but it's been here for a while."

I closed and locked the door and watched Beyers through the peephole. He stood thinking for a moment, and then he knocked on Mr. Wolesky's door. He showed Morelli's picture and asked a few questions. He thanked Mr. Wolesky, gave him his card, and backed away.

I returned to the window, but Beyers didn't appear in the lot. "He's going door-to-door," I said.

We continued to watch from the window, and eventually Beyers limped to his car. He drove a late-model dark blue Ford Escort equipped with a car phone. He left the lot and turned toward St. James.

Morelli was in the kitchen with his head in my refrigerator. "Beyers is going to be a real pain in the ass. He's going to check on the van plates and put it together."

"What's this going to do for you?"

"It's going to knock me out of Trenton until I get a different vehicle." He took a carton of orange juice and a loaf of raisin bread. "Put this on my tab. I've got to get out of here." He stopped at the door. "I'm afraid you're going to be on your own for a while. Stay locked up in the apartment here, don't let *anyone* in, and you should be okay. The alternative is to come with me, but if we get caught together, you'll be an accessory."

"I'll stay here. I'll be fine."

"Promise me you won't go out."

"I promise! I promise!"

Some promises are meant to be broken. This was one of them. I had no intention of sitting on my hands, waiting for Ramirez. I wanted to hear from him yesterday. I wanted the whole ugly affair to be done. I wanted Ramirez behind bars. I wanted my apprehension money. I wanted to get on with my life.

I looked out the window to make sure Morelli was gone. I got my pocketbook and locked up after myself. I drove to Stark Street and parked across from the gym. I didn't have the nerve to move freely on the street without Morelli backing me up, so I stayed in the car with the windows closed and the doors locked. I was sure by this time Ramirez

knew my car. I figured it was better than no re-
minder at all.

Every half hour I ran the air-conditioning to get
the temperature down and break the monotony. Several times I'd looked up at Jimmy Alpha's office
and seen a face at a window. The gym windows
showed less activity.

At twelve-thirty Alpha trotted across the street
and knocked on my window.

I powered it down. "Sorry to have to park here,
Jimmy, but I need to continue my surveillance for
Morelli. I'm sure you understand."

A wrinkle creased his brow. "I don't get it. If I
was looking for Morelli, I'd watch his relatives and
his friends. What's this thing with Stark Street and
Carmen Sanchez?"

"I have a theory about what happened. I think
Benito abused Carmen just like he abused Lula.
Then I think he panicked and sent Ziggy and some
other guy over to Carmen's to make sure she didn't
make noise. I think Morelli walked in on it and
probably shot Ziggy in self-defense just like he said.
Somehow Carmen and the other guy and Ziggy's
gun managed to disappear. I think Morelli's trying
to find them. And I think Stark Street is the logical
place to look."

"That's crazy. How'd you come up with such a
crazy idea?"

"From Morelli's arrest statement."

Alpha looked disgusted. "Well what'd you expect Morelli to say? That he shot Ziggy for the hell of it? Benito's an easy target. He has a reputation for being a little too aggressive with the ladies, and Ziggy worked for him, so Morelli took it from there."

"How about the missing witness? He must have worked for Benito, too."

"I don't know anything about the missing witness."

"People tell me he had a nose that looked like it had been smashed with a frying pan. That's pretty distinctive."

Alpha smiled. "Not in a third-rate gym. Half the bums who work out here have noses like that." He looked at his watch. "I'm late for a lunch. You look hot in there. You want me to bring something back for you? A cold soda? A sandwich, maybe?"

"I'm okay. I think I'm going to break for lunch soon, too. Have to use the little girls' room."

"There's a john on the second floor. Just get the key from Lorna. Tell her I said it was okay."

I thought it was decent of Alpha to offer the use of his facilities, but I didn't want to take a chance on Ramirez cornering me while I was on the toilet.

I took one last look up and down the street and drove off in search of fast food. A half hour later I was back in the very same parking space, feeling much more comfortable and twice as bored. I'd brought a book back with me, but it was hard to read and sweat at the same time, and sweating took precedence.

By three my hair was wet against my neck and face and had frizzed out to maximum volume. My shirt was plastered to my back, and perspiration stained over my chest. My legs were cramped, and I'd developed a nervous twitch to my left eye.

I still hadn't seen a sign of Ramirez. Pedestrian traffic was restricted to pockets of shade and had disappeared into smoky air-conditioned bars. I was the only fool sitting baking in a car. Even the hookers had disappeared for a midafternoon crack break.

I palmed my defense spray and got out of the Cherokee, whimpering as all my little spine bones decompressed and realigned themselves. I stretched and jogged in place. I walked around the car and bent to touch my toes. A breeze trickled down Stark Street, and I felt inordinately blessed. True, the air index was lethal and the temperature hovered at blast-furnace range, but it was a breeze all the same.

I leaned against the car and pulled the front of my shirt away from my sweaty body.

Jackie emerged from the Grand Hotel and lumbered down the street toward me, en route to her corner. "You look like heat stroke," she said, handing me a cold Coke.

I popped the tab, drank some soda, and held the cold can against my forehead. "Thanks. This is great."

"Don't think I'm getting soft on your skinny

white ass," she said. "It's just you're gonna die sitting in that car, and you're gonna give Stark Street a bad name. People gonna say it a race murder, and my white trash pervert business'll get ruined."

"I'll try not to die. God forbid I should ruin your pervert business."

"Fucking A," she said. "Them little white perverts pay fine money for my big nasty ass."

"How's Lula?"

Jackie shrugged. "She's doing as good as she can. She appreciated that you sent flowers."

"Not much activity here today."

Jackie slid her eyes up to the gym windows. "Thank sweet Jesus for that," she said softly.

I followed her gaze to the second floor. "You better not be seen talking to me."

"Yeah," she said. "I gotta get back to work, anyway."

I stood there for a few minutes longer, enjoying the soda and the luxury of being fully vertical. I turned to get back in the car and gasped at the sight of Ramirez standing next to me.

"Been waiting all day for you to get out of this car," he said. "Bet you're surprised at how quiet I move. Didn't even hear me come up on you, did you? That's how it's always gonna be. You're never gonna hear me until I pounce. And then it's gonna be too late."

I took a slow breath to quiet my heart. I waited a moment longer to steady my voice. When I felt some control, I asked him about Carmen. "I want to know about Carmen," I said. "I want to know if she saw you coming."

"Carmen and me, we had a date. Carmen asked for what she got."

"Where is she now?"

He shrugged. "Don't know. She split after Ziggy got offed."

"What about the guy that was with Ziggy that night? Who was he? What happened to him?"

"Don't know nothing about that either."

"I thought they worked for you."

"Why don't we go upstairs and talk about this? Or we could go for a ride. I got a Porsche. I could take you for a ride in my Porsche."

"I don't think so."

"See, there you go again. Refusing the champ. You're always refusing the champ. He don't like that."

"Tell me about Ziggy and his friend . . . the guy with the smashed nose."

"Be more interesting to tell you about the champ. How he gonna teach you some respect. How he gonna punish you so you learn not to refuse him." He stepped closer, and the heat coming off his body made the air feel cool by comparison. "Think maybe I'll make you bleed before I fuck you. You like that? You want to get cut, bitch?"

That's it. I'm out of here. "You're not going to

do anything to me," I said. "You don't scare me, and you don't excite me."

"You lie." He wrapped his hand around my upper arm and squeezed hard enough to make me cry out.

I kicked him hard in the shin, and he hit me. I never saw his hand move. The crack rang in my ears and my head snapped back. I tasted blood and blinked hard several times to clear the cobwebs. When most of the stars faded, I shot him square in the face with the Sure Guard.

He howled in pain and rage and reeled into the street with his hands to his eyes. The howling metamorphosed to choking and gasping, and he went down on all fours like some monstrous animal—a big, pissed-off, wounded buffalo.

Jimmy Alpha came running from across the street, followed by his secretary and a man I'd never seen before.

The man went down on the ground with Ramirez, trying to calm him, telling him he'd be okay in a minute, to take deep breaths.

Alpha and the secretary rushed over to me.

"Jesus," Jimmy Alpha said, pressing a clean handkerchief into my hand. "Are you okay? He didn't break anything, did he?"

I put the handkerchief to my mouth and held it there while I ran my tongue over my teeth to see if any were missing or loose. "I think I'm okay."

"I'm really sorry," Jimmy said. "I don't know what's the matter with him, the way he treats women. I apologize for him. I don't know what to do."

I wasn't in the mood to accept an apology. "There are lots of things you can do," I said. "Get him psychiatric help. Lock him up. Take him to the vet and get him neutered."

"I'll pay for a doctor," Jimmy Alpha said. "Do you want to go to a doctor?"

"The only place I'm going is to the police station. I'm pressing charges, and nothing you can say is going to stop me."

"Think about it for a day," Jimmy pleaded. "At least wait until you're not so upset. He can't take another assault charge now."

TWELVE

I WRENCHED THE DRIVER'S DOOR OPEN AND jammed myself behind the wheel. I eased away from the curb, being careful not to run over anyone. I drove at a moderate speed, and I didn't look back. I stopped for a light and assessed the damage in the rearview mirror. My upper lip was split on the inside and still bleeding. I had a purple bruise forming on my left cheek. My cheek and my lip were beginning to swell.

I was holding tight to the wheel, and I was using every strength I possessed to stay calm. I drove south on Stark to State Street and followed State to Hamilton. When I reached Hamilton I felt as if I was safe in my own neighborhood and could allow myself to stop and think. I pulled into a convenience store lot and sat there for a while. I needed to go to the police station to report the assault, but I didn't want to leave the security and comfort of home turf, and I wasn't sure how the police would regard this latest incident with Ramirez. He'd threatened me, and then I'd deliberately provoked him by parking across from the gym. Not smart.

I'd been on adrenaline overdose ever since Ramirez appeared at my side, and now that the adrenaline was slacking out, exhaustion and pain were creeping in. My arm and my jaw ached and my pulse rate felt like it had dropped to twelve.

Face up, I said to myself, you're not going to make it to the police station today. I shuffled through my shoulder bag until I found Dorsey's card. Might as well keep some continuity and whine to Dorsey. I dialed his number and left a message to call back. I didn't specify the problem. I didn't think I could go through it twice.

I hauled myself into the store and got myself a grape popsicle. "Hadda akthident," I said to the clerk. "My lip ith thwollen."

"Maybe you should see a doctor."

I ripped the paper off the popsicle and put the ice to my lip. "Ahhh." I sighed. "Thas bedda."

I returned to the car, put it into gear, and backed into a pickup truck. My whole life flashed in front of me. I was drowning. Please God, I prayed, don't let there be a dent.

We both got out and examined our cars. The

pickup didn't have a scratch. No dent, no paint chipped, not even a smudge in the wax. The Cherokee looked like someone had taken a can opener to its right rear fender.

The guy driving the pickup stared at my lip. "Domestic quarrel?"

"A akthident."

"Guess this just isn't your day."

"No day ith my day," I said.

Since the accident had been my fault, and there'd been no damage to his car, we didn't do the ritual of trading insurance information. I took one last look at the damage, shuddered violently, and slunk away, debating the value of suicide as opposed to facing Morelli.

The phone was ringing as I came through my front door. It was Dorsey.

"I haf an assault charge againth Ramireth," I said. "He hit me in the mouff."

"Where'd this happen?"

"Thark Threet." I gave him the details and refused his offer to come to my apartment to get my statement. I didn't want to chance his running into Morelli. I promised I'd stop in tomorrow to complete the paperwork.

I took a shower and had ice cream for supper. Every ten minutes I'd look out the window to see if there was any sign of Morelli in the lot. I'd parked in a far corner where the lighting was poor. If I could just get through the night, tomorrow I'd take the Cherokee to Al at the body shop and see if he could do an instant repair. I had no idea how I'd pay for it.

I watched television until eleven and went to bed, lugging Rex's cage into the bedroom to keep me company. There'd been no phone calls from Ramirez and no sign of Morelli. I wasn't sure if I was relieved or disappointed. I had no idea if Morelli was listening, protecting me as agreed, so I slept with my defense spray, my portable phone, and my gun on the nightstand.

My phone rang at six-thirty. It was Morelli.

"Time to get up," he said.

I checked my bedside clock. "It's practically the middle of the night."

"You'd have been up hours ago if you had to sleep in a Nissan Sentra."

"What are you doing in a Sentra?"

"I'm having the van painted a different color and the antennae removed. I've managed to 'find' a new set of plates. In the meantime, the body shop gave me a loaner. I waited until dark and then parked on Maple, just behind the lot."

"So you could guard my body?"

"Mostly I didn't want to miss hearing you get undressed. What was that weird squeaking sound all night?"

"Rex on his wheel."

"I thought he lived in the kitchen."

I didn't want Morelli to know I'd been scared

and lonely, so I lied. "I cleaned the sink, and he didn't like the smell of the cleanser, so I brought him into the bedroom."

The silence stretched for a couple beats.

"Translation," Morelli said. "You were scared and lonely, and you brought Rex in for company."

"These are difficult times."

"Tell me about it."

"I suppose you need to get out of Trenton before Beyers returns."

"I suppose I do. I'm too visible in this car. I can get the van at six tonight, and then I'll be back."

"Catch you later."

"Ten-four, Captain Video."

I went back to bed, and two hours later I was jolted awake by the car alarm blaring away in the lot below me. I flew out of bed, rushed to the window, and threw the curtains open in time to see Morty Beyers smash the alarm to smithereens with his gun butt.

"Beyers!" I bellowed from my open window. "What the hell do you think you're doing?"

"My wife left me, and she took the Escort."

"So?"

"So I need a car. I was gonna rent one, and then I thought of Morelli's Jeep sitting here, and I figured it'd save me some money to use it until I tracked Mona down."

"Christ, Beyers, you can't just come into a lot

and take someone's car! That's stealing. You're a goddamn car thief."

"So?"

"Where'd you get the keys?"

"Same place you did. Morelli's apartment. He had an extra set in his dresser."

"You won't get away with this."

"What are you gonna do, call the police?"

"God will get you for this."

"Fuck God," Beyers said, sliding behind the wheel, taking time to adjust the seat and fiddle with the radio.

Arrogant bastard, I thought. Not only is he stealing the damn car, but he's sitting there flaunting his ability to take it. I grabbed my defense spray and bolted out the door and down the stairs. I was barefoot, wearing a Mickey Mouse nightshirt and a pair of Jockey string bikinis, and I could have cared less.

I was through the back door with my foot on the pavement when I saw Beyers turn the key and step on the accelerator. A split second later the car exploded with a deafening blast, sending doors flying off into space like Frisbees. Flames licked up from the undercarriage and instantly consumed the Cherokee, turning it into a brilliant yellow fireball.

I was too astonished to move. I stood openmouthed and speechless while parts of the roof and fender reversed their trajectory and clanked down to earth.

Sirens sounded in the distance, and tenants

poured from the building to stand beside me and
stare at the burning Jeep. Clouds of black smoke
boiled into the morning sky, and searing neat rippled across my face.

There'd never been any possibility of saving
Morty Beyers. Even if I'd immediately responded,
I couldn't have gotten him out of the car. And probably he was dead from the blast, not the fire. It
occurred to me that chances of this being an accident were slim. And that chances of this being
meant for me were large.

On the positive side, I didn't have to sweat Morelli finding out about yesterday's accident damage.

I backed away from the fire and eased my way
through the small crowd that had formed. I took the
stairs two at a time and locked myself in my apartment. I'd carelessly left the front door wide open
when I'd dashed out after Beyers, so I did a thor-
ough search with my gun drawn. If I came on the
guy who roasted Morty Beyers, I wasn't going to
fool around with his neurotransmitters—I was going to go for a bullet in the gut. The gut made a
nice big target.

When I was sure my apartment was secure, I got
dressed in shorts and shirt. I took a fast bathroom
break and checked my appearance in the bathroom
mirror. I had a purple bruise on my cheekbone and
a small gash in my upper lip. Most of the swelling
had gone down. As a result of the morning's fire,
my complexion looked like it had been sunburned

and sandblasted. My eyebrows and the hair around my face had gotten singed and stuck out in spikes about an eighth of an inch long. Very attractive. Not that I was complaining. I could have been dead and missing a few body parts that had landed in the azaleas. I laced up my Reeboks and went downstairs to take another look.

The parking lot and adjoining streets were filled with fire trucks and police cars and ambulances. Barricades had been set up, holding the curious away from the smoldering remains of Morelli's Jeep. Oily, sooty water slicked the blacktop, and the air smelled like charred pot roast. I didn't want to pursue that train of thought. I saw Dorsey standing on the perimeter, talking to a uniform. He looked up and caught my eye and headed over.

"I'm getting a bad feeling about this," he said.

"You know Morty Beyers?"

"Yeah."

"He was in the Jeep."

"No shit. Are you sure?"

"I was talking to him when it blew."

"I guess that explains your missing eyebrows. What were you talking about?"

"Vinnie had only given me a week to bring Morelli in. My week was up, and Morty took up the hunt. We were sort of talking about Morelli."

"You couldn't have been talking too close or you'd be hamburger."

"Actually I was right about where we're standing

now, and we were yelling at each other. We were sort of . . . disagreeing."

A uniform came over with a twisted license plate. "We found this over by the Dumpster," he said. "You want me to run an ID?"

I took the plate. "Don't bother. The car belongs to Morelli."

"Oh boy," Dorsey said. "I can hardly wait to hear this."

I figured I'd embellish the truth a little, since the police might not be up on the finer points of bounty hunterism and might not understand about commandeering. "It's like this," I said. "I went to see Morelli's mother, and she was very upset that no one was running Joe's car. You know how bad it is for the battery to let a car sit. Well one thing led to another and next thing I'd agreed to drive the car around for her."

"So you've been driving Morelli's car as a favor to his mother?"

"Yes. He'd asked her to take care of it, but she didn't have time."

"Very noble of you."

"I'm a noble person."

"Go on."

So I did. I explained about Beyers's wife leaving him, and about how he tried to steal the car, and how he made the mistake of saying "fuck God," and then the car blew up.

"You think God got pissed off and fried Beyers?"

"That would be one theory."

"When you come to the station to complete the report on Ramirez, we might want to talk further on this."

I watched for a few more minutes and then went back to my apartment. I didn't especially want to be around when they scooped up the ashes that had been Morty Beyers.

I sat in front of the television until noon, keeping my windows closed and my curtains drawn to the crime scene below. Every once in a while I'd wander into the bathroom and stare at myself in the mirror to see if my eyebrows had grown back yet.

At twelve o'clock I parted my curtains and braved a peek at the lot. The Cherokee had been removed, and only two patrolmen remained. From my window it appeared they were filling out property damage forms for the handful of cars that had been pelted with debris from the explosion.

A morning of television had anesthetized me sufficiently that I felt ready to cope, so I took a shower and got dressed, being careful not to dwell on thoughts of death and bombings.

I needed to go down to the police station, but I didn't have a car. I had a few dollars in my pocket. Nothing in my checking account. My credit cards were in collection. I had to make another apprehension.

I called Connie and told her about Morty Beyers.

"This is going to make a serious hole in Vinnie's

dike," Connie said. "Ranger's recovering from gun-shot and now Morty Beyers is out of the picture. They were our two best agents."

"Yeah. It sure is a shame. I guess Vinnie's left with me."

There was a pause at the other end of the phone. "You didn't do Morty, did you?"

"Morty sort of did himself. You have anything easy come in? I could use some fast money."

"I have an exhibitionist gone FTA on a $2,000 bond. He's been kicked out of three retirement homes. He's currently living in an apartment some-where." I could hear her shuffling through papers. "Here it is," she said. "Ommigod, he's living in your building."

"What's his name?"

"William Earling. He's in apartment 3E."

I grabbed my pocketbook and locked up. I took the stairs to the third floor, counted off apartments, and knocked on Earling's door. A man answered, and right off I suspected I had the right person be-cause he was old and he was naked. "Mr. Earling?"

"Yup. That's me. I'm in pretty good shape, huh chickie? You think I've got some fearful equip-ment?"

I gave myself a mental command not to look, but my eyes strayed south of their own volition. Not only wasn't he fearful, but his doodles were wrin-kled. "Yeah. You're pretty fearful," I said. I handed him my card. "I work for Vincent Plum, your bond agent. You failed to appear for a court hearing, Mr. Earling. I need to take you downtown so you can reschedule."

"Damn court hearings are a waste of time," Earling said. "I'm seventy-six years old. You think they're gonna send some seventy-six-year-old guy to prison because he flashed his stuff around?"

I sincerely hoped so. Seeing Earling naked was enough to make me turn celibate. "I need to take you downtown. How about you go put some clothes on."

"I don't wear clothes. God brought me into the world naked, and that's the way I'm going out."

"Okay by me, but in the meantime I wish you'd get dressed."

"The only way I'm going with you is naked."

I took out my cuffs and snapped them on his wrists.

"Police brutality. Police brutality," he yelled.

"Sorry to disappoint you," I said. "I'm not a cop."

"Well what are you?"

"I'm a bounty hunter."

"Bounty hunter brutality. Bounty hunter brutality."

I went to the hall closet, found a full-length raincoat, and buttoned him into it.

"I'm not going with you," he said, standing rigid, his hands cuffed under the coat. "You can't make me go."

"Listen, Grandpa," I said, "either you go peaceably or I'll gas you and drag you out by your heels."

I couldn't believe I was saying this to some poor senior citizen with a snail dick. I was appalled at myself, but what the hell, it was worth $200.

"Don't forget to lock up," he said. "This neighborhood's going to heck in a handbasket. The keys are in the kitchen."

I got the keys, and one of them had a little Buick insignia on it. What a break. "One more thing," I said. "Would you mind if I borrowed your car to take you downtown?"

"I guess that'd be okay as long as we don't use too much gas. I'm on a fixed income, you know."

I buzzed Mr. Earling through in record time and took care not to run into Dorsey. I stopped at the office on the way home to pick up my check and stopped at the bank to cash it. I parked Mr. Earling's car as close to the door as possible to cut down on his streaking distance when he got out of jail. I didn't want to see any more of Mr. Earling than was absolutely unavoidable.

I jogged upstairs and called home, cringing at the thought of what I was about to do.

"Is Daddy out with the cab?" I asked. "I need a ride."

"He's off today. He's right here. Where do you need to go?"

"An apartment complex on Route 1." Another cringe.

"Now?"

"Yeah." Very large sigh. "Now."

"I'm having stuffed shells tonight. Would you like some stuffed shells?"

Hard to believe how much I wanted those stuffed shells. More than good sex, a fast car, a cool night, or eyebrows. I wanted temporary respite from adult-hood. I wanted to feel unconditionally safe. I wanted my mom to cluck around me, filling my milk glass, relieving me of the most mundane re-sponsibilities. I wanted to spend a few hours in a house cluttered with awful overstuffed furniture and oppressive cooking smells. "Stuffed shells would be good."

My father was at the back door in fifteen minutes. He gave a start at the sight of me.

"We had an accident in the parking lot," I said. "A car caught fire, and I was standing too close." I gave him the address and asked him to stop at K-Mart on the way. Thirty minutes later he dropped me off in Morelli's parking lot.

"Tell Mom I'll be there by six," I said to him.

He looked at the Nova and the case of motor oil I'd just purchased. "Maybe I should stay to make sure it runs."

I fed the car three cans and checked the dipstick. I gave my father an A-okay sign. He didn't seem impressed. I got behind the wheel, gave the dash a hard shot with my fist, and cranked her over. "Starts every time," I yelled.

My father was still impassive, and I knew he was thinking I should have bought a Buick. These indignities never befell Buicks. We pulled out of the lot together, and I waved him off on Route 1, pointing the Nova in the direction of Ye Olde Muffler Shoppe. Past the orange-peaked roof of the Howard Johnson Motel, past the Shady Grove Trailer Park, past Happy Days Kennels. Other drivers were giving me a wide berth, not daring to enter into my thundering wake. Seven miles down the road I cheered at the sight of the yellow and black muffler shop sign.

I wore my Oakleys to hide my eyebrows, but the counterman still did a double take. I filled out the forms and gave him the keys and took a seat in the small room reserved for the parents of sick cars. Forty-five minutes later I was on my way. I only noticed the smoke when I stopped at an intersection, and the red light only blinked on occasionally. I figured that was as good as I could expect.

My mother started as soon as I hit the front porch. "Every time I see you, you look worse and worse. Bruises and cuts and now what happened to your hair, and ommigod you haven't got eyebrows. What happened to your eyebrows? Your father said you were in a fire."

"A car caught fire in my parking lot. It wasn't anything."

"I saw it on the TV," Grandma Mazur said, elbowing her way past my mother. "They said it was a bombing. Blew the car sky high. And some guy was in the car. Some sleazoid named Beyers. Except there wasn't much left of him."

Grandma Mazur was wearing a pink-and-orange-print cotton blouse with a tissue wadded up in the sleeve, bright blue spandex shorts, white tennies, and stockings rolled just above her knee.

"I like your shorts," I said to her. "Great color."

"She went like that to the funeral home this afternoon," my father yelled from the kitchen. "Tony Mancuso's viewing."

"I tell you it was something," Grandma Mazur said. "The VFW was there. Best viewing I've been to all month. And Tony looked real good. They gave him one of those ties with the little horse heads on."

"We got seven phone calls so far," my mother said. "I told everyone she forgot to take her medicine this morning."

Grandma Mazur clacked her teeth. "Nobody knows fashion around here. You can't hardly ever wear anything different." She looked down at her shorts. "What do you think?" she asked me. "You think these are okay for an afternoon viewing?"

"Sure," I said, "but if it was at night I'd wear black."

"Just exactly what I was thinking. I gotta get me some black ones next."

By eight o'clock I was sated with good food and overstuffed furniture and ready to once again take up the mantle of independent living. I staggered out of my parents' house, arms loaded with leftovers, and motored back to my apartment.

For the better part of the day I'd avoided thinking about the explosion, but it was time to face facts. Someone had tried to kill me, and it wasn't Ramirez. Ramirez wanted to inflict pain and hear me beg. Ramirez was frightening and abhorrent, but he was also predictable. I knew where Ramirez was coming from. Ramirez was criminally insane.

Planting a bomb was a different kind of insanity. A bombing was calculated and purposeful. A bombing was meant to rid the world of a particular, annoying person.

Why me? I thought. Why would someone want me dead? Even articulating the question sent a chill through my heart.

I parked the Nova in the middle of my lot and wondered if I'd have the courage to step on the accelerator tomorrow morning. Morelli's car had been shoveled away and there was little evidence of the fire. The macadam was pocked and cracked where the Jeep had burned, but there was no crime scene tape or charred debris to further mark the spot.

I let myself into my apartment and found my answering machine light furiously blinking. Dorsey had called three times requesting a call back. He didn't sound friendly. Bernie had called to say they were having a storewide sale and I should drop by.

Twenty percent off blenders and a complimentary bottle of daiquiri mix to the first twenty customers. My eyes glazed over at the thought of a daiquiri. I still had a few dollars left, and blenders had to be pretty cheap in the overall scheme of things, right? The last call was from Jimmy Alpha with another apology and his hopes that I hadn't been badly hurt by Ramirez.

I looked at my watch. It was almost nine. I couldn't get to Bernie before closing. Too bad. I was pretty sure if I had a daiquiri I could think much more clearly and probably figure out who tried to send me into orbit.

I turned the television on and sat in front of it, but my mind was elsewhere. It was scanning for potential assassins. Of my captures only Lonnie Dodd was a possibility, and he was in jail. More likely this had to do with the Kulesza murder. Someone was worried about me poking around. I couldn't imagine anyone being worried enough to want to kill me. Death was very serious shit.

There had to be something I was missing here. Something about Carmen or Kulesza or Morelli . . . or maybe the mystery witness.

An ugly little thought wriggled around in a back corner of my brain. So far as I could see, I was a genuine, mortal threat to only one person. That person was Morelli.

The phone rang at eleven, and I caught it before the machine picked up.

"Are you alone?" Morelli asked.

I hesitated. "Yes."

"Why the hesitation?"

"How do you feel on the subject of murder?"

"Whose murder are we talking about?"

"Mine."

"I feel warm all over."

"Just wondering."

"I'm coming up. Watch for me at the door."

I tucked the defense spray into the waistband of my shorts and covered it with my T-shirt. I glued my eye to the peephole and opened the door when Morelli strolled down the hall. Every day he looked a little bit worse. He needed a haircut, and he had a week's worth of beard that probably had only taken him two days to grow. His jeans and T-shirt were street-person quality.

He closed and locked the door behind himself. He took in my scorched, bruised face and the bruises on my arm. His expression was grim. "You want to tell me about it?"

"The cut lip and the bruises are from Ramirez. We had a tussle, but I think I won. I gassed him and left him throwing up in the road."

"And the singed eyebrows?"

"Mmmm. Well, that's a little complicated."

His face darkened. "What happened?"

"Your car blew up."

There was no reaction for several beats. "You want to run that by me again?" he finally said.

"The good news is . . . you don't have to worry about Morty Beyers anymore."

"And the bad news?"

I took his license plate from the kitchen counter and handed it to him. "This is all that's left of your car."

He stared down at the plate in shocked silence.

I told him about Morty Beyers's wife leaving him, and the bomb, and the three phone calls from Dorsey.

He drew the same conclusion I'd drawn. "It wasn't Ramirez."

"I made a mental list of people who might want me dead, and your name was at the top."

"Only in my dreams," he said. "Who else was on the list?"

"Lonnie Dodd, but I think he's still in prison."

"You ever get death threats? How about ex-husbands or ex-boyfriends? You run over anyone recently?"

I had no intention of dignifying that question with a reaction.

"Okay," he said. "So you think this is associated with the Kulesza murder?"

"Yes."

"Are you scared?"

"Yes."

"Good. Then you'll be careful." He opened my refrigerator door, pulled out the leftovers my mom had sent home with me, and ate them cold. "You need to be careful when you talk to Dorsey. If he finds out you've been working with me, he could charge you with aiding and abetting."

"I have this very disturbing suspicion that I've been talked into an alliance that's not in my best interest."

He cracked a beer open. "The only way you're going to collect that $10,000 is if I allow you to bring me in. And I'm not going to allow you to bring me in if I can't prove myself innocent. Any time you want to call the deal off, just let me know, but you can kiss your money good-bye."

"That's a rotten attitude."

He shook his head. "Realistic."

"I could have gassed you any number of times."

"I don't think so."

I whipped the spray out, but before I could aim he'd knocked the canister from my hand and sent it flying across the room.

"Doesn't count," I said. "You were expecting it."

He finished his sandwich and slid his dish into the dishwasher. "I'm always expecting it."

"Where do we go from here?"

"We keep doing more of the same. Obviously we're hitting a nerve."

"I don't like being a target."

"You aren't going to whine about this, are you?" He settled himself in front of the television and started working the channel changer. He looked tired, sitting with his back against the wall, one leg bent at the knee. He locked in a late-night show and closed his eyes. His breathing grew deep and even and his head slumped to his chest.

"I could gas you now," I whispered.

He raised his head, but he didn't open his eyes. A smile played at the corners of his mouth. "It's not your style, Cupcake."

HE WAS STILL SLEEPING ON THE FLOOR IN FRONT of the television when I got up at eight. I tiptoed past him and went out to run. He was reading the paper and drinking coffee when I returned.

"Anything in there about the bombing?" I asked.

"Story and pictures on page three. They're calling it an unexplained explosion. Nothing especially interesting." He looked over the top of the paper at me. "Dorsey left another message on your machine. Maybe you should see what he wants."

I took a fast shower, dressed in clean clothes, slathered some aloe cream on my blistered face, and followed my scaly nose to the coffeepot. I drank half a cup while I read the funnies, and then I called Dorsey.

"We've got the analysis back from the lab," he said. "It was definitely a bomb. Professional job. Of course, you can get a book out of any library will tell you how to do a professional bombing. You could build a fucking nuke if you wanted to. Anyway, I thought you'd want to know."

"I suspected as much."

"You have any ideas who would do such a thing?"

"No names."

"How about Morelli?"

"That's a possibility."

"I missed you at the station yesterday."

He was fishing. He knew there was something screwy about all of this. He just hadn't figured it out yet. Welcome to the club, Dorsey. "I'll try to get there today."

"Try real hard."

I hung up and topped off my coffee. "Dorsey wants me to come in."

"Are you going?"

"No. He's going to ask questions I can't answer."

"You should put in some time on Stark Street this morning."

"Not this morning. I have things to do."

"What things?"

"Personal things."

He raised an eyebrow.

"I have some loose ends to tie up . . . just in case," I said.

"Just in case what?"

I made an exasperated gesture. "Just in case something happens to me. For the past ten days I've been stalked by a professional sadist, and now I'm on the happy bomber's hit list. I feel a little insecure, okay? Give me a break, Morelli. I need to see some people. I have a few personal errands to run."

He gently peeled a strip of loose skin off my nose. "You're going to be okay," he said softly. "I understand that you're scared. I get scared, too. But we're the good guys, and the good guys always win."

I really felt like a jerk, because here was Morelli being nice to me, and what I actually wanted to do was hop on over to Bernie's to buy a blender and get my free daiquiri mix.

"How were you planning on running these errands without the Jeep?" he asked.

"I retrieved the Nova."

He winced. "You didn't park it in the lot, did you?"

"I was hoping the bomber wouldn't know it was my car."

"Oh boy."

"I'm sure I have nothing to worry about," I said.

"Yeah. I'm sure, too. I'll go down with you just to make double sure."

I collected my gear, checked the windows, and reset the answering machine. Morelli was waiting for me at the door. We walked downstairs together, and we both paused when we reached the Nova.

"Even if the bomber knew this was your car, he'd have to be stupid to try the same thing twice," Morelli said. "Statistically the second hit comes from a different direction."

Made perfect sense to me, but my feet were stuck

to the pavement and my heart was rocketing around in my chest. "All right. Here I go," I said. "Now or never."

Morelli had dropped to his belly and was looking under the Nova.

"What do you see?" I asked him.

"A hell of an oil leak." He crawled out and got to his feet.

I raised the hood and checked the dipstick. Wonder of wonders, the car needed oil. I fed it two cans and slammed the hood down.

Morelli had taken the keys from the door handle and angled himself behind the wheel. "Stand back," he said to me.

"No way. This is my car. I'll start it up."

"If one of us is going to get blown apart it might as well be me. I'm as good as dead if I don't find that missing witness, anyway. Move away from the car."

He turned the key. Nothing happened. He looked at me.

"Sometimes you have to smack it around," I said.

He turned the key again and brought his fist down hard on the dash. The car coughed and caught. It idled rough and then settled in.

Morelli slumped against the wheel, eyes closed. "Shit."

I looked in the window at him. "Is my seat wet?"

"Very funny." He got out of the car and held the door for me. "Do you want me to follow?"

"No. I'll be fine. Thanks."

"I'll be on Stark Street if you need me. Who knows . . . maybe the witness will show up at the gym."

When I got to Bernie's store I noticed people weren't standing in line to go through the door, so I assumed I was in good shape for the daiquiri mix.

"Hey," Bernie said, "look who's here."

"I got your message about the blender."

"It's this little baby," he said, patting a display blender. "It chops nuts, crushes ice, mashes bananas, and makes a hell of a daiquiri."

I looked at the price affixed to the blender. I could afford it. "Sold. Do I get my free daiquiri mix?"

"You bet." He took a boxed blender to the register, bagged it, and rang it up. "How's it going?" he asked cautiously, his eyes fixed on the singed stumps of hair that had once been eyebrows.

"It's been better."

"A daiquiri will help."

"Without a shadow of a doubt."

On the other side of the street, Sal was Windexing his front door. He was a pleasant-looking man, thick-bodied and balding, wrapped in his white butcher's apron. So far as I knew, he was a small-time bookie. Nothing special. I doubted he was connected. So why would a guy like Kulesza, whose entire life centered on Stark Street, drive all the way across town to see Sal? I knew a few of Kulesza's vital statistics, but I didn't know anything of his personal life. Shopping at Sal's was the only moderately interesting piece of information I had about Kulesza. Maybe Ziggy was a betting man. Maybe he and Sal were old friends. Maybe they were related. Now that I thought about it, maybe Sal would know about Carmen or the guy with the flat nose.

I chatted with Bernie for a few more minutes while I settled in to the idea of interviewing Sal. I watched a woman enter the shop and make a purchase. This seemed like a good approach to me. It would give me an opportunity to look around.

I promised Bernie I'd be back for bigger and better appliances and walked across the street to Sal's.

THIRTEEN

I PUSHED THROUGH SAL'S FRONT DOOR AND WENT to the long case filled with steaks and ground meat patties and twine-bound roasts.

Sal gave me a welcoming smile. "What can I do for you?"

"I was at Kuntz's, buying a blender. . . ." I held the bag up for him to see. "And I thought I'd get something for supper while I was here."

"Sausage? Fresh fish? Nice piece of chicken?"

"Fish."

"I got some flounder just caught off the Jersey shore."

Probably it glowed in the dark. "That'll be fine. Enough for two people."

Somewhere in the back a door opened, and I

could hear the drone of a truck motor. The door clanged shut, and the motor noise disappeared.

A man entered from the hallway beside the walk-in, and my heart jumped into triple time. Not only was the man's nose smashed, but his entire face looked as if it had been pressed flat . . . as if it had been hit with a frying pan. I couldn't know for sure until Morelli took a look, but I suspected I'd found the missing witness.

I was torn between wanting to jump up and down and make sounds of excitement and wanting to bolt and run before I was hacked up into chops and roasts.

"Got a delivery for you," the man said to Sal. "You want it in the lockup?"

"Yeah," Sal said. "And take the two barrels set by the door. One of them's heavy. You'll need the dolly."

Sal's attention turned back to the fish. "How you gonna cook these fillets?" he asked me. "You know you can pan fry them, or bake them, or stuff them. Personally, I like them fried. Heavy batter, deep fat."

I heard the back door close after the guy with the flat face. "Who was that?" I asked.

"Louis. Works for the distributor in Philly. He brings up meat."

"And then what does he take back in the barrels?"

"Sometimes I save up trim. They use it for dog food."

I had to grit my teeth to keep from flying out the door. I'd found the witness! I was sure of it. By the time I got to the Nova I was dizzy with the effort of restraint. I was saved! I was going to be able to pay my rent. I'd succeeded at something. And now that the missing witness was found, I'd be safe. I'd turn Morelli in and have nothing more to do with Ziggy Kulesza. I'd be out of the picture. There'd be no reason for anyone to want to kill me . . . except, of course, Ramirez. And hopefully Ramirez would be implicated sufficiently to put him away for a long, long time.

The old man across from Carmen's apartment had said he'd been bothered by the noise from a refrigerator truck. Dollars to donuts it had been a meat truck. I couldn't know for sure until I did another check on the back of Carmen's apartment building, but if Louis had parked close enough he might have been able to ease himself down onto the roof of the refrigerator truck. Then he put Carmen on ice and drove away.

I couldn't figure the connection with Sal. Maybe there was no connection. Maybe it was just Ziggy and Louis working as cleanup for Ramirez.

I had a decent view of Sal's from where I sat. I shoved the key into the ignition and took one last look. Sal and Louis were talking. Louis was cool. Sal was agitated, throwing his hands into the air. I decided to watch awhile. Sal turned his back on Louis and made a phone call. Even from this distance I could see he wasn't happy. He slammed the receiver down, and both men went into the walk-in freezer and reappeared moments later rolling out the trim drum. They shunted the drum down the hallway leading to the back exit. Louis reappeared a short while later with what appeared to be a side of beef slung over his shoulder. He deposited the meat in the freezer and rolled out the second drum. He paused at the back hallway and stared toward the front of the store. My heart skipped in my chest, and I wondered if he could see me snooping. He walked forward, and I reached for my Sure Guard. He stopped at the door and turned the little OPEN sign to CLOSED.

I hadn't expected this. What did this mean? Sal was nowhere in sight, the store was closed, and so far as I knew it wasn't a holiday. Louis left through the back hallway, and the lights went out. I got a bad feeling in the pit of my stomach. The bad feeling escalated to panic, and the panic told me not to lose Louis.

I put the Nova in gear and drove to the end of the block. A white refrigerator truck with Pennsylvania plates eased into traffic ahead of me, and two blocks later we turned onto Chambers. I would have liked nothing better than to drop the whole thing in Morelli's lap, but I hadn't a clue how to get in touch with him. He was north of me on Stark Street, and

I was heading south. He probably had a phone in the van, but I didn't know the number, and besides, I couldn't call him until we stopped somewhere.

The refrigerator truck picked up Route 206 at Whitehorse. Traffic was moderately heavy. I was two car lengths back, and I found it fairly easy to stay hidden and at the same time keep sight of Louis. Just past the junction of Route 70 my oil light went on and stayed on. I did some vigorous swearing, screeched to a stop on the shoulder, poured two cans of oil with breakneck precision, slammed the hood, and took off.

I pushed the Nova up to eighty, ignoring the shimmy in the front end and the startled looks of other drivers as I rattled past them in my pussy-mobile. After an agonizing couple of miles I caught sight of the truck. Louis was one of the slower drivers on the road, holding his speed down to only ten miles an hour over the limit. I breathed a sigh of relief and fell into place. I prayed he wasn't going far. I only had a case and a half of oil in the backseat.

At Hammonton Louis left-turned onto a secondary road and drove east. There were fewer cars on this road, and I had to drop farther back. The countryside was rolling farmland and patches of woods. After about fifteen miles, the truck slowed and pulled into a gravel drive that led to a corrugated metal warehouse-type building. The sign on the front of the building said this was the Pachetco Inlet

Marina and Cold Storage. Beyond the building I could see boats and beyond the boats the glare of sun on open water.

I sailed by the lot and made a U-turn a quarter mile up the road where it dead-ended at the Mullico River. I returned and did a slow drive-by. The truck was parked at the board walkway that led to the boat slips. Louis and Sal were out of the truck, leaning against the back step bumper, looking like they were waiting for something or someone. They were alone in the lot. It was a small marina, and it seemed that even though it was summer, most of the activity was still weekend-based.

I'd passed a gas station a few miles back. I decided it would be an inconspicuous place to wait. If Sal or Louis left the marina they'd go in this direction, back to civilization, and I could follow. There was the added advantage of a public phone and the possibility of getting in touch with Morelli.

The station was pre-computer age with two old-fashioned gas pumps on a stained cement pad. A sign propped on one of the pumps advertised live bait and cheap gas. The single-level shack behind the pumps was brown shingle patched with flattened jerry cans and assorted pieces of plywood. A public phone had been installed next to the screen door.

I parked, partially hidden, behind the station, and walked the short distance to the phone, happy for the opportunity to stretch my legs. I called my own number. It was the only thing I could think to do.

The phone rang once, the machine answered, and I listened to my own voice tell me I wasn't home. "Anybody there?" I asked. No reply. I gave the public phone number and suggested if anyone needed to get in touch with me I'd be at that number for an indeterminate number of minutes.

I was about to get back into my car when Ramirez's Porsche sped by. This is curiouser and curiouser, I thought. Here we have a butcher, a shooter, and a boxer, meeting at the Pachetco Inlet Marina. It seemed unlikely that they were just three guys going fishing. If it had been anyone other than Ramirez who had driven down the road, I might have ventured closer to take a peek. I told myself I was holding back because Ramirez might recognize the Nova. This was only part of the truth. Ramirez had succeeded in his goal. The mere sight of his car sent me into a cold sweat of terror that left serious doubts about my ability to function through another confrontation.

A short time later, the Porsche hummed past me, en route to the highway. The windows were tinted, obscuring vision, but at best it could only seat two men, so that left at least one man at the marina. Hopefully, that one man was Louis. I made another call to my answering machine. This message was more urgent. "CALL ME!" I said.

It was close to dark before the phone finally rang.

"Where are you?" Morelli asked.

"I'm at the shore. At a gas station on the outskirts

of Atlantic City. I've found the witness. His name is Louis."

"Is he with you?"

"He's down the road." I briefed Morelli on the day's events and gave him directions to the marina. I bought a soda from an outside machine and went back to do more waiting.

It was deep twilight when Morelli finally pulled up next to me in the van. There'd been no traffic on the road since Ramirez, and I was sure the truck hadn't slipped by. It had occurred to me that Louis might be on a boat, possibly spending the night. I couldn't see any other reason for the truck to still be in the marina lot.

"Is our man at the marina?" Morelli asked.

"So far as I know."

"Has Ramirez come back?"

I shook my head no.

"Think I'll take a look around. You wait here."

No way was I doing any more waiting anywhere. I was fed up with waiting. And I didn't entirely trust Morelli. He had an annoying habit of making beguiling promises and then waltzing out of my life.

I followed the van to the water's edge and parked beside it. The white refrigerator truck hadn't been moved. Louis wasn't out and about. The boats tied up to the wharf were dark. The Pachetco Inlet Marina was not exactly a bustling hub of activity.

I got out of the Nova and walked around to Morelli.

"I thought I told you to wait at the gas station," Morelli said. "We look like a fucking parade."

"I thought you might need help with Louis."

Morelli was out of the van and standing beside me, looking disreputable and dangerous in the dark. He smiled, and his teeth were startlingly white against his black beard. "Liar. You're worried about your $10,000."

"That too."

We stared at each other for a while, making silent assessments.

Morelli finally reached through the open window, snatched a jacket off the front seat, pulled a semiautomatic from the jacket pocket, and shoved it into the waistband of his jeans. "I suppose we might as well look for my witness."

We walked to the truck and peered inside the cab. The cab was empty and locked. No other cars were parked in the lot.

Nearby, water lapped at pilings, and boats groaned against their moorings. There were four board docks with fourteen slips each, seven to a side. Not all of the slips were in use.

We quietly walked the length of each dock, reading boat names, looking for signs of habitation. Halfway down the third dock we stopped at a big Hatteras Convertible with a flying bridge, and we both mouthed the boat's name. "Sal's Gal."

Morelli boarded and crept aft. I followed several feet behind. The deck was littered with fishing gear,

long-handled nets and gaffs. The door to the salon
was padlocked on the outside, telling us Louis was
probably not on the inside. Morelli pulled a penlight
from his pocket and shone it into the cabin window.
The largest portion of the boat interior appeared to
have been stripped down for serious fishing, similar
to a head boat, with utilitarian benches in place of
more luxurious accommodations. The small galley
was cluttered with crushed beer cans and stacks of
soiled paper plates. The residue from some sort of
powder spill glittered under the penlight.

"Sal's a slob," I said.

"You sure Louis wasn't in the car with Ramirez?" Morelli asked.

"I have no way of knowing. The car has tinted
glass. But it only seats two, so at least one person
is left here."

"And there were no other cars on the road?"

"No."

"He could have gone in the other direction," Morelli said.

"He wouldn't have gone far. It dead-ends in a
quarter mile."

The moon was low in the sky, spilling silver dollars of light onto the water. We looked back at the
white refrigerator truck. The cooler motor hummed
quietly in the darkness.

"Maybe we should take another look at the
truck," Morelli said.

His tone gave me an uneasy feeling, and I didn't

want to voice the question that had popped into my head. We'd already determined Louis wasn't in the cab. What was left?

We returned to the truck, and Morelli scanned the outside thermostat controls for the refrigeration unit.

"What's it set at?" I asked.

"Twenty."

"Why so cold?"

Morelli stepped down and moved to the back door. "Why do you think?"

"Somebody's trying to freeze something?"

"That would be my guess, too." The back door to the truck was held closed by a heavy-duty bolt and padlock. Morelli weighed the padlock in the palm of his hand. "Could be worse," he said. He jogged to the van and returned with a small hacksaw.

I nervously looked around the lot. I didn't especially want to get caught hijacking a meat truck. "Isn't there a better way to do this?" I stage whispered over the rasp of the saw. "Can't you just pick the lock?"

"This is faster," Morelli said. "Just keep your eyes peeled for a night watchman."

The saw blade lunged through the metal, and the lock swung open. Morelli threw the bolt back and pulled on the thick, insulated door. The interior of the truck was stygian black. Morelli hauled himself up onto the single-step bumper, and I scrambled after him, wrestling my flashlight out of my shoulder bag. The frigid air pressed against me and took my breath away. We both trained our lights on the frost-shrouded walls. Huge, empty meathooks hung from the ceiling. Nearest the door was the large trim barrel I'd seen them roll out earlier in the afternoon. The empty barrel stood nearby, its lid slanted between the barrel and the truck wall.

I slid my spot of light farther to the rear and dropped it lower. My eyes focused, and I sucked in cold air when I realized what I was seeing. Louis was sprawled spread-eagle on his back, his eyes impossibly wide and unblinking, his feet splayed. Snot had run out of his nose and frozen to his cheek. A large urine stain had crystallized on the front of his work pants. He had a large, dark dot in the middle of his forehead. Sal lay next to him with an identical dot and the same dumbstruck expression on his frozen face.

"Shit," Morelli said. "I'm not having any luck at all."

The only dead people I'd ever seen had been embalmed and dressed up for church. Their hair had been styled, their cheeks had been rouged, and their eyes had been closed to suggest eternal slumber. None of them had been shot in the forehead. I felt bile rise in my throat and clapped a hand over my mouth.

Morelli yanked me out the door and onto the

gravel. "Don't throw up in the truck," he said. "You'll screw up the crime scene."

I did some deep breathing and willed my stomach to settle.

Morelli had his hand at the back of my neck. "You going to be okay?"

I nodded violently. "I'm fine. Just t-t-took me b-b-by surprise."

"I need some stuff from the van. Stay here. Don't go back in the truck and don't touch anything."

He didn't have to worry about me going back into the truck. Wild horses couldn't drag me back into the truck.

He returned with a crowbar and two pairs of disposable gloves. He gave one pair to me. We snapped the gloves on, and Morelli climbed up the step bumper. "Shine the light on Louis," he ordered, bending over the body.

"What are you doing?"

"I'm looking for the missing gun."

He stood and tossed a set of keys at me. "No gun on him, but he had these keys in his pocket. See if one of them opens the cab door."

I opened the passenger side door and searched the map pockets, the glove compartment, and under the seat, but I didn't come up with a gun. When I went back to Morelli he was working at the sealed drum with a crowbar.

"No gun up front," I said.

The lid popped off, and Morelli flicked his flash-light on and looked inside.

"Well?" I asked.

His voice was tight when he answered. "It's Car-men."

I was hit with another wave of nausea. "You think Carmen's been in Sal's freezer all this time?"

"Looks like it."

"Why would he keep her around? Wouldn't he be afraid someone would discover her?"

Morelli shrugged. "I suppose he felt safe. Maybe he's done this sort of thing before. You do something often enough, and you become complacent."

"You're thinking about those other women who've disappeared from Stark Street."

"Yeah. Sal was probably just waiting for a con-venient time to take Carmen out and dump her at sea."

"I don't understand Sal's connection."

Morelli hammered the lid back on. "Me either, but I feel pretty confident Ramirez can be persuaded to explain it to us."

He wiped his hands on his pants and left smudges of white.

"What's with all this white stuff?" I asked. "Sal got a thing with baby powder or cleanser or some-thing?"

Morelli looked down at his hands and his pants. "I hadn't noticed."

"There was powder on the floor of the boat. And

now you picked some up from the drum and wiped it on your pants."

"Jesus," Morelli said, staring at his hand. "Holy shit." He flipped the lid off the drum and ran his finger around the inside rim. He put the finger to his mouth and tasted it. "This is dope."

"Sal doesn't strike me as a crackhead."

"It's not crack. It's heroin."

"Are you sure?"

"I've seen a lot of it."

I could see him smiling in the dark.

"Sweet Pea, I think we've just found ourselves a drop boat," he said. "All along I've been thinking this was about protecting Ramirez, but now I'm not so sure. I think this might be about drugs."

"What's a drop boat?"

"It's a small boat that goes out to sea to rendez-vous with a larger ship engaged in drug smuggling.

"Most of the world's heroin comes from Afghan-istan, Pakistan, Burma. It's usually routed through northern Africa, then up to Amsterdam or some other European city. In the past, the favored method of entry for the northeast has been to body-pack it through Kennedy. For a year now, we've been get-ting tips that the stuff is traveling big time on ships coming into Port Newark. The DEA and Customs have been working overtime and coming up empty." He held his finger in the air for inspection. "I think this could be the reason. By the time the ship sails into Newark, the heroin's already been off-loaded."

"Onto a drop boat," I said.

"Yeah. The drop boat snags the dope from the mother ship and brings it back to a small marina like this where there are no customs inspectors.

"My guess is they load the stuff into these barrels after it's handed down, and one of the bags broke last time out."

"Hard to believe someone would be that sloppy about leaving incriminating evidence."

Morelli grunted. "You work with drugs all the time and they become commonplace. You wouldn't believe what people leave in full view in apartments and garages. Besides, the boat belongs to Sal, and chances are Sal wasn't along for the ride. That way if the boat gets busted, Sal says he loaned it to a friend. He didn't know it was being used for illegal activities."

"You think this is why there's so much heroin in Trenton?"

"Could be. When you have a drop boat like this you can bring in large quantities and eliminate the couriers, so you have good availability at low overhead. The cost on the street goes down and the purity goes up."

"And addicts start dying."

"Yeah."

"Why do you think Ramirez shot Sal and Louis?"

"Maybe Ramirez had to burn some bridges."

Morelli played his light over the back corners of the truck. I could barely see him in the dark, but I could hear the scrape of his feet as he moved.

"What are you doing?" I asked.

"I'm looking for a gun. In case you haven't noticed I'm shit out of luck. My witness is dead. If I can't find Ziggy's missing gun with an intact latent, I'm as good as dead, too."

"There's always Ramirez."

"Who may or may not be feeling talkative."

"I think you're overreacting. I can place Ramirez at the scene of two execution-type killings, and we've uncovered a major drug operation."

"Possibly this casts some doubt about Ziggy's character, but it doesn't alter the fact that I appeared to have shot an unarmed man."

"Ranger says you've got to trust in the system."

"Ranger *ignores* the system."

I didn't want to see Morelli in jail for a crime he didn't commit, but I also didn't want him living the life of a fugitive. He was actually a pretty good guy, and as much as I hated to admit it, I'd become fond of him. When the manhunt was over I'd miss the teasing and the late-night companionship. It was true that Morelli still touched a nerve every now and then, but there was a new feeling of partnership that transcended most of my earlier anger. I found it hard to believe he would be sent to jail in light of all the new evidence. Possibly he would lose his job on the force. This seemed like a minor disgrace to me when compared to spending long years in hiding.

"I think we should call the police and let them sort through this," I said to Morelli. "You can't stay in hiding for the rest of your life. What about your mother? What about your phone bill?"

"My phone bill? Oh shit, Stephanie, you haven't been running up my phone bill, have you?"

"We had an agreement. You were going to let me bring you in when we found the missing witness."

"I hadn't counted on him being dead."

"I'll be evicted."

"Listen, Stephanie, your apartment isn't all that great. Besides, this is wasted talk. We both know you aren't capable of bringing me in by force. The only way you're going to collect your money is by my permission. You're just going to have to sit tight."

"I don't like your attitude, Morelli."

The light whirled, and he lunged toward the door. "I don't much care what you think of my attitude. I'm not in a good mood. My witness is dead, and I can't find the damn murder weapon. Probably Ramirez will squeal like a pig, and I'll be exonerated, but until that happens I'm staying hidden."

"The hell you are. I can't believe it's in your best interest. Suppose some cop sees you and shoots you? Besides, I have a job to do, and I'm going to do it. I should never have made this deal with you."

"It was a good deal," he said.

"Would you have made it?"

"No. But I'm not you. I have skills you could only dream about. And I'm a hell of a lot meaner than you'll ever be."

"You underestimate me. I'm pretty fucking mean."

Morelli grinned. "You're a marshmallow. Soft and sweet and when you get heated up you go all gooey and delicious."

I was rendered speechless. I couldn't believe just seconds before I'd been thinking friendly, protective thoughts about this oaf.

"I'm a fast learner, Morelli. I made a few mistakes in the beginning, but I'm capable of bringing you in now."

"Yeah, right. What are you going to do, shoot me?"

I wasn't soothed by his sarcasm. "The thought isn't without appeal, but shooting isn't necessary. All I have to do is close the door on you, you arrogant jerk."

In the dim light I saw his eyes widen as understanding dawned a nanosecond before I swung the heavy, insulated door shut. I heard the muffled thud of his body slam against the interior, but he was too late. The bolt was already in place.

I adjusted the refrigeration temperature to forty. I figured that would be cold enough to keep the corpses from defrosting, but not so cold I'd turn

Morelli into a popsicle on the ride back to Trenton. I climbed into the cab and cranked the motor over— compliments of Louis's keys. I lumbered out of the lot and onto the road and headed for the highway.

Halfway home I found a pay phone and called Dorsey. I told him I was bringing Morelli in, but I didn't provide any details. I told him I'd be rolling into the station's back lot in about forty-five minutes and it'd be nice if he was waiting for me.

I swung the truck into the driveway on North Clinton right on time and caught Dorsey and two uniforms in my headlights. I cut the engine, did some deep breathing to still my nervous stomach, and levered myself out of the cab.

"Maybe you should have more than two uniforms," I said. "I think Morelli might be mad."

Dorsey's eyebrows were up around his hairline. "You've got him in the back of the truck?"

"Yeah. And he isn't alone."

One of the uniforms slid the bolt, the door flew open, and Morelli catapulted himself out at me. He caught me midbody, and we both went down onto the asphalt, thrashing and rolling and swearing at each other.

Dorsey and the uniforms hauled Morelli off me, but he was still swearing and flailing his arms. "I'm gonna get you!" he was yelling at me. "When I get outta here I'm gonna get your ass. You're a goddamn lunatic. You're a menace!"

Two more patrolmen appeared, and the four uniforms wrestled Morelli through the back door. Dorsey lagged behind with me. "Maybe you should wait out here until he calms down," he said.

I picked some cinders out of my knee. "That might take a while."

I gave Dorsey the keys to the truck and explained about the drugs and Ramirez. By the time I was done explaining, Morelli had been moved upstairs, and the coast was clear for me to get my body receipt from the docket lieutenant.

It was close to twelve when I finally let myself into my apartment, and my one real regret for the evening was that I'd left my blender at the marina. I truly needed a daiquiri. I locked my front door and tossed my shoulder bag onto the kitchen counter.

I had mixed feelings about Morelli . . . not sure if I'd done the right thing. In the end, it hadn't been the retrieval money that had mattered. I'd acted on a combination of righteous indignation and my own conviction that Morelli should surrender himself.

My apartment was dark and restful, lit only by the light in the hall. Shadows were deep in the living room, but they didn't generate fear. The chase was over.

Some thought needed to be given to my future. Being a bounty hunter was much more complicated than I'd originally assumed. Still, it had its high points, and I'd learned a lot in the past two weeks.

The heat wave had broken late in the afternoon

and the temperature had dropped to a lovely seventy degrees. My curtains were closed, and a breeze played in the lightweight chintz. A perfect night for sleeping, I thought.

I kicked my shoes off and sat on the edge of my bed, suddenly feeling mildly uneasy. I couldn't pinpoint the source of the problem. Something seemed off. I thought about my pocketbook far away on the kitchen counter, and my apprehension increased. Paranoia, I told myself. I was locked in my apartment, and if someone tried to come through the window, which was highly unlikely, I'd have time to stop them.

Still, the ripple of anxiety nagged at me.

I looked over at the window, at the gently billowing curtains, and cold understanding struck like a knife slice. When I'd left my apartment the window had been closed and locked. The window was open now. Jesus, the window was *open*. Fear skittered through me, snatching my breath away.

Someone was in my apartment . . . or possibly waiting on my fire escape. I bit down hard on my lower lip to keep from wailing. Dear God, don't let it be Ramirez. Anyone but Ramirez. My heart beat with a ragged thud, and my stomach sickened.

As I saw it, I had two choices. I could run for the front door or dive down the fire escape. That was assuming my feet would move. I decided chances were greater that Ramirez was in the apartment than on the fire escape, so I went to the window. On a sharp intake of breath I ripped the curtains open and stared at the latch. It was secure. A circle of glass had been removed from the top window, allowing Whoever to slip an arm through and open the lock. The cool night air whistled softly through the neatly cut circle.

Professional, I thought. Maybe not Ramirez. Maybe just your garden-variety second-story man. Maybe he'd gotten discouraged by my poverty, decided to move on to fatter pickings, and locked up after himself. I looked through the opening at the fire escape. It was empty and felt benign.

Call the police and report the break-in, I told myself. The phone was at bedside. I punched it on and nothing happened. Shit. Someone must have disconnected it in the kitchen. A little voice in my head whispered to get out of the apartment. Use the fire escape, it said. Move fast.

I turned back to the window and fumbled with the latch. I heard movement behind me, felt the intruder's presence. In the window's reflection I could see him standing in the open bedroom door, framed by the weak light from the hall.

He called my name, and I felt my hair stand on end like the cartoon version of an electrocuted cat.

"Close the curtains," he said, "and turn around nice and slow so I can see you."

I did as I was told, squinting in the dark in blind confusion, recognizing the voice but not understanding the purpose. "What are you doing here?" I asked.

"Good question." He flipped the light switch. It was Jimmy Alpha, and he was holding a gun. "I ask myself that question all the time," he said. "How did it come to this? I'm a decent man, you know? I try to do what's right."

"Doing what's right is good," I told him.

"What happened to all your furniture?"

"I had some hard times."

He nodded. "Then you know what it's like." He grinned. "That why you started working for Vinnie?"

"Yeah."

"Vinnie and me, we're sort of alike. We do what we have to do to hang in there. I guess you're like that, too."

I didn't like being lumped in with Vinnie, but I wasn't about to argue with a guy who was holding a gun. "I guess I am."

"You follow the fights?"

"No."

He sighed. "A manager like me waits a whole lifetime for a decent fighter to come along. Most managers die without ever getting one."

"But you got one. You have Ramirez."

"I took Benito in when he was just a kid. Fourteen years old. I knew right away he was gonna be different from the others. There was something about him. Drive. Power. Talent."

Insanity, I thought. Don't forget insanity.

"Taught him everything he knows about boxing. Gave him all my time. Made sure he ate right. Bought him clothes when he had no money. Let him sleep in the office when his mother was crazy on crack."

"And now he's champ," I said.

His smile was tight. "It's my dream. All my life I've worked for this."

I was beginning to see the direction of the conversation. "And he's out of control," I said.

Jimmy sagged against the doorjamb. "Yeah. He's out of control. He's gonna ruin everything . . . all the good times, all the money. I can't tell him anything, anymore. He don't listen."

"What are you going to do about it?"

"Ahh," Alpha sighed. "That's the big question. And the answer to the question is diversify. I diversify, I make a shitload of money, excuse my language, and I get out.

"You know what it means to diversify? It means I take the money I make on Ramirez, and I invest it in other businesses. A chicken franchise, a laundromat, maybe even a butcher shop. Maybe I can get a butcher shop real cheap because the guy who owns it can't make good on some bad bets he took."

"Sal."

"Yeah. Sal. You got Sal real upset today. Bad timing, the way you walked in just when Louis got there, but I guess in the end it's gonna work out okay."

"I didn't realize Sal knew me."

"Honey, you're not hard to recognize. You don't got no eyebrows."

"Sal was worried that I spotted Louis."

"Yeah. So, he called me, and I said we should all meet at the marina. Louis was going to the marina anyway. There's a drop coming in tomorrow, and I'm thinking maybe I'm going to have to do Louis because he's such a fuck-up. The guy can't do anything right. He lets people see him at Carmen's, then he has to take care of them. He only gets two out of three. He can't score Morelli. The dumb shit found Morelli's car in your parking lot and didn't stop to think maybe Morelli wasn't driving it, so he ends up roasting Morty Beyers. Now you've got Louis fingered. I figure his time is up.

"So I borrow Benito's car, and I go to the marina, and on the way I see you at the gas station, and I get a brilliant idea. Jimmy, I say to myself, this is your way out."

I was having a hard time following. I still didn't completely understand Jimmy's involvement. "Out of what?" I asked.

"Out of the whole fucking mess. See, there's something you got to understand about me. I gave up a lot for the fight game. I never got around to getting married or to having a family. All my life I never had anything but boxing. When you're young, you don't mind. You keep thinking there's time. But then one day you wake up, and you find out there's no more time.

"I've got a fighter who likes to hurt people. It's a sickness. There's something messed up in his head, and I can't make it better. I know he's not gonna go the count on his career, so I take the money we make, and I buy a couple properties. Next thing I know I meet this Jamaican guy says he's got a better way to make money. Drugs. I make the buy, his organization does the distribution, I wash the money through my businesses and Ramirez. We do this for a while and it works real good. All we have to do is keep Ramirez out of jail so we can launder.

"Problem is, I've got a lot of money now, and I can't get out. The organization's got me by my gonads, you know what I mean?"

"Striker."

"Yeah. Big motherfucking Jamaican posse. Greedy, nasty beggars.

"So I'm going down the road to whack Louis, I see you sitting there, and I get a plan. The plan is that I execute Sal and Louis Striker style. Then I leave some high-quality H spilled in the boat and on the barrel so the cops figure out the operation and shut it down. Now no one's left to talk about me behind my back, and I'm too risky for Striker to use for a while. And the beauty of it is that Sal and Louis get pinned on Ramirez, thanks to you.

I'm sure when you made your statement to the cops you told them all about Ramirez buzzing by you at the gas station."

"I still don't understand why you're here, holding me at gunpoint."

"I can't take a chance on Ramirez talking to the cops and maybe they come to the conclusion he's really as dumb as he looks. Or maybe he tells them I borrowed his car, and they believe him. So I'm going to have you put a bullet in him. Then there's no Benito, no Sal, no Louis."

"What about Stephanie?"

"There's not going to be any Stephanie, either." He had the phone base shoved into his slacks. He plugged it into my bedroom wall jack and dialed. "My man," he said when the connection was made. "I've got a girl here wants attention."

Something was said at the other end.

"Stephanie Plum," Jimmy answered. "She's at home, waiting for you. And Benito, make sure no one sees you. Maybe you better come up the fire escape."

The conversation was severed and the phone discarded.

"Is this what happened to Carmen?" I asked.

"Christ, Carmen was a mercy killing. I don't know how she ever made it home. By the time we heard about it she'd already called Morelli."

"Now what?"

He leaned back against the wall. "Now we wait."

"What happens when Ramirez gets here?"

"I turn my back while he does his thing, then I shoot him with your gun. By the time the police show up, you'll both have bled to death, and there'll be no more loose ends."

He was deadly serious. He was going to watch while Ramirez raped and tortured me, and then he was going to make sure I was mortally injured.

The room swam in front of me. My legs wobbled, and I found myself sitting on the edge of the bed. I dropped my head between my knees and waited for the fog to clear. A vision of Lula's battered body flashed into my mind, feeding my terror.

The dizziness faded, but my heart pounded hard enough to rock my body. Take a chance, I thought. Do something! Don't just sit here and wait for Ramirez.

"You okay?" Alpha said to me. "You don't look good."

I kept my head down. "I'm going to be sick."

"You need to go to the can?"

My head was still between my knees. I shook it, no. "Just give me a minute to catch my breath."

Nearby, Rex ran in his cage. I couldn't bear to look over, knowing it might be the last time I'd see him. Funny how a person can get so attached to a little creature like that. A lump formed in my throat at the thought of Rex being orphaned, and the message came back to me. Do something! *Do something*!

I said a short prayer, gritted my teeth, and bucked forward, lunging at Alpha, catching him off guard, nailing him in the gut with a head butt.

Alpha let out a *woof!* of air, and the gun discharged over my head, shattering my window. If I'd had any cool at all I would have followed up with a good hard kick to the crotch, but I was operating on thoughtless energy, with adrenaline pumping into my system at warp speed. I was in fight-or-flight mode, and flight was the hands-down choice.

I scrambled away from him, through the open bedroom door, into the living room. I was almost to the front hall when I heard another crack from his gun, and an electric stab of heat shot down my left leg. I yelped in pain and surprise, whirling off balance, into the kitchen. I grabbed my shoulder bag off the counter with two hands and searched for my .38. Alpha moved into the kitchen doorway. He aimed his gun and steadied it. "Sorry," he said. "There's no other way."

My leg was on fire and my heart was banging in my chest. My nose was running and tears blurred my vision. I had both hands on the little Smith and Wesson, still in my pocketbook. I blinked the tears away and fired.

FOURTEEN

RAIN PATTERED GENTLY ON MY LIVING ROOM WIN-
dow, competing with the sound of Rex running in
his wheel. It had been four days since I'd been shot,
and the pain was down to an annoying but manage-
able ache.

The mental healing would be slower. I still had
night terrors, still found it difficult to be alone in
my apartment. After shooting Jimmy Alpha, I'd
crawled to the phone and called the police before
I'd passed out. They'd arrived in time to catch Ramirez halfway up my fire escape. Then they'd trundled him off to jail and me off to the hospital.
Fortunately, I'd fared better than Alpha. He was
dead. I was alive.

Ten thousand dollars had been deposited in my

bank account. Not a cent of it had been spent yet. I was slowed down by seventeen stitches in my butt. When the stitches came out I figured I'd do something irresponsible like fly to Martinique for the weekend. Or maybe I'd get a tattoo or dye my hair red.

I jumped at the sound of someone knocking on my door. It was almost seven P.M., and I wasn't expecting company. I cautiously made my way to the foyer and looked out the peephole. I gasped at the sight of Joe Morelli in sports coat and jeans, clean shaven, hair freshly trimmed. He stared directly at the peephole. His smile was smug. He knew I was looking at him, wondering if it would be wise to open the door. He waved, and I was reminded of a time two weeks earlier when our positions had been reversed.

I unlocked the two dead bolts but left the chain in place. I cracked the door. "Yes?"

"Take the chain off," Morelli said.

"Why?"

"Because I brought you a pizza, and if I tip it on end to give it to you the cheese will slide off."

"Is it a Pino's pizza?"

"Of course it's a Pino's pizza."

I shifted my weight to ease my left leg. "Why are you bringing me pizza?"

"I don't know. I just felt like it. Are you going to open the door or what?"

"I haven't decided."

This brought a slow, evil smile. "Are you afraid of me?"

"Uh . . . yes."

The smile stayed fixed in place. "You should be. You locked me in a refrigerator truck with three dead people. Sooner or later, I'm going to get you for it."

"But not tonight?"

"No," he said. "Not tonight."

I closed the door, slid the chain free, and opened the door to him.

He put the white pizza box and a six-pack on the kitchen counter and turned to me. "Looks like you're walking a little slow. How are you feeling?"

"Okay. Fortunately, Alpha's bullet tore through some fat and did most of its damage to the wall in the hallway."

His smile had faded. "How are you really feeling?"

I'm not sure what it is about Morelli, but he never fails to strip my defenses. Even when I'm on guard, being watchful, Morelli can piss me off, turn me on, make me question my judgment, and, in general, provoke inconvenient emotions. Concern pinched the corners of his eyes, and there was a seriousness to his mouth that belied the casual tone of his question.

I bit down hard on my lip, but the tears came anyway, silently spilling down my cheeks.

Morelli gathered me into his arms and held me

close. He rested his cheek against the top of my head and pressed a kiss into my hair.

We stood like that for a long time, and if it hadn't been for the pain in my butt I might have fallen asleep, finally comforted and at peace, feeling safe in Morelli's arms.

"If I ask you a serious question," Morelli murmured against my ear, "will you give me an honest answer?"

"Maybe."

"Do you remember that time in my father's garage?"

"Vividly."

"And when we went at it in the bakery . . ."

"Uh huh."

"Why did you do it? Are my powers of persuasion really that strong?"

I tipped my head back to look at him. "I suspect it had more to do with curiosity and rebellion on my part." Not to mention hormones on the rampage.

"So you're willing to share some of the responsibility?"

"Of course."

The smile had returned to his mouth. "And if I made love to you here in the kitchen . . . how much of the blame would you be willing to assume?"

"Jesus, Morelli, I've got seventeen stitches in my ass!"

He sighed. "Do you think we could be friends after all these years?"

This from the person who had tossed my keys into a Dumpster. "I suppose it's possible. We wouldn't have to sign a pact and seal it in blood, would we?"

"No, but we could belch over beer."

"My kind of contract."

"Good. Now that we have that settled, there's a ball game I'd like to see, and you have my television."

"Men always have ulterior motives," I said, carting the pizza into the living room.

Morelli followed with the beer. "How do you manage this sitting business?"

"I have a rubber doughnut. If you make any cracks about it, I'll gas you."

He shrugged out of his jacket and shoulder holster, hung them on the doorknob to my bedroom door, buzzed the TV on, and searched for his channel. "I got some reports for you," he said. "Are you up to it?"

"A half hour ago I might have said no, but now that I have this pizza I'm up to anything."

"It's not the pizza, darlin'. It's my masculine presence."

I raised an eyebrow.

Morelli ignored the eyebrow. "First of all, the medical examiner said you were due for the Robin Hood sharpshooter award. You got Alpha with five rounds to the heart, all within an inch of each other.

Pretty amazing, considering you also shot the shit out of your pocketbook."

We both chugged some beer, since neither of us was sure yet how we felt about me killing a man. Pride seemed out of place. Sorrow didn't quite fit. There was definitely regret.

"Do you think it could have ended any other way?" I asked.

"No," Morelli said. "He would have killed you if you hadn't killed him first."

This was true. Jimmy Alpha would have killed me. There was no doubt in my mind.

Morelli leaned forward to see the pitch. Howard Barker struck out. "Shit," Morelli said. He turned his attention back to me. "Now for the good part. I had a recorder attached to the utility pole on the far side of your parking lot. I was using it for backup when I wasn't around. I could check it at the end of the day and catch up if I'd missed anything. The damn thing was still working when Jimmy dropped in on you. Recorded the whole conversation, the shooting and everything, clear as a bell."

"Dang!"

"Sometimes I'm so slick I scare myself," Morelli said.

"Slick enough not to be locked up in jail."

He selected a piece of pizza, losing some green pepper and onion slices in the process, scooping them back on with his fingers. "I've been cleared of all charges and reinstated in the department, pay retroactive. The gun was in the barrel with Carmen. It had been refrigerated all this time, so the prints were clear, and forensics found traces of blood on it. DNA hasn't come back yet, but preliminary lab tests suggest the blood is Ziggy's, proving Ziggy was armed when I shot him. Apparently, the gun jammed when Ziggy fired at me, just as I'd suspected. When Ziggy hit the floor, the gun fell out of his hand, and Louis picked it up and took it with him. Then Louis must have decided to get rid of it."

I took a deep breath and asked the question that had been uppermost in my mind for the last three days. "What about Ramirez?"

"Ramirez is being held without bail pending psychiatric evaluation. Now that Alpha is out of the picture, several very creditable women have come forward to testify against Ramirez."

The sense of relief was almost painful.

"What are your plans?" Morelli asked. "You going to keep working for Vinnie?"

"I'm not sure." I ate some pizza. "Probably," I said. "Almost definitely probably."

"Just to clear the air," Morelli said. "I'm sorry I wrote that poem about you on the stadium wall when we were in high school."

I felt my heart stutter. "On the stadium wall?"

Silence.

Color rose to Morelli's cheekbones. "I thought you knew."

"I knew about Mario's Sub Shop!"

"Oh."

"Are you telling me you wrote a poem about me on the *stadium wall*? A poem detailing what transpired behind the éclair case?"

"Would it help any if I told you the poem was flattering?"

I wanted to smack him, but he was on his feet and moving before I could get out of my rubber tube.

"It was years ago," he said, dancing away from me. "Shit, Stephanie, it's unattractive to hold a grudge."

"You are scum, Morelli. *Scum*."

"Probably," Morelli said, "but I give good . . . pizza."

Introducing the first ever "Plumography"— your guide to the world of all things Plum!

*"There are some men who enter a woman's life
and screw it up forever. Joseph Morelli did
this to me—not forever, but periodically."*

ONE FOR THE MONEY

Meet Stephanie Plum. The Trenton native just got
laid off as discount lingerie buyer for E.E. Martin's
in Newark, but the worst part is, she lost her cher-
ished Mazda Miata to the repo man. Replacement:
a used Nova with a bad muffler. A visit to her parents and her Grandma Mazur, who lives with them,
leads to a light at the end of the Jersey Tunnel: a
job with her cousin Vinnie at Vincent Plum Bail
Bonding Company. Ten thousand a pop for hauling
in the bad guys—guys like Joe Morelli, Stephanie's childhood nemesis-turned-hunky-vice-cop
now wanted on a murder rap. Still as sexy and dangerous as ever, the heat is on—and working with
just-as-hot fellow bondsman and mentor, Ranger,
Stephanie could get burned. The bright side? Stephanie's junked her Nova and hijacked Morelli's
Jeep Cherokee. Unfortunately, it's soon blown to
smithereens. Packing pepper spray and a .38 Special, and with two new men in her life, it looks like
a promising new career for Stephanie Plum . . .

1) Historic Moment: First book in the series.
2) New Characters Introduced: Stephanie Plum,

Grandma Mazur, Cousin Vinnie, Joe Morelli, Ranger, Lula
3) Automotive Factoid: Stephanie drives a Nova and Jeep Cherokee.

"Morelli and I had done battle before. With only short-lived victories on both sides, I suspected this would be another war of sorts. And I figured I'd have to learn to live with it."

TWO FOR THE DOUGH

Stephanie Plum is trying to ease into her new job with a level head. It appears Joe Morelli is around for good—and bad—and she's resigned to it. Her loose professional relationship with Ranger ends in a platonic night together with no strings attached, and her new set of wheels, a secondhand Jeep Wrangler, suits her needs. Until it's stolen out from under her. How is she supposed to nab Kenny Mancuso, her new bail jumper and a distant relative of Morelli's? In a burst of misguided good intentions, she's strong-armed into accepting as a gift a 1953 Buick passed down from Grandma Mazur's brother, Sandor. It may look like a beluga whale but it's a car built to last—much to Stephanie's chagrin. Meanwhile, Morelli, whose libido has been stuck on overdrive ever since he met Stephanie years ago, is ready to make the moves on the resistant bounty hunter. Will she cave? Not on her Grandma's life— which happens to be in danger from an ice pick– wielding goon . . .

1) Historic Moment: Morelli's intentions become known, and the battle of the sexes begins.
2) New Characters Introduced: Kenny Mancuso, Eddie Gazarra, Mary Lou Stankovic
3) Automotive Factoid: Stephanie drives a Jeep Wrangler and a '53 Buick.

"I wasn't sure why I was still working for Vinnie. I suspected it had something to do with the title. Bounty hunter. It held a certain cachet. Even better, the job didn't require panty hose."

THREE TO GET DEADLY

Uncle Mo Bedemier may have a reputation as a kindly old candy-store owner but all that changes when he skips bail on a very minor charge. Bounty hunter Stephanie Plum needs to know why and that means scouting Uncle Mo's neighborhood. And no one knows Stark Street better than the new file clerk, Lula, a former hooker with an attitude—and better yet, a Nissan in working order. This seamier side of Jersey is where Stephanie comes to after a knock on the head, a corpse at her heels, and Joe Morelli on her tail as the possible murderer. Before the investigation is over, Ranger loses his Beemer, no thanks to Stephanie; the Nissan ends up in the shop for repairs; and Stephanie winds up with a green Mazda as loaner and red highlights in her hair. It certainly gets Morelli's attention because it prompts a first kiss on the back of Stephanie's very vulnerable neck . . .

1) Historic Moment: Morelli finally kisses Stephanie—and she's all for it.

2) New Characters Introduced: Uncle Moses Bedemier, Joyce Barnhardt, Stuart Baggett
3) Automotive Factoid: Stephanie drives a Nissan,
a Mazda, and a '53 Buick.

*"From here on out, Morelli was erotica non grata.
'Look but Don't Touch,' that was my motto."*

FOUR TO SCORE

It's been months since Joe Morelli made his move
on Stephanie Plum, and true to form, it's been
months since she's heard from him again. But the
minute he returns, the rugged vice cop again proves
irresistible—for at least one more night. She'd kick
herself for giving in if she wasn't so preoccupied
with a bail jumper: a waitress on the run for stealing
her boyfriend's car. To make matters even worse,
Vinnie's hired Joyce Barnhardt, Stephanie's high
school rival and eventual home-wrecker, to join the
bounty-hunting team as a skip tracer. Now, with the
help of Lula riding shotgun in Stephanie's new
Honda CRX, and a transvestite named Sally Sweet,
Stephanie becomes embroiled in a game of murder,
extortion, and kidnapping. Where it all leads is back
into Morelli's arms—wrapped up on a motorcycle
powered with 109 horses taking her to places she'd
promised she'd never go again.

1) Historic Moment: Stephanie and Morelli "do the
   deed."

2) New Characters Introduced: Sally Sweet, Edward Kuntz

3) Automotive Factoid: Stephanie drives a Honda CRX and a '53 Buick.

"When I was a little girl I used to dress Barbie up without underpants . . . And being a bail enforcement agent is sort of like being a bare-bottom Barbie. It's about having a secret."

HIGH FIVE

With her Honda CRX now just a memory of blown-up cinders, Stephanie's back in her '53 Buick—a "classic", she defends, with *no* authority. But with absolute conviction she's on the hunt for a vanishing relative. According to Grandma Mazur, Uncle Fred's gone missing. Seventy years old, just left the bank, and an easy mark. It doesn't look good. Whatever link the disappearance has to the rough beating of her friend, Lula, Stephanie's determined to find it. By way of a Porsche, garbage truck, and a BMW, past a nasty, vertically-challenged bookie and a stun-gun-toting Grandma Mazur, and through a Mafia wedding, Stephanie's bound and determined to make it out alive. But whether she ends up with Ranger or Morelli—both of whom make their intentions known—is a fate that she leaves to the heavens . . . and a simple draw of the name.

1) Historic Moment: Stephanie gets the hots for Ranger.

2) New Characters Introduced: Uncle Fred, Aunt
   Mabel, Randy Briggs
3) Automotive Factoid: Stephanie drives a Porsche,
   a BMW, and a '53 Buick.

"Two of the men on my list of desirables actually desire me back. The problem being that they both sort of scare the hell out of me."

HOT SIX

Stephanie Plum's career as a bounty hunter may finally be taking its toll—on both her used Civic Honda and her emotions. Ranger has just been arrested by a rookie cop on a concealed weapons charge. Simple enough, until Ranger disappears. It seems he's also wanted in connection with the murder of a gun-trader's son. Now Stephanie wants Ranger in the worst way while Joe Morelli wants Stephanie in the *best* way. But Joe's private time is cramped by Grandma Mazur who moves in with Stephanie for the forseeable future. That's not the only surprise Grandma has: a suitor, Eddie DeChooch, hints at an exquisite night of sin. Stephanie's not so lucky. After her car is torched, she ends up with a one-of-a-kind Rollswagon that's drawing stares, and a sideline as a dog-sitter. But her biggest concern—next to finding Ranger—is Grandma Mazur's bid for a driver's license. With the streets endangered and Stephanie's life turned upside down, Morelli offers what he can to help. To Stephanie's surprise it's a proposal of marriage . . .

1) Historic Moment: Grandma Mazur moves in
   with Stephanie, Morelli proposes, and Ranger's
   secret past is alluded to.
2) New Character Introduced: Eddie DeChooch
3) Automotive Factoid: Stephanie drives a Civic
   Honda and a custom-built "Rollswagon" (and a
   '53 Buick).

"Morelli's still trouble ... but now he's the kind of trouble a woman likes."

SEVEN UP

Joe Morelli? Marriage? Sharing a bathroom? He must be desperate. But is Stephanie? At least, desperate to put her new bounty hunt to rest, anyway. After getting caught smuggling a truckload of bootleg cigarettes up from Virginia, Eddie DeChooch missed his court date. Stephanie doesn't want to have anything to do with it. After all, Eddie not only left behind a bullet-riddled corpse in his garden, but he's dating her Grandma Mazur. It's all hitting a little too close to home—so does the bombshell news leveled by Stephanie's sister, Valerie: a marriage break-up that's brought the depressed wife back to her roots. While Stephanie's considering her own marriage to Morelli, two of her childhood friends vanish. For answers she turns to the only man who can help. Ranger's deal? He'll give Stephanie everything she needs—if she gives him everything he wants. Trouble is, what he wants, Stephanie wants just as bad! With divided attention between the two men in her life, Stephanie finally relents, and grants Ranger his wish, leaving Morelli behind. How big a mistake could it be? She's about to find out ...

1) Historic Moment: Stephanie's sister Valerie moves in with the Plum family after her marriage fails.
2) New Characters Introduced: Valerie, Mooner, Ziggy and Benny
3) Automotive Factoid: Stephanie drives a Harley (and a '53 Buick).

*"A few months ago Ranger and I made a dea
that has haunted me—another one of those
jumping off the garage roof things, except thi
deal involved my bedroom . . ."*

HARD EIGHT

Stephanie Plum is on the hunt for a mother and child on the run who have left behind an angry ex-husband. He's eager to collect on a child custody bond. When local thug and businessman Eddie Abruzzi warns Stephanie to lay off of the case, she's only more intrigued. And a little scared, especially when she finds a bag of snakes on her doorknob and tarantulas in her car. What Stephanie needs is back-up, and Ranger's more than available—for the bounty hunt, and for Stephanie. Soon, a stalker in a bunny suit is on Stephanie's tail, her CRV is blown to bits, and a corpse winds up on her couch. That's just one body too many in Stephanie's house, considering her Grandma Mazur and sister, Valerie, have moved in, leaving little room for Joe Morelli who wants back into Stephanie's life. Before the case closes, she's sure to find her man. It's the other two men Stephanie has to contend with that are putting the perplexed and love-sick bounty hunter's heart at risk . . .

1) Historic Moment: Stephanie knows that she must decide on her future with Morelli once and for all.
2) New Characters Introduced: Eddie Abruzzo, Mrs. Markowitz, Carol Nadich, Evelyn Soder, Albert Kloughn
3) Automotive Factoid: Stephanie drives a Honda CR-V (not to mention a '53 Buick).